I0606462

VIDA ROSE

Things We Tried to Bury

Copyright © 2026 by Vida Rose

All rights reserved. No part of this publication may be reproduced, stored, or transmitted in any form or by any means, electronic, mechanical, photocopying, recording, scanning, or otherwise without written permission from the publisher. It is illegal to copy this book, post it to a website, or distribute it by any other means without permission.

This novel is entirely a work of fiction. The names, characters, and incidents portrayed in it are the work of the author's imagination. Any resemblance to actual persons, living or dead, events, or localities is entirely coincidental.

First edition

ISBN: 979-8-9944508-0-2

This book was professionally typeset on Reedsy.
Find out more at reedsy.com

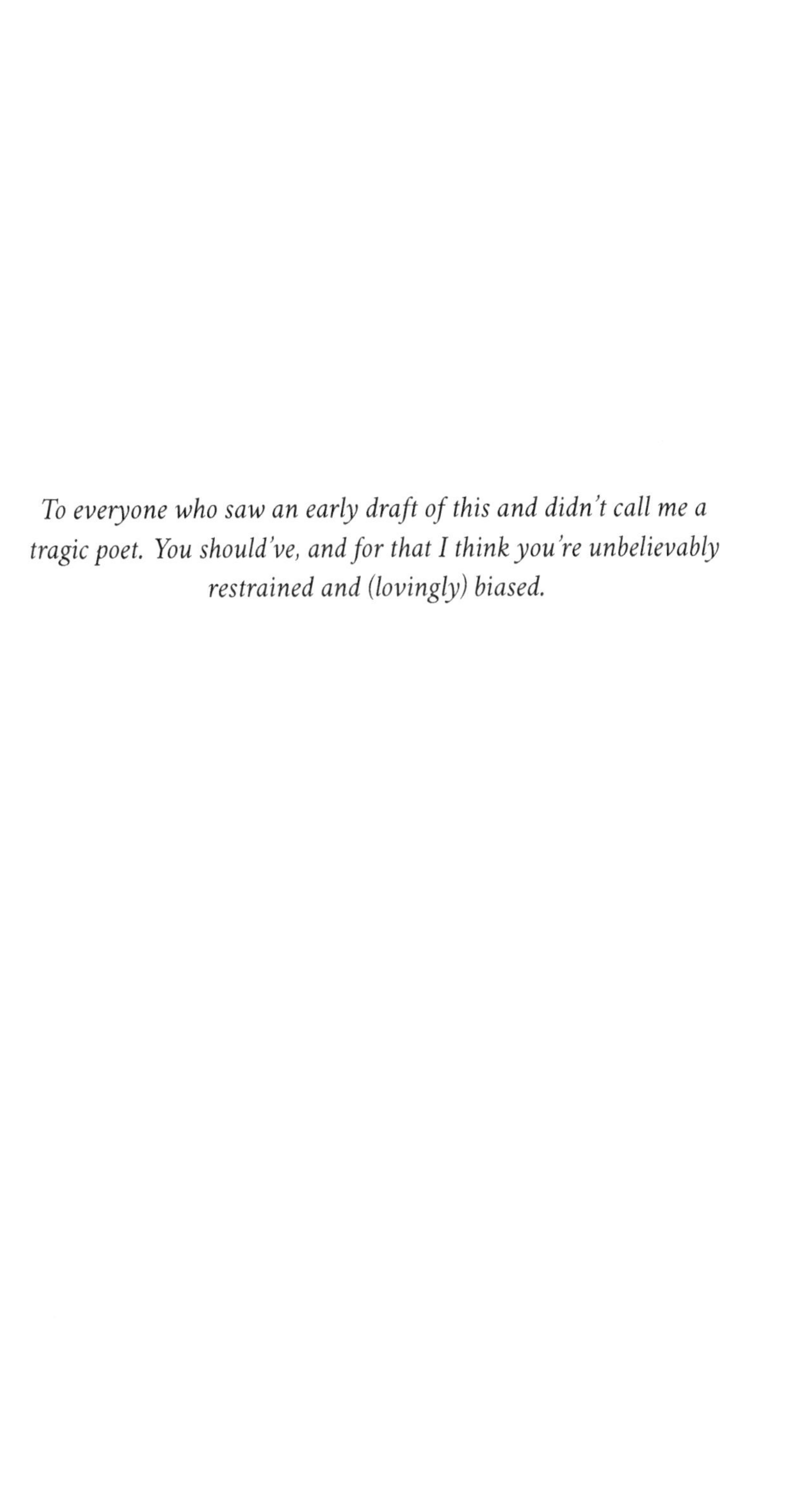

To everyone who saw an early draft of this and didn't call me a tragic poet. You should've, and for that I think you're unbelievably restrained and (lovingly) biased.

Contents

Preface

For the longest time, I've been fascinated with the concepts of loss and nostalgia. I spent a lot of time in my adolescence with books hundreds of years old, stories woven into culture, into people, becoming someone worthy of writing my own. I grew up surrounded by literary-motivated parents and mountains of books, toiling over the written word for as long as I remember. I've always been drawn to horror, even more when life changed in my late teen years.

I won't detail any of it, but to feel trapped and consumed by something out of your own control is this all-encompassing thing. It uproots you in a way that leaves you changed forever. It was about this time that I began having nightmares where I'd wander a quiet collection of rooms until they filled with water or electrocuted me or ended me in some other form. These rooms weren't like the ones at Greystone, not quiet, but old hotels or tunnels… inherently transitory places transformed into prisons. I grew sharper, I learned how to fix elevators in these hotels, I found keys in walls, but it was never enough. Greystone ballroom came to me in a dream one night after escaping the reality of it, and I remembered dancing in it, how it felt to be free in this darkened space.

What followed was a year of prying my memory open to find the things that felt so threatening about it and still haunted me. You'll find a lot of these things on paper here as I sort through them myself, using fiction as a form of healing. It's my own journey towards dancing in that ballroom, finding the lighter spots in the darkest of human cruelty. This is not a book about what the world takes from you, but how we survive it or, at least, the ways love can grow from it.

I want to thank my own supporters, especially the inspiration for Eleanor, Valory Pierce. Without you involved in this project, and all the late night tangents about how she might take her tea, Eleanor would never have had a voice to reference dialogue from and wouldn't have had so much life breathed into her. I also can't forget the involvement of Serena, Cippy, Taylor, Sydney, and Adey for all the words of encouragement and delusions of grandeur it took to finish this and not light it on fire as soon as it hit print. Last but not least, my parents, with whom I would not have had the encouragement to actually publish.

I hope we can all take back our manors for ourselves. Paint the walls, sort the documents, but know that sometimes starting over is the best way to reclaim ourselves from the things that haunt us. You just need to close your eyes, escape the halls, and trust yourself enough to make your way back to the sunlight.

I

Part One

1

Belle Epoque

"The past is never dead. It's not even past. All of us labor in webs spun long before we were born, webs of heredity and environment, of desire and consequence, of history and eternity."
— William Faulkner (from Requiem for a Nun)

* * *

Elias preferred the evenings that demanded nothing from him.

The fire had been lit early, though the hour did not require it, and the room was already warm with the slow, indulgent heat that crept into the bones and asked nothing in return. He had removed his coat and draped it with care over the back of the chair, smoothing the velvet as if wrinkles might invite some unnamed disorder. The teapot rested nearby, steeping longer than necessary. He liked it strong, almost bitter. It reminded him that some things were meant to be endured.

Outside, London softened under fog. The windows admitted only a pale, incandescent glow that remained in the streetlamps that refused to fade into night. Elias sat with a novel open in his lap, though he had not turned the page in some time. His mind was elsewhere. The house felt too quiet. Not lonely, but quiet.

He had learned, over the years, to recognize the moments when memory waited just beyond reach, poised like a guest at the threshold. Tonight, he refused it. He lifted the cup, breathed in the steam, and let the heat scald his tongue just enough to anchor him. A soft knock sounded from the hall, familiar and restrained.

"Come in," He said, lazily, placing his cup in its saucer.

Eleanor entered without hurry, her steps measured, her presence altering the room in a way that had nothing to do with sound. She wore a gown of dove-grey wool, practical and well-cut, her gloves still on as if she did not intend to linger. Her hair was pinned neatly back, dark and glossy, not a strand out of place. She looked as she always did in the evenings: composed, thoughtful, prepared for weather that might change its mind.

"You'll ruin your tea," she commented, a playful smile at her lips. He smiled faintly, placing his cup back into its saucer.

"It's survived worse," he replied, his eyes equally playful and resigned. She crossed the room, pulling out a chair across from him and still not too close, her respectful sort of distance.

"I've had a letter from my father," she said at last. "Nothing of note. He asks after your health."

"As always."

"As always." A pause. "He hopes the winter has not unsettled you." She smirked, pulling a cup from the tray on his desk and holding it out to be filled. He graciously obliged, shutting the book into his lap and placing it beside the lamp.

"The winter and I have an unspoken understanding," he mused, pouring her a generous helping of black tea from the silver pot.

Eleanor inclined her head, as if accepting this. Her eyes moved, briefly, to the mantel — to the small, unremarkable objects arranged there. Elias followed her gaze despite himself. The memory came then, sharp and sudden.

A long corridor, sunlit and echoing. The sound of laughter, not his own, ricocheting off stone walls. A man's voice, indulgent, warning them not to run. Dust motes dancing like they had been invited. His chest felt caved in as he heard a smaller version of himself, coaxing his friend inside. It faded as suddenly as it came in, the room returning to him.

The fire cracked softly. Eleanor was watching him now, not with alarm, but with the quiet attentiveness of someone who noticed when a door had been left ajar. "You were elsewhere," she said gently.

He looked down, standing as he did so. The air hummed with the memory.

"Briefly," he said, flatly.

"I thought so." She reached for her gloves and stood, the matter settled without interrogation. "I'll have supper sent up shortly. You've a tendency to forget when you're… preoccupied."

He nodded. He was grateful, though he wasn't sure he could have placed why. As she turned to leave, Elias became acutely aware of a hollow anticipation in his chest. It wasn't urgent, but instead the sense that the world had begun to arrange around him, patient and unseen. Nothing had happened. The architecture still began to take shape around him, fragile and icy.

Elias crossed the room and nudged the fire with the poker, though it did not require tending. Sparks lifted briefly, then settled. He watched them until they vanished, counting without realizing he had begun. The clock on the mantel ticked on, undisturbed, each second falling into place with reassuring precision.

He told himself the sensation would pass. It always did. Winter had a way of pulling memories loose, as if cold stiffened the mind's joints and made it careless. He had work enough to occupy him; obligations enough to keep the hours aligned. There was no reason for old corridors to surface now, of all times.

Those firelight, hungry hollows, carried forever in their expanses. Elias, ten or eleven, his hand clasped in the sure hand of the blond beside him, his golden aura shocking in the summer sun flooding from the windows. It was violently brilliant, the way everything turned orange just before it set. The summer heat was breathless, and they glanced once at each other before bounding down the halls, all action and no forethought; how quickly childhood wonder was made sharp. The grandfather clock at the end of the hall counted their steps, falling over one another in laughter in the end.

He shook his head, ignoring the flash of fire dancing towards him in the hearth. He refused to believe it was anything but his seasonal overwork, his records and documents pulling him to madness. At times, his home was too alive with the pull of energies so beyond him it barely registered in the daylight. He had learned, over time, that most discomforts passed if you did not dignify them. He refused to, having become a scholar in this particular avoidance.

The door opened again, this time without hesitation.

Eleanor crossed the threshold with a quiet assurance. The hem of her skirt whispered against the rug as she moved, the sound precise and deliberate, a counterpoint to the fire's low crackle. She had removed her gloves somewhere between leaving and returning; her hands were bare now, pale against the darker fabric of her sleeves. She did not look at Elias at first.

Her gaze went instead to the small table by the window. The teacup sat where she had left it, steam long since vanished, the surface filmed with a thin, unbroken skin. The chair opposite remained untouched, angled slightly away as if it had been considered and dismissed. One of the lamps had not been lit; the corner of the room nearest the shelves lay in shadow, the books there half-swallowed by it. She lingered on it, not confused but instead taking log of it all.

"There's a note from your aunt," she continued, smoothing a crease from the tea towel that had not truly needed it. "Nothing of consequence. A dinner she hopes you'll attend next week. I declined on your behalf." A pause, then, "We can revisit it if you wish."

He did not answer immediately. She noticed, following his eyes to the teacup on his desk. She seemed to consider it only as far as he had, lifting it to weigh it in her hands. Then, she replaced it wordlessly, as though restoring a small imbalance to the room. She turned to Elias without concern, only assessment.

"Tomorrow," she said. "You'll have a visit with investors at ten. I'll see that the carriage is ordered early. The streets will be thick with frost." She waited just long enough for the words to land. Then she inclined her head, once, and moved back toward the door, leaving behind the faintest impression that something had been set in motion—not by urgency, but by design. Always by design.

The door shut softly behind her, the latch catching with a sound scarcely louder than a breath. The room settled in her absence, as if it had been waiting for permission to exhale. Elias remained where he was, the echo of her presence lingering in the careful order she had restored. He moved softly to the window and rested his palm on the crisp glass. Outside, the light was already thinning, the sky paling into something brittle and pale. The city went on as it always did— carriages passing, voices rising and falling, a life continuing with or without him.

2

December, 1879

It was a long, cold month in London. Elias buried himself in work, refusing to do much of anything in the winter months. They were icy and cold, and his home offered a fire and all the treats his heart could desire. He lost himself in fine teas, home-baked sweets, and an excess of Christmas gifts that no one had thought through enough for them to be heartfelt. These sorts of gifts came from obligation, not care, but he certainly never minded it. It was an odd thought, but he rather liked being ignored for his personality; he liked the surface-level sorts of sweets the holidays brought.

From time to time, his thoughts wandered — to his fiancée Eleanor, to Alaric, which he didn't know what to call, to the states of things. Elias buried himself in work, though not out of duty. The days were short, the nights unreasonably long, and the roaring fire within his home had become a fixture of safety. It was easier to drown in meaningless indulgences than to sit with his thoughts for too long.

And yet, they still wandered.

The oncoming holiday party was truly no different than

any before it, but these things always shook him. They were so lavish, yet so isolating. Every year, it was something new. He strongly remembered the year Alaric had shown up in bright red, the year he had screamed so loud at his rival he became a laughing stock for a few weeks, the time Alaric had stolen all the apple tarts and he'd thrown a fit of sorts — in his defense, they were only sixteen during that event. This was to be his first holiday party bringing his betrothed, and as to be expected, she had hardly called on him all month. That is, until the end of December.

She rushed in dressed entirely in a royal blue — a color so striking against the gray of winter that it seemed reverent. However, her expression was far more striking still. The lady looked disheveled — at least, as much as she perhaps was capable of. It was impossible for her to look too human, in a way, always slightly detached — an air of composure she refused to break. Yet... right now she was close to looking manic. She stopped before his desk, composing herself on the other side of the furniture as Elias tilted his head in concern.

Her eyes held a fervor Elias had never seen come from even her most excitable moments.

"You've always been accompanied by a servant." He remarked, his voice steady, but his mind running with a silent urgency. He couldn't think of a single precedent for this, aside from perhaps something surprising. He studied her for a sign of harm. Nothing. No visible wounds, no indications of distress aside from the wildness in her eyes. If it hadn't been danger... then what?

"I do pardon my manners, Elias," She responded, her voice breathy and pleading. "There's been a terrible accident and I'm afraid I needed to get ahead of your family regarding the news… should that be alright."

An accident?

He thought of his family, wondering who it had been and what the severity of it was. It could be his uncle; the old curmudgeon was pushing seventy and frequently refused help in his house maintenance. If not him, likely his mother, who did nothing but crochet and stare out the window in melancholy for some undisclosed reason. Perhaps his grandfather, who locked himself in his study many years ago and wasn't seen frequently anywhere else. So much of his family was cagey and suspicious about most things that it could truly be just about anyone.

"So… who?" Elias said aloud, his thoughts spilling aloud.

Eleanor sighed and allowed herself to relax slightly, hanging her head. Her fingers laced with the wrinkles of her skirt at her hip, tangling as if she needed something tangible to hold onto, knowing Elias would provide no such comfort.

Then, finally, she looked at him. Her voice, when it came, was small.

"You."

The word landed between them, hollow, final.

It didn't make sense.

This was a joke. It had to be. He was in no danger.

His mind searched for an answer — his childhood rival's face, Alaric, his childhood, his dealings of all kinds. He was an honest man. He swore it.

Yet Eleanor's face remained unreadable, her knuckles white where they clutched her fabrics.

"What?" He murmured, his voice barely above a whisper.

As if saying it again would make it any less absurd. What on earth had he done to find himself in immediate danger.

"Lord Edwin Greystone has passed. He's left his manor to Alaric, naturally, and… well, you. You are to both leave home immediately and live there for a full year, and… something was said about clearing your name of greed should you succeed. Though, Elias, I never found you to be greedy. I know what they say of you, but I—"

She faltered, her fingers gripping the folds of her skirt, as if searching for the words to say. Elias barely heard them.

"Enough." Elias retorted, his voice sharp but unsteady as it cut through the air between them. His head had fallen into his hands, his fingers pressed into his temples.

Greystone. Of course it was Edwin Greystone. The manor had been lurking at the edges of his life for years, always threatening to reappear. And now by some cruel joke, it had claimed him too.

A breath of incredulous laughter escaped him, muffled by his palms.

"So that's it, then? I play house with Alaric for a year and suddenly I'm a good man again?"

Eleanor was meek but sure as she spoke. "You know it was never about the truth, Elias."

And that much he did know. He had stolen, supposedly, from Alaric in their childhood, though no one could agree on exactly what had happened. All Elias remembered clearly was the day a small snuffbox appeared quietly among his things, a weighted accusation he never fully understood but could never forget. The flash of shock, then disappointment, then anger and heartbreak as Edwin cast him from the manor. The way the summers ended there ensured he was never welcomed back, and the bitterness of it had remained on Alaric's tongue, assuming all Elias wanted was the legacy he desperately clung to.

The Thornes bore their burdens heavily, but the Greystones carried a different kind of weight, one of honor and expectation, whispered of even in the darkest corners of London. Elias's mother had grown pale with melancholy, her smiles rare and fleeting. His father was a shadow of a man, broken and destitute after a reckoning with the Greystone legacy. His grandfather, once strong and proud, had slipped into madness and suspicion, haunted by ghosts no one else could see. And Greystone, the distant lord, remained an untouchable enigma, a storm cloud that neither helped nor hindered but always loomed.

For Elias, the name was both a prison and a promise. He had fought with every ounce of himself to reclaim his place, to prove that he was more than a pawn in a family's long, bitter game. But no matter how fiercely he struggled, the past clung to him like a second skin, a shadow he could neither outrun nor shed.

The manor, once a sanctuary in his childhood, a place where he dreamed of belonging and becoming something more, had become a cold reminder of what he had lost. Worthiness, recognition, even love, all seemed just out of reach, slipping away like smoke through his fingers. And beneath his carefully composed exterior, Elias carried a quiet, burning ache.

And people were certain he must have been guilty of something for it all to collapse.

His fingers curled into his palms. "And if I refuse?"

Eleanor hesitated. Then, carefully, "Then you will never be free of it."

Of course. That was the only possible answer.

The weight of Greystone was already settling over him, and

he had yet not left his chair.

Elias could do nothing but stare at his betrothed, the weight of her words pressing against his chest and the silence suffocating them both. The fire in the hearth crackled, though the warmth did not reach him. The room felt far bigger than it really was, bending in all sorts of impractical ways. He could feel the pull of the manor even from here, threatening him as if it were a rain cloud past the mountains on a clear summer's day. Struggling to compose himself, he took a deep breath and desperately attempted to ground himself in the present.

He wanted to argue, deny any hold the legacy of either family had on him. Even moreso, he wanted to denounce the role Edwin had cast him in. A sad clown on a stage, a tool in a generations—long rivalry, and now a pawn who once believed the hatchet was buried with every party, every charity, every goddamn public chess move. No, it had always followed him, waiting for the right moment to claim him too. As a Thorne, it was his fate that he had truly, truly thought he could trade and deal and schmooze his way out of.

The lady watched him carefully, her fingers still twisting the fabric of her skirt. Equally crestfallen, her voice was softer now, a warning rather than a plea.

"You know what they'll say if you refuse." She spoke, her voice hardly audible. There was something almost pitiful in her expression.

He knew. And then, a foreboding thought threatened him.

Alaric will be waiting for him. The thought tightened around his ribs like a vice. He pictured the blond at the front entrance, laughing at him. He would be boastful and obnoxious as ever, and unrealistically beautiful, and it would consume him with rage. Or worse— he would be indifferent, as if he knew all along that Greystone was the shadow cast eternally over the Thorne legacy. He ran his hands through his hair, as if to pull off some of the weight pressing down on him. He knew, even before he spoke, that there was no true choice.

"Fine." The word tasted bitter, final.

Lady Draven nodded once, but did not look relieved. It was as if she understood without speaking a word.

"You should leave soon." The words carried an urgency she did not elaborate on as she spoke. It was the most serious and least anxious he'd ever seen his betrothed. She knew.

He looked past her, then turned to look out the window. The night air stretched beyond the glass and straight on to Greystone Manor. It was almost as if he could hear it growl in the dark. He wondered if it was Alaric pulling him into his fate, or if it was simply destiny. It hardly mattered.

The fire crackled. The flames licked the logs, desperate to burn, but it suddenly felt very, very cold.

* * *

Across town, Alaric was awoken by the sound of knocking.

He groaned, rolling over in his sheets, tangled in the feeling of silk and smelling of perfume. Not his own, of course. Never his own. The knocking came again, more insistent now. He squinted at the clock — far too late for visitors.

"Go away" he called, his voice coated with the gruffness of sleep. The knocking did not stop.

His stomach twisted. That kind of knocking only came from the kinds of people he had no desire to meet.

Ever curious, however, he forced himself out of his bed, pushing a hand through his blond hair, still tangled with product from the day before. The cold from the floor on his bare feet shocked him awake as he lumbered to the door. He flung it open, annoyed.

And then he saw her.

His mother stood before him in the hallway wrapped in a dark robe over a darker still nightdress. Her posture was perfectly straight — but her eyes were red. Alaric's words died in his throat. She did not cry — ever. Or at least, as long as he could remember. Something was terribly wrong.

"Mother," He said slowly, cautious, "I—"

She said not a word, but held out a letter to him. It was hardly ornate, sent in urgency and obligation. He was used to stationary and ornate wax seals, but this had nothing of the sort — just his own name on the front and a broken, nondescript wax seal.

Alaric hesitated before taking it. The paper was heavy in his hands, dripping with something.. .foreboding, almost. He wasn't sure, but it felt wrong somehow. His gaze flickered up at his mother, but she said nothing, just waited. He took the paper from its envelope, scanning it.

Lord Edwin Greystone. Dead.

And then, an obligation.

"Oh, you're joking." He glanced up, a dry, humorless laugh leaving his lips. "Tell me you're joking."

His mother did not smile. Not even a twitch from her stoic face.

"Why the hell would he leave me anything?" His voice came out irritated and louder than he meant it to. "He barely spoke to me after that day with the Thorne kid."

A pregnant pause stretched between them.

"It was not a request, Alaric." His mother said curtly. Oh, she was serious. He hated the way she said it.

He shifted, running a hand through his hair uncomfortably. "No, no, no, this— this doesn't make any sense. Edwin practically abandoned me. Barely tolerated me. And now he's leaving me a house?"

"It is not just a house." She added, quiet.

"What else, then?"

"It's a chance to earn your place in our lineage. You're only Greystone because of my brother's generosity."

Alaric went quiet. One of the great mysteries of his life was his parentage; it had always only been his mother and himself, her obsession with their legacy, and Edwin keeping all her secrets.

"And," she began, "You are not the only heir."

He blinked. His pulse quickened. His blood ran hot. A terrible pit formed in his stomach.

"Then who?" He asked, though he already knew. He searched his mother's eyes for anything that could betray the reality of it. There was nothing. He was certain before she opened her mouth and the second she met his gaze.

"Elias."

The silence that fell between them was heavier than the snow outside. It was too thick, too final. He knew it was his turn to speak, but the chill that ran down the back of his neck made that difficult. Somewhere in the room behind him, a candle flickered.

His mother did not move.

For the first time in years, Alaric had nothing to say.

He glanced down at the letter in his hands, a cold sheet of

finality. When he glanced back up, his mother had disappeared as if she had never been there at all. Though the door to his room was still wide open and her words hung heavy in the air, she had indeed slipped into the night. Alaric was left alone with this reality. Though there was no hint of a breeze or a draft, the candle on his desk snuffed out behind him. He ignored it.

He turned, letting out a sharp exhale as he shut the door to his bedroom. Climbing into bed once more, he turned the letter over in his hands absentmindedly, tracing the edges in his fingers. As he ran his hands over the letter once more, it seemed unreasonably warm in his hands. It felt as though it had been written only this hour, and he had no answers for the way the ink even appeared to shine in the candlelight as if still wet.

More than anything, he was caught in a moment that held stale in the air. His mouth began to taste of copper — the way it would if he had bitten his lip, but there wasn't a trace of blood. Or of biting.

A stillness settled over him — not the quiet of sleep, but the kind that holds just before something shifts. The calm before the storm.

Elias.

He understood that part. He had always hoped Elias would one day escape him. Yet their families had always been entwined, their stories written in the same ink, bound by things older than the both of them. He had known Elias' mother before grief hollowed out her face, and had seen his father as madness took him. He had watched as the shadow of Greystone drew in the Thornes — until it had simply swallowed them whole, like a beast.

It had never been a fate he had wished on Elias.

He sometimes imagined them in another world, one where history had no claim over either of them. But history was relentless.

Alaric was a Greystone. Elias was a Thorne. And that seemed to mean something.

Elias.

The name echoed in his head, not in his mother's voice, not in his own, but in a much younger one. It was edged with laughter and echoed in the halls.

The manor's corridors had seemed so vast then — so winding and gilded, filled with shadows that never introduced themselves as he and Elias tore through the halls. The two of them had made worlds of it. Edwin, their elder, led them through hidden doors and passageways they'd never find on their own. Elias, wide-eyed and eager, trusted the Greystones to lead him where he was not yet confident enough to go.

Alaric hadn't thought about those summers in years.

The memory flickered with the candlelight, warm at the edges but threatening to burn him if he were too close. He could still see Edwin, taller than them both and wise, eyes almost too knowing even for his mid age. Edwin had all these stories about Greystone Manor. He had once told them then that the house had a heartbeat—that it had a memory.

Alaric had scoffed then, but Elias—Elias had believed.

He shut his eyes, setting the letter in his lap and pressing his fingers to his temples until the memory blurred. Edwin was dead. Yet even now, it was as if he could hear him calling from the manor all across London.

The night passed too slowly for comfort after that. He supposed at one point that he had fallen asleep, but he could not place when or how. What he did know is that when he woke up, the letter was no longer in his lap but instead on the nightstand, and that the dawn had already broken hours before. The day felt different somehow, almost as if the air were stagnant, as if the day were waiting with an open maw to consume.

Peering out of eyes still full of sleep, he noticed the light shine on the letter from the night before, still present as if written only a few minutes ago. It disturbed him, to say the least. Before he could process this fully or even fully wake up, a knock at the door shook him. This knock was normal, poised, in proper time; a bit of routine.

"Come in.." He grumbled, suspicious but longing for some normalcy. In walked a servant, small and wrapped in the hush of morning, with a silver tray of tea and a damp towel. She set it softly onto his nightstand to accompany the letter with little fanfare, perhaps less than felt appropriate. She never hesitated in her work, which he found comfort in—consistency in a world that had begun unraveling. "Good morning, Susie." He added with a small smile, as if greeting a childhood friend.

"Good morning, master." She replied, curt and serious but never unkind.

Her mouse brown hair was tied back in a braid in the back of her head, carefully lifted from her face. She was dressed as well as any household member, clean in clothing free of wrinkles or marks. She bowed before she spoke. "The morning's tea is Earl Grey, accompanied by a dash of cream and sugar to your taste. Please take it at your leisure. Today, you will join your mother at breakfast, followed by a meeting with the estate regarding the Greystone Manor…" a pause. "My condolences, master." She added, too quickly, as if hurrying past something she wished she hadn't had to say at all.

Alaric stiffened. Greystone. His last name had begun feeling like ink spilled on a page, dark and irreversible. The tea's steam curled into the air, warm and fragrant, but the weight in his chest did not lift. It felt as if the manor had been watching him sleep.

Feeling suddenly a bit lightheaded, he leaned forward, placing his fingers to his temples. "Yes, I… suppose the matter should be dealt with." The words felt foreign and far, as if spoken by another. He lifted his gaze to Susie, seeking anything that might anchor him. "I don't suppose you know anything more than we did last night, do you?"

Susie hesitated, the barest flicker of uncertainty crossing her face.

"I know very little, master. I'd bargain less than you've heard. I am not family, after all." She offered, failing to comfort him in doing so. Alaric studied her — the slight shift in her stance, the way her hands were clasped together just a little tighter than usual. Something was off.

"Maybe, but if you told me the opposite, I would be far from surprised." He mused, reaching for his tea. It was a welcome normal moment in an array of strange ones. The tea settled on his tongue, the warmth soothing him in any way it could. Everything was so ordinary and yet he couldn't shake the feeling that something was changed forever. His grip tightened on the porcelain handle, threatening to crack the cup.

"Thank you, Susie." He forced an exhale. "You're dismissed."

The woman nodded, bowing before making haste towards the direction of the kitchen.

And just like that, he was alone. His mouth tasted of copper again, despite the Assam. It couldn't cover up the taste of Greystone Manor.

After composing himself enough to face reality, Alaric descended the grand staircase. His footsteps echoed in the vastness of the house, hollow. Morning light poured through the tall windows and onto his skin, casting everything in an almost ethereal glow. The house was quiet, but in a way that felt composed, rather than peaceful. An imposed silence took over, rather than a natural one, one he had never known.

The main dining room had already been set. Silverware gleamed. Crystal glittered. A fresh arrangement of flowers sat at the center of the dining table, their fragrance fleeting and delicate. At the head of the table was his mother, straight backed as ever and dressed in soft grays that spoke of neither mourning or indifference but something in—between. Her expression was unreadable as she lifted a porcelain teacup to her lips.

"Sit." She ordered, without looking up.

Alaric slid into his chair, watching as a servant placed a plate in front of him. Eggs over easy, toast, and a single cut of ham — his usual, though he doubted she ordered it out of sentimentality or anything of the sort.

"I trust you slept well." His mother continued, no ounce of concern behind her words.

"As well as one does after receiving a letter from the dead." He muttered, reaching for his tea.

His mother sighed, a small, measured thing, before placing her cup back on its saucer. It made no sound as she did so. "Mind your dramatics. We have much to discuss."

A familiar irritation fluttered in his chest. She always did this — treated emotions as if they were things to be tidied, rather than things to be cared for. She spoke as if it were vulgar to react to death in a normal, human manner. Alaric set down his tea with an unnecessary, much louder, clink.

"Why did he name me in the will?" He demanded. The air grew heavier with the question. She didn't flinch. She simply buttered her toast with careful, even, measured strokes.

"You know as much as I do."

He scoffed. "That would be a first."

Her gaze flickered up, sharp as a knife. "Do not be petulant. We are Greystones. We handle matters as they come."

Something about her measured response made his stomach twist. He had always suspected she knew more about Edwin than she let on, more about that manor.

"Then tell me, Mother dearest," he mocked, much to her annoyance, "what, exactly, are we handling?"

She studied him for a moment before speaking. "You are expected at Greystone Manor within the following month." She said, voice smooth as ever. "And so is Elias Thorne."

Alaric's grip on his teacup tightened along with his chest. There it was again. Elias. His mother took another sip of her tea as if the world was not shifting around him.

"It is time you made peace with the past, Alaric." She added, betraying the only ounce of sentiment she had shown all year. Though the words were heavy, she said them so easily, as if advising him to brush his teeth more thoroughly or eat more vegetables. She spoke as if it were a fact of life that he would end up there eventually. Perhaps that was true. Alaric's eyes shifted to his tea, examining his reflection as if trying to memorize his own face before he would be changed by whatever the manor had in store.

* * *

The morning found Elias sitting rigid in the armchair by his window, watching as the sunlight bled over the rooftops. He had not slept. The letter sat on the table beside him, its wax seal broken but its presence far more heavy in the air. Lord Edwin Greystone. Dead. His fingers tapped absentmindedly on the armrest, his body utterly still but his mind anything but. The manor would want him back now. Of course, it did. The thought crept in, unwelcome and inescapable. It was something one never truly left behind. It waited, patient, knowing those bound to it would one day return. And now it had called for him.

The knock on his door was soft, but insistent as it woke him from his trance. He did not answer at first, staring at the flickering candlelight that threatened to go out by the door. He already knew who it would be. He knew before he even rose from his chair. Before he crossed the room with slow, measured steps. Before he opened the door.

His mother stood at the door to his office, dressed in a dark gown that pooled at her feet like ink. She looked smaller than he remembered — frailer, even — but her eyes were distant and unreadable and held all her weight. In her hands, she clutched a letter, already unsealed as if she had debated reading the contents herself. She did not greet him. She did not explain. She simply held the letter out to him.

Elias grasped it, the paper feeling heavy as it brushed his fingers. He glanced up at her, expecting… something — an explanation, a warning, anything. She only watched him, tired and distant, as she often did. It was as if she had seen this moment before. Finally, she spoke, breaking the silence.

"Read it." She commanded, soft but firm.

Elias walked with it into the room, his fingers lingering around the edge of the envelope as his mother followed silently. He felt the paper grow warmer as he lifted it from its confines, reading it and seeing it confirmed. Lord Edwin really was dead. Greystone manor really was in his hands, with a terrible catch. It really was all his responsibility. His eyes narrowed.

"You knew." He said quietly, turning to study the sharp lines of his mother's face. She inhaled, slow and steady.

"I suspected." She admitted, soft and quiet but never meek. Something in the way she said it made Elias feel ill. She had expected this all along. She had been waiting for it. He exhaled sharply, folding the letter back up and tossing it onto his desk.

"And now?"

Her eyes met his. "Now, you go back, Elias."

He did not immediately respond, instead walking to the letter and lifting it once more. His eyes scanned for anything that might make this all go away. He hoped the ink would shift beneath his gaze, that it might change.

His mother watched him for a long moment, lingering by the door. It was as though she were soaking in the moment with him, however cold it felt. Somehow, it felt final when she turned and began to disappear down the hall, saying something so barely audible that it nearly disappeared into the air between them.

"Be careful."

Elias did not ask why. He knew she would not tell him.

* * *

25

The chapel smelled faintly of cold stone and lingering incense, the air thick with unsaid things. Elias sat stiffly in the polished pew, fingers pressed tight against the wood, as if gripping it might anchor him against the currents swirling beneath the surface of this quiet room. Morning light filtered in, fractured through stained glass— reds and purples pooling unevenly at his feet. The colors felt like bruises, sharp and unsettling.

Ahead, the coffin rested, black and final. The minister's voice was steady and low, reciting prayers that seemed to wash over the procession in a way they didn't for Elias. As he glanced over to Eleanor beside him, her eyes remained fixed and somber, but she did not cry alongside the other women in the room. Every now and then, she would swallow and her gaze would slip briefly to her hands, but not once did she bring the handkerchief in her lap to her eyes; it appeared to be merely for show.

Alaric sat several rows away, shoulders squared, jaw tight— his posture the very image of control. Elias resisted the urge to look, but the tension between them was a tangible thing, a current humming just beneath the surface of this muted space. When he did finally look at the other man, he found himself stilled by the sight. Where one normally found life and brightness in the curve of his jaw, the curl of his honey-colored hair, there was now a perceivable dullness. Peeking out of his coat pocket, a monogrammed handkerchief, pressed flat.

He thought of the letter; they both carried the same cruel summons. The will. The inheritance that would unravel everything.

Elias felt the weight of it press into his ribs and swirl the muscle there like a worm. The moment was closing in on them, shrinking the air until all that remained was the slow, steady ticking of the clock in the back of the church. Somewhere deep beneath the cool calm, Elias knew they were tethered to each other in ways they refused to acknowledge. The same storm gathered just beyond the chapel doors.

The prayers ended. A hush fell, heavier now, like the calm before a tempest. The mourners rose slowly, their movements stiff and careful. He remained seated for a moment longer, chest tight with a feeling other than just grief. Elias's gaze flicked involuntarily toward Alaric as he passed, earning the slightest tightening around his eyes. Their eyes met for a fraction of a second, a flash of something fierce and fragile passing between them, and then he lost the other in the procession, his golden head disappearing into a throng of family members.

The heavy doors creaked open to an unforgiving, cold English morning. Damp fog clung to the cemetery grounds, curling in a slow, spectral spiral. The air smelled of wet earth and decayed leaves, familiar and suffocating. The hearse greeted them, and two mourners' deep black cloaks danced in the wind as they lifted the coffin into its unforgiving shape. The chill outside seemed to seep into bones, his own breath spinning a horrifying waltz in the winter air. Eleanor joined him then, only paces behind, her arm slipping in the crook of Elias' with not a single word between them. He gave her a rather sullen smile, unsure if her presence was a comfort or simply another thing to account for.

The procession began its slow march forward, a long line of black and gray weaving through the crumbling path between crooked gravestones and tangled undergrowth. Elias's footsteps echoed unevenly on the dirt beneath him, his breath shallow and uneven. Alaric was still close, his presence like a shadow on a storming night. They moved within the crowd as two parts of a fractured whole, each tied to their respective family lines.

Elias' mother remained at the back of the parade, her perpetual mourning black adorned on this day as well. He couldn't help but think that it suited her, as she linked her arm uncertainly with his father, whose own state prevented him from keeping up without the help. His gaze was miles away, and he hadn't said a word to Elias since he arrived; Elias wasn't certain that the man was lucid enough anymore to do so. He only knew that when he was a boy, Edwin had been the closest thing his father had to a best friend, but since his mind began to fracture, the two stopped writing. Eventually his father became simply a body without a soul. He wondered if his father even recognized Edwin's death as a reality.

Every step felt heavier, weighted with years of bitterness and unspoken history. His gaze locked forward, trying to ignore the tight coil in his chest and the heat of Alaric's eyes burning beside him.

The grave yawned before them after some time, an abyss threatening to swallow the morning light. As the coffin was lowered, he could feel the weight of it pressing on his chest, heavy with the reality of it.

Mourners shoveled dirt onto the coffin, its hopeful mahogany glimmer slowly dulling as shovelful after shovelful combined. He watched his father's hands idly strike earth, carelessly throwing it onto his own confidante. Death struck Elias as a cruel reality, but he'd never been so close to it before. Somewhere between the icy English winter and Eleanor's still unfamiliar hand on his elbow, his anxieties turned to confusion, then grief. Those summers in Greystone Manor and his once idol, both lied compacted under worms and roots — forever. His hands clenched, nails biting into his palms. Somewhere from behind his shoulder, a woman's choking sob hidden in her gloves could be heard.

Then, Alaric again, more to himself than anyone else. "Not done with us yet, huh?"

Elias hated how his body responded, with a flicker of recognition, of shared dread, like two boys hiding in a dark corridor again. The words churned in Elias's gut, twisting painfully. Grief and fear were indistinguishable to him; both tasted metallic, both clawed up his throat the way his father's madness had clawed into him as a child. He swallowed hard, bile and sour acid burning his throat, his mouth suddenly dry and metallic.

The mourners began to drift toward the church once more, their footsteps muted on the damp grass. Elias stayed rooted a moment longer, stomach still churning, the bitter taste of bile still heavy at the back of his throat. He caught one last glance of Alaric's frame, his shadow drifting towards the church's distant light like a ghost.

Inside, the muted clamor of voices awaited. Soft condolences and the polite hum of restrained grief clung to the walls, foreign chatter as Elias lumbered through it. The heaviness in his chest had settled into a cold knot, and the nausea had not subsided, clipping his responses and coloring his attitude. Eleanor had followed him in quietly, but chose this moment to make her presence insistent once more, unlinking her arm from his elbow to reach for a glass of champagne. She handed one to Elias, who merely watched the bubbles play in the light, as if they'd also do something unexpected.

Her voice, when it came, came low and firm. "Elias, I think it's time you consider that you shouldn't handle this alone."

Elias' eyes flickered up from the glass, meeting hers with an urgent disapproval. "Eleanor, you can't." He felt his stomach twist again.

She held his gaze, calm but unyielding. "I'm not asking. I'm telling you." She paused, letting him connect the unholy pieces on his own before, "I am coming with you."

He looked away, fingers tightening around the stem of the glass, knuckles pale. The room seemed to tilt slightly, and the weight in his chest grew heavier. "Greystone manor is not a place for you." *It isn't a place for me, either.* She set down her glass with a quiet clink as his breath shallowed.

Her eyes softened, but she did not back down. "I know you. You'll shut yourself in some corner and forget the world. I'd rather not receive the news of it secondhand." She paused, her gloved hand finding Elias' own — shaking, cold. Her brow furrowed briefly at the observation, but she didn't comment on it. Instead, "I'm not going for the house. I'm going for you. You can glower about it all you like, but I'll be there."

Elias studied her as their hands clasped — her quiet resolve, the set of her mouth. It unnerved him; he couldn't name why. "You don't know what it's like," he said finally. "It's—"

"What? Haunted?" she asked, dryly. "I thought you didn't believe in such things."

He hesitated. "I don't."

"Then it's only dust and memory and obligation, and I've lived with worse." She said, firm.

After a long while, she said quietly, "You don't have to like that I'm coming. But you should know I'm not going to be left behind."

Elias did not respond, simply nodding.

The rest of the morning was a blur of handshakes and trying his best not to vomit. Eleanor left first, her carriage door closing with a finality and speeding away too quickly. Alaric disappeared in the crowd, and he was left alone too soon. His mother attempted to straighten his coat out and reassure him as she said goodbye, but he couldn't help but try to unsuccessfully make final desperate eye contact with his father, begging for any reaction that might show him the man was still real. When he did, there wasn't anything behind his eyes but that same vacancy that haunted him since his own childhood. They climbed into their own carriages, disappearing into fog and lamplight down the path. He stood a while longer by the curb, his breath ghosting in the air. When his own carriage arrived, he climbed in without a word.

The ride home was silent but for the wheels on cobblestone. London passed by in faint smears of gold and gray, the fog dampening the city's pulse. Elias sat rigid, hands folded in his lap. Across from him, the empty seat reflected dimly in the window. In it, for one disoriented heartbeat, he caught a faint flash of golden hair. Then, as quickly as it had appeared, it was gone. He leaned his head back against the cushion, closing his eyes, drifting into something that wasn't quite sleep or thought.

Tomorrow, the solicitors would expect their signatures. After that, the manor.

He exhaled, long and quiet. The carriage turned a corner, vanishing into fog.

3

January,1880

Brown, thick mud crawled up the hem of Elias Thorne's velvet overcoat, a vulgar reminder that even New Years' cheer could not shield one from the indignities of London — or from Lord Alaric Greystone. The two stood at the edge of the festivities exchanging insults in place of gifts, their usual holiday tradition. Once, people had watched them for a very different reason — two boys glued together by summer mischief, too young to understand the fault line growing between them. Now, while Elias threw insults at Alaric, the taller man sipped a red wine with an enraging smirk on his face, admiring the distinct splatter of filth on the other's clothing as if it were paint. Onlookers, unfortunately, knew this would go on for a while and left the noblemen to it, unsure if any of it was intentional or simply a happy accident.

Every event was the same in this manner. Since adolescence, the two men had endlessly bickered while the room watched the drama unfold as entertainment. Their stature and their reputations had changed over time, but notably not their bitterness towards one another. Alaric and Elias were entertainment of their own, to everyone but perhaps the more recent addition of Lady Eleanor Draven, dutifully in tow with the Thorne man and never betraying a single word of insight. The three were simply a facet of London's messier nobility. Eleanor watched in horror from the other side of the room, awaiting the end of the argument that continued in vain.

Both were men of a younger twenty-three, each holding a particular degree of sway outside of this very room. Elias Thorne, despite his vulgarity around his unwilling companion, was the more mature and stoic of the two. His hair was the color of autumn leaves in November, catching warmth in the light but giving way to shadow. His eyes followed suit, holding restrained, though unmistakable intensity. He remained steady, even now — restrained intensity behind every breath. His presence made one feel seen-through, but not understood, betraying little of his own thoughts for the world to analyze itself. It was clear that his mind was simply always at work, for better or for worse.

Elias' hands, though unnervingly still, occasionally clenched at his sides. It was the tell he hated most — the little twitch that revealed he was losing his grip on composure. Alaric always noticed it. Of course he did.

Alaric Greystone stood beside him, half listening and half sipping wine with a smug smile on his youthful lips. His sun-kissed blond hair fell in unruly waves, catching light from the chandelier that made it look almost too bright, too alive. Every moment was a performance for him, especially apparent in the manner of dress he'd chosen for himself with an array of luxurious fabrics and bold colors. His glacial blue eyes seemed to always sparkle with mischief, constantly shifting as if he was always looking for his next scandal. Alaric boasted a certain feminine charm, betraying an air of confidence that bordered on playful arrogance, thriving both on attention and subversion. Every fold of silk and every dramatic flourish was intentional — armor stitched from color and spectacle.

His energy was equal parts infectious and sharp — an underlying awareness that gave way to a certain complexity that he shrugged off frequently. Alaric's laughter was often too loud, as if created from bells. His icy eyes never focused on Elias for long — always flitting, like a butterfly unwilling to rest. When they did, there was a flash of something unreadable, bordering on curiosity, rather than rage or even annoyance.

Eleanor Draven, though removed, watched the two men bicker while occasionally staring into her small plate of macrons as she traced the ornate rim. It was as if she wished she could disappear into the sweetness, though her gaze never met either fully. She watched them with the quiet resignation of someone who had long realized that being loved by Elias meant being tolerated by his ghosts.

Having been engaged to Thorne for over a year, it was hardly anything new and her expression was hardly that of a bride-to-be. Her cool brown eyes were rounded like a child's, despite being of a respectable age of twenty-one, and held no malice. However, they betrayed a certain depth to them — something unspoken, a quiet longing for a life that might have been and perhaps could never be. She shifted uncomfortably, her ethereal pastel ballgown catching the light of the room and shimmering, making her appear nearly angelic. She was a reserved, graceful woman, a perfect match for the somber Elias, and yet seemed entirely removed from him as she simply observed the party. It was as if she were waiting for someone or something to draw her in.

Tonight, she had tied her deep black hair into an understated style, her heart-shaped face impossibly pale and soft lips curved into a shape that never quite reached a smile. Any emotion that did betray her was covert, a perpetually distant ghost in her own life even as the rustling of her gown suggested that she was, in fact, still alive.

As onlookers avoided the scene, the ever-blunt Elias chewed into Alaric with a force unseen to any of his company. The taller man betrayed no sign of annoyance, laughing off a rather cutting remark to request a refill of his drink. Confidently, he strode behind the array of sweets and succulent meats to the door of the terrace, presumably to get some distance and some fresh air. Elias followed with naught more than an eye roll and other soft, chiding remarks. Eleanor turned, her dress rustling as she took a seat on the edge of the expansive ballroom.

The air outside was frigid, betraying a cold known only to Englishmen without any warmth in their own hearts. Alaric, warmed by his light drunkenness, leaned casually on the railing and gazed into the expanse of the night. It was snowing this night, the soft flakes landing on the stone surface of the terrace and casting a sort of light of their own onto it. The night sky above them was devoid of stars, leaving only fluffy clouds that could do naught more but deliver cold to the two men. As both men stepped out into the night, the air chilled them, causing Alaric to pull his overcoat into his chest tighter and Elias to shiver slightly, the most reaction he had shown in ages. Alaric swirled his wine in his overfilled glass, admiring its color before smiling down his nose at the approaching Elias.

"You show me so much passion, old friend" He offered

languidly, bringing the glass toward his lips.

Elias sneered, his face retracting in part due to the temperature and in part due to the comment.

"One would be gravely mistaken. You insist upon making my life difficult." He remarked. He stood rigidly in the December cold, his muddied overcoat offering far less warmth than he'd hoped. He gazed upon the blond, his confident stature and intense eyes staring right back at him. Despite the frigid air, the two were locked in this moment with one another as the party continued behind them both. The raucous sound of joy and holiday cheer offset the dark, tense confrontation on its fringes.

Alaric snickered, turning to gaze out towards the falling snow. How peaceful the scene was, and how calm the falling snow made the courtyard. It made the night air practically silent as the tension cut through with its sudden noise.

"I insist upon nothing, aside perhaps enjoying my evening." The blond replied, swishing his wine audibly in its ornate glass. "I had come here hoping to perhaps share a dance with a beautiful woman, maybe fill myself with sweets, maybe even have a conversation with an old friend." He elaborated, turning his head to look back towards his companion and quickly roll his eyes. "You are, in fact, none of those things. Actually, I think you must be the furthest thing from a sweet that I can picture. You're all bones and look like you might taste more akin to dust." He added with another infuriating snicker.

Elias balked, his fists close to his sides, uttered briefly speechless at the other man's audacity.

"I abhor you." He uttered, in a tone angrier than any he would speak in wider company.

"Oh, I'm aware." Alaric stepped closer, carrying impossible warmth beneath his coat. "If only your engagement brought you this much passion. Poor Lady Draven, forced to endure your silences while you pour all of your energy into me." Alaric uttered without missing a beat, taking another nonchalant sip of his wine, red as blood.

Elias tore through with anger, alight with rage that bubbled under the surface. He could think of a million ways to respond, but none of them felt right. Poor Lady Draven? He scoffed internally, as if the man could understand the burden of duty that bound them. The man poured every moment of spare time he had on Lady Draven. They were betrothed on duty alone, perhaps, but he did everything possible to make himself the picture of a decent future husband for her. She was simply prone to melancholy, he convinced himself, and none of his gifts or letters could cheer her in these colder seasons. She had talked endlessly about this party since the harvest season; of course he had nothing to do with her current mood. At least, he could convince himself of this, which justified his following his rival around the party, something he could admit was bordering on obsession.. Meanwhile, Eleanor was left all on her own while her betrothed pursued this distraction. He couldn't help but to think, begrudgingly, Alaric may have a point. He could never admit that aloud.

Elias finally broke the silence, his voice sharp and cutting. "And what would you know of duty? Of commitment? Perhaps passion — you flit from one meaningless indulgence to another."

Alaric's lips curved into a sly, seductive smile. "Meaningless, is it?" He remarked, his smile absolutely maddening. "Here you are, trailing after me like a shadow. Tell me, what does that make you, then?"

Elias stiffened, his fists curling at his sides, untwisting to brush the comfort of the velvet there to self-soothe. "It makes me a man bound by honor and obligations you could never begin to understand."

The taller man laughed, low and rich, and stepped towards his rival, his wine glass sloshing as he did so. "Obligations. Honor. Such charming words for your shackles that you willingly wear. Tell me. Does Lady Draven know that she's just another link in your chain?"

"That's enough." Elias snapped, his voice low and growling. "You do not get to speak about her."

"Why not?" The blond toyed, Elias his prey. "Because it's the truth? Because it stings? Or simply because it's easier to blame her for your misery than to admit your pursuits are no more meaningful than mine?"

Elias' breath hitched in his throat. He turned sharply, eyes on the falling snow. "You're insufferable." He said, his voice barely audible over the freezing wind.

"And yet," Alaric began, stepping beside him and allowing their shoulders to nearly brush. The tension between them crackled with electricity. "You can't seem to walk away."

With that, the blond attempted to continue his step, only to be caught by Elias' hand on his upper arm. He wasn't entirely sure what compelled him to do it, aside from a desperate need to trap him in his storm. As if by the hand of karma itself, his blood red wine sloshed violently all over his chest. It stained the white of his undershirt with its deep red color, narrowly missing the rest of his clothing. The liquid clung to the ensemble like a spreading wound, the contrast stark and damning.

Elias froze for a fraction of a second, his hand still clutching his rival's arm. He hadn't expected his own hand to betray him. He was stalled too by the sudden, desperate grip as if pulling Alaric back might also pull himself back from unraveling. He could feel the heat building beneath his collar as the wine soaked through Alaric's overcoat. A pulse of unwanted familiarity rang between them as their gaze caught.

Whether thankfully or otherwise, there was little of it left in the glass and what had been in the goblet was now decorating his clean appearance. To Elias' dismay and shock, the other man laughed through his nose, dropping his face to the snowy ground and pushed back a strand of golden locks over his own ear as if to compose himself.

"Well," he drawled, his voice rich with irony. "It seems I've become a canvas for your frustrations." Alaric remarked, almost amused. "How very fitting."

Elias expected anger. He almost wanted it. Instead, Alaric placed a steadying hand over his own wine-soaked chest. "I'll tell them it was my fault." He leaned in just enough for his breath to ghost Elias's cheek. "We both know your desperation is saved only for me."

The blond strode back into the party, met by a few gasps immediately and raucous laughter as he explained. He shrugged it off so wonderfully, Elias thought, as he looked down to his own hands. He had hated those hands since he was a boy. They were too eager, too clumsy, too honest. They gave him away every time. Alaric had once held those same hands steady in a dark hallway when Elias was crying over a nightmare. Now they trembled for entirely different reasons.

With a dismissive wave of his hand and a self-deprecating remark or two, he had the crowd under his spell. He wore the humiliation like a badge of honor, firmly affixed to his chest. Elias could see how the room bent towards him with a magnetic charm that made him seem untouchable.

He was still lightly shaking from the cold and something untraceable. What had possessed him to grab the man in the first place? Was it rage? His brief moment of a broken facade left him confused and, oddly, lonely. How was it that the other man could be covered in wine and win friends, and he could be covered in mud and stared at and muttered about? He knew they would always be so different it hurt, his passion saved for negativity and Alaric's saved for acceptance. Just as when they were kids, Elias felt like a clumsy monstrous outsider, and Alaric could present as a king despite his faults. Defeated, he slowly slipped back into the holiday cheer in an attempt to find Eleanor. Perhaps if nothing else, her presence could provide a sense of purpose, a reprieve.

Yet even as he moved through the crowd, his thoughts lingered on Alaric — his laugh, his charm, the way he could shrug off the incident as if it were nothing. Elias couldn't decide if he hated him for it — or envied him. However invisible he felt, the crowd still parted for him to find the Draven daughter dutifully poised to wait for him. She was a vision in pastel blue as always, and while his feelings for her were more honor-bound, he couldn't help but be relieved as her light smile graced those gentle lips. The sound of Alaric's laugh clung to Elias's ribs long after he'd moved away—bright, careless, and unbearably familiar.

"Oh dear… you are absolutely red." She commented, her wine-stained lips fashioning into an understated pout at the sight of his face. Their arms linked, and Elias moved to escort her out, but she refused, stopping in the pale blue of the moonlight on the front porch. The snow lightly graced her shoulders, unnoticed in her razor-sharp focus. The night swallowed them. Behind them, Alaric's laughter echoed from the ballroom — too bright, too hollow, too familiar.

Eleanor's gaze flicked back toward the spill of warm light behind them. Someone near the far wall—she couldn't place the name, only the cut of a dark coat and the unmistakable stillness of someone listening too closely—had been watching Elias for several minutes. Not watching the two of them leave, but watching him, the way people look when they think they've just witnessed something worth repeating. A small crease formed between her brows. Attention like that rarely meant anything kind. Elias was only made aware of this far later, when the dust had settled and Eleanor felt it relevant.

"Ironically, it seems someone else is redder." He grumbled, reluctantly turning back to look into the party once more. The whole room seemed to bend towards his rival, a silent approval of anything he did or didn't do in company. Elias' eyes narrowed before a soft, gloved hand sent a rush of cold through his head. Eleanor turned his face to lock her eyes on his, a rare moment of genuine affection.

"Let's get you home. Earl Grey tea?" She offered, her warm smile returning and provoking a mirrored one from the man. Despite their arrangement, there was a crumb of honesty between them; she knew all his favorites and his habits. She often used them in these persuasive ways, but he could forgive it if it meant one less moment in this stuffy holiday party. Her hand on his cheek was steadier than her pulse through it but she offered it the way a pragmatist offered olive branches.

"With a bit of lavender."

* * *

The weeks that followed were a blur. Preparations were made in just as much haste as was reserved for a funeral or large family names.. Lady Draven insisted on joining the party bound for Greystone, as she'd said. Though there was an echo of affection between them, it was practicality that spurred her forward. A year apart was both inefficient and downright foolish.

Eleanor had no intention of being shut out of whatever came next. She was to be in charge of finances and of marital comfort; she would stand at the doors beside her fiance as it opened its great maw, ready to look the past in the eye with him. Her tone left little for argument. She'd taken to asking questions about the manor — its size, its history, the extent of its inheritance, and never of Edwin himself. Elias found that telling.

His mother hadn't objected to this decision. A betrothal meant unity, and appearance mattered. Still, Elias had his own suspicions and Eleanor had her own reasons— she often did. Perhaps she hoped to understand the place before it swallowed them both. Perhaps she only wanted to see what it would make of him. She didn't ask why the letter still sat on his desk, days later, or why he touched it like something alive. But he caught her looking at it once—just long enough to wonder what it said that he hadn't told her.

Elias, while appreciative, recognized this meant that both households would spend the month in quiet, rushed flurry. Before he could even take a full breath, he was pressed down again by the weight of what was to come. Time felt hollow

— measured not in obligations but in anticipations. By the seventh morning of the final week, the carriage was ready and Elias found himself waiting by the window once more, unsure if he was headed towards the past or a far more horrifying future. Everything felt foreboding and electric somehow. Then, before he could collect his thoughts, they were off.

The expanse of trees rolled past them expectantly as they made their way to the jaws of Greystone manor. Elias was pensive, quiet. Eleanor was nervous, almost shivering in anticipation. The manor called from a distance, a great inhale that was expectant and hungry. Somehow, the air felt thinner here, as if life had been sucked out of it. Their bags had been packed in such a hurry that neither knew if they had everything they would need. Yet, Elias was certain he could never be truly prepared as he clung to the edge of the carriage and said goodbye to his old life.

Then, they were at the feet of the beast, staring up at the foreboding building from the carriage.

He stepped down cautiously, gripping onto the side of his carriage as if it would help him in the slightest. His boots crunched the gravel beneath his feet with uncertain finality. His legs felt weak and his stomach uneasy as he locked eyes with it. It was an aging manor, the stones weathered and torn by the vines that crawled along the sides, but it was somehow still… alive. Vibrating with eagerness to consume. He couldn't place what it was that was so inviting and still terrifying. There was something familiar in its ruin, as though a once-beloved family dog had dug itself from the grave and returned to the hearth—loyal, wrong, uncanny. Elias slowly walked forward as if pulled by the procession of a dream. There, on the stone steps, stood Alaric. He was turned slightly away from the doors, taking in the grounds, when his eyes caught Elias's. They held each other's gaze like a lock had turned between them.

A requiem. Every step Elias took toward the steps sounded like it had been composed for something neither of them could yet name. The two kept their gaze fixed as they reunited, the manor between them, expecting, waiting.

"You're late." The blond broke the silence, his smile threatening to break his composure as he kept his back turned to the doors themselves. For a moment — one terrible, suspended heartbeat — Elias felt fourteen again, staring at the boy he once trusted more than anyone. He seemed almost comforted by the appearance of his rival. His voice was a touch softer than Elias remembered.

"I did not wish to come." The darker haired man admitted, crossing his hands nervously. He felt Eleanor behind him, her steps echoing his own reluctance—every one of them heavy, deliberate.

"Nor I." Alaric replied, his voice tinged with amusement, or perhaps exhaustion. He laughed, just once, to himself.

They turned their eyes to the doors then, as they creaked open with a breathless groan—though neither man had touched them. The house had made its choice. It remembered them, and that was the worst part.

Elias's stomach turned cold.

It was beginning.

4

February (I) , 1880

laric had forgotten how the manor breathed—slow, deliberate, like something ancient remembering how to wake. No one spoke or breathed as its jaws opened to swallow the three of them whole. The threshold felt like the opening to another realm; once they passed it, they would be at the mercy of Greystone Manor. He could say he was feeling nothing simpler than irritation, but it was far deeper in his body, some sort of deep memory wrapped in nostalgia. In the air wafting from the doorway was the faintest scent of damp roses, and of blood.

Alaric stepped aside to allow his rival into the manor as if offering it to him, a gesture laced with irony, Eleanor followed dutifully behind Elias, her expression unreadable, the lines of her mouth held tightly shut. She lifted the hem of her skirt with precision, not grace—neither hesitant nor entirely at ease, as if already measuring the weight of the house against herself. Alaric watched her, just long enough to wonder what, exactly, she hoped to find here.

As Elias took the first steps across that barrier, Alaric's stomach twisted into knots—recognition, regret, and something unnamed.

It was a long way from what it had been once upon a time. Years ago, those summers, they had crossed the threshold when it had been their kingdom. It had been a vast, crumbling stage upon which he and Elias had ruled as wild, unsupervised boys with dirt-stained knees and their secrets pressed into the mortar of the walls. The memories came back in pieces — half there and strangely vivid. Elias laughing at something just out of frame. The distant sounds of Lord Greystone's piano. Their tutor smacking their hands with a ruler as they intentionally mispronounced silly French words. The way Elias' face looked when he argued with him. The way he believed in goodness. He wondered if Elias still did.

Now, the home was far more grim in appearance. It was as if he were trespassing on something half-dead and sacred. He wondered if the house remembered him, too. The air around the threshold pressed tighter against his chest, as if the manor were sniffing him out — wondering what he had become. The manor had become darker in his absence; what once was so bright and inviting was now foreboding and eerie. It was a living creature, having gone neglected and mangy without the proper love and care put into it.

What he knew of Lord Greystone's final years were wrapped in secrecy, as most things in their family were. However, what he did know was that the man had not passed in a good state. He had learned over the course of the week, in hushed tones among his staff, that the man had spent many long nights wandering the halls of this very structure whispering to himself. Driven mad in his isolation, perhaps, he frequently scribbled notes all over the place and hid them from himself as though playing a game on his own. Perhaps, he considered, this was the reason for the inconvenient custody of the building, or perhaps it was one last sick game from dear Lord Greystone himself. Either way, his own first step past the threshold felt final, and it felt fated. Elias locked eyes with him and they caught a glimmer of real fear between them before it fell away into pomp and circumstance once more.

"It's quite cold and dark, isn't it?" Alaric remarked, straightening his thick gray overcoat and forcing a nervous smile. The darker man returned the expression, his gaze briefly falling to the floor.

"That's how we know he's really gone." Elias noted, leaning into his own warmer memory of the place. "Edwin never let a room go cold."

Just then, as if on command, a fire flickered up in the base of the fireplace by the stairs. The flames lit up the grandiosity of the main room, exposing it for its true glory, hidden by the pallor of time. The main room was composed of a vast entrance and two connected staircases on each side that led to a second level hall. A crystal chandelier hung from the ornate ceiling, adorned with candles that now only welcomed dust and cobwebs. To the right of the main entry, there was the parlor where the men would go to smoke after every vapid, boring dinner among the wealthy for generations. It remained dark, much like the dining hall to the left. This whole entry was once bathed in light at all hours of the day; at night it was busy with servants and glazed with candlelight. It was a difficult sort of nostalgia, all bite and no bark and complicated with his present fears and complexities. Before he could explore his thoughts on the matter, the figure of a woman emerged from the dark beside the fireplace, standing and walking into view as if she were a vision.

It was as if she were a fixture of the house. She blended in with its melancholy, her dress dusting the floor with dark ivory lace, blended into a dark gray striped pattern that crawled up her sylphlike figure. At the top of her head rested a worn bonnet, an item more of duty than aesthetics as it pushed her hair back and kept her suspiciously vulpine face clear of auburn hair. She must have been in her mid 20s — not much older than the crew, but carried herself as if she were wiser. She bowed as she stopped before the three, hands clasped in front of her.

"Winifred Vane. Pleased to make your acquaintance." The waifish figure bowed, a light smile on her lips. "Winnie, if it pleases you. I'll be your guide and your company."

Alaric peeled his eyes from her finally, glancing down to the floor briefly to collect his thoughts. He cleared his throat — a gesture of formality. He would be nothing but welcoming to the home before him, even if it made his stomach turn on impulse and smelled of rot.

"Alaric Greystone. Pleased to make your acquaintance."

The silence that followed was too long to be natural, thick with tension as Winifred's eyes found him. They didn't falter, and they seemed to already know him. Her smile didn't seem too off, but didn't reach her eyes either. There was something unreadable about them, as though she was not regarding just the group before her, but their echoes — their lineages, their legacies, and their sins. The fire behind her crackled louder than before, flaring for a moment with an eerie, almost reverent warmth.

Suddenly, he felt so young and small under her gaze. He felt spotlighted out of the three, walking onto a stage made for the sins of Greystone. He hated how familiar the sensation was — being watched, being assessed, being found wanting. There he'd perform, all dressed in ruffles and white, a sad clown for his elders. They'd all done the song and dance for many generations before him, and now it would be his turn. Though, as a small boy, this house had not felt so suffocating to him. Once, it was a playground of their wildest dreams, his stage bright and colorful, the director of the play. Greystone Manor had grown so cold since; the cobwebs warped around the curtains of the stage, reflecting light.

Perhaps the choking feeling he was locked into was just grief, or perhaps his nerves. He hadn't realized he'd been silent for such a long time until Eleanor, ever the peacemaker, subtly tapped his hand. Alaric simply nodded in response, awkwardly lowering his eyes to the floor. Elias shifted beside him, his brow furrowed slightly, gaze trained not on Winifred, but the hearth. The fire had dimmed again, the warmth receding as quickly as it had come. Alaric's pulse jumped. The manor had always breathed like this—soft inhales, sharp exhalations—though he'd never admitted that aloud. "Odd," he murmured to no one in particular. "I thought I saw it— never mind."

When he finally looked at Winifred, it was with curiosity — cool, tempered, and brittle at the edges. She turned her head toward him, and her eyes met his with a softness that did not feel earned. She held the look a little longer than Alaric had, searching for something human, something familiar. But the longer he stared, the more he felt like he was being stared through. There was no fear in her. No uncertainty.

It unsettled him. Not because she was strange, but because she looked at him like she knew what he feared most.

Eleanor stood between the two men now, her posture fluid and polite, ever the diplomat. Her eyes had been on Winifred the entire time. Not with suspicion, exactly, but with interest. A quiet calculation behind a demure smile.

Winifred turned, her skirts brushing the marble floor like fog. She gestured down the long corridor with a sweep of her hand. "Shall I show you around?" she asked. Her tone was light, even pleasant, but none of them missed the echo her words left behind — something older than hospitality.

No one noticed the fire had gone out again.

* * *

The three of them hesitated to follow, as if doing so would lock them into a fate none of the three wanted. Elias, in particular, stilled. His eyes found a portrait in the main staircase, caught between nostalgia and something heavier. It was enormous, spanning from just above the floor to nearly the ceiling. Furthermore, it was odd, even absurd, to see a portrait of himself in a manor that never had, technically, belonged to him.

The painting captured a day they both remembered, though never spoke of. There, a canvas depiction of he and Alaric at the age of perhaps fourteen, when they had fallen out with one another. In the strokes of oil, the two of them laughed together in the forest just beyond the manor — Elias knew the spot, with its crypts and gazebos, as if it functioned as a labyrinth. Something in his chest tightened. He knew this day. The lightness in his limbs, the weightlessness of it… it was a memory he hadn't let himself touch in years.

In the painting, two boys laughed in the garden just beyond the manor grounds, half-collapsed in each other's arms. He couldn't remember the last time he'd heard himself laugh like that. Alaric had stolen many things from him over the years, but that loss hurt most unexpectedly. Alaric's blond hair was a messy halo. Elias's smile — a real one, unburdened — glowed beneath the canopy of green. A book lay open between them, pages mid-flutter in the breeze. He recognized it. Shakespeare, or maybe Alice in Wonderland. Always Alice.

"If I were Alice—" Elias heard, a voice from memory, bright with youth.

"I'd simply never come home!" The other completed, resulting in raucous laughter between the two. Memory rose with the draft. They rolled in the soft tufts of green grass and daisies, their tan trousers streaked with green grass as their ties lay strewn over tree branches nearby like forgotten flags. The heat caressed their backs, heavy with the weight of summer, boyhood welcoming them back from high society as an old friend.

"Now, picture this, Eli! I shrink like Alice and end up swimming in your morning tea!" Young Alaric joked, eyes fervent with glee. Young Elias returned the sentiment, smiling wide enough to make even the caterpillars chuckle.

"You'd hate it. 'Oh no, Eli, it smells dreadful! There's no lavender!'" He teased back, dropping the book to roll onto his back and fling a hand over his face dramatically, only to burst into laughter a second later. Alaric joined him, the two boys side by side in the fresh summer grass. It was a bright, sunny day and the two had snuck off into the garden after their lessons to read together, something they often did, though it was likely Edwin had figured them out long ago. It was their time away from everyone else, from the world, from their families… Just them, and perhaps Alice. Suddenly, the laughter came to a quiet rest as Alaric gazed skyward.

"I often wish that wasn't the case, Eli… As a Greystone, certain things are expected of me. Of you. Of Alice." His voice had lowered, the way it sometimes did when he said something truer than usual. He sighed, his hand finding Elias' in the weeds, seeking human connection for but a moment. "I think if I could decide, really decide, we'd just run. As far as we could. Paris. Or anywhere. Where we're not Greystone or Thorne. Just… Alice and the White Rabbit, maybe."

Young Elias didn't respond immediately, just stared at the blond beside him as his eyes wandered the sky. He agreed, but saying anything felt too loud all of a sudden. It felt like it would shatter this moment, as his hand felt the softness of his friend's palm and the consistency of his heartbeat. Alaric was the one thing that truly felt real, felt human, among obligations and studies and hallways and inheritance. The blond closed his eyes and Elias watched the shine of his skin as it reflected the sunshine; Alaric simply glowed under the sunlight. He watched as the sunshine turned his friend golden, played on his cheek like an old friend. How he wished he weren't so dull.

The sunlight faded, the heat cooled, the grasp numbed.

Elias blinked, and the warmth of that summer day gave way to cold stone and silence. Alaric stood beside him now — no joy, no gleam in his eye. Just a grimace.

"How tacky," he muttered.

Elias followed his gaze back to the painting. The colors had dulled. The faces were faded. Even the joy looked ghostly.

"You'd think the old man might've burned it when we stopped speaking. Meaningless keepsake…" Alaric added, his voice harsh. A joke, maybe. Or maybe not. Elias' eyes dropped to the floor. Eleanor noticed, her gaze sharply turning to Winifred as she spoke.

"Winifred, do you happen to know who painted this? It's… rather evocative," Eleanor offered gently, trying and perhaps failing to defuse the moment. The silence from the two men was louder than it should have been.

Winifred's eyes flicked to the canvas.

"A local artist, I believe. Commissioned by the baron some years back, Miss Draven." she said. She turned then, gliding a few paces ahead, her voice drifting back like a wisp of smoke.

"Though some pieces," she mused, "feel as though they paint themselves, don't they?" she added, barely above a whisper.

Alaric muttered something beneath his breath, the words lost to the shadows. His eyes lingered on the portrait a moment longer before he swept past Elias, the hem of his coat brushing close enough to stir the air. Elias's skin prickled as though touched by memory itself.

Still, he didn't move. He stood, rooted before the painting, his fingers—slender, searching—tracing the intricate edge of the frame. He seemed to be committing it to memory, or perhaps trying to read some hidden truth in its gilded borders. Behind him, Eleanor paused. Her face betrayed little, but her eyes lingered on him, quietly troubled. She hesitated, then turned, her steps soft as she followed the others down the corridor.

Elias remained behind.

The cold seeped in through the stone, sharp as breath on glass. Just then, from the depths of the house, a sound rose — a thin, distant echo of laughter. Faint and high, a sound committed only to memory. His breath caught. It faded before he could place it, leaving behind only the hush of an old house holding its breath. As if by command, he wandered alongside the group, dazed and somehow colder.

As he walked alongside the others, Elias let his gaze drift from frame to frame, each portrait more severe than the last. Long-dead Greystones loomed from their gilded cages, all draped in velvet and pride, their eyes oil—dark and unblinking. Every few faces, a Thorne would appear — less adorned, more subdued, tucked in like afterthoughts or offerings. Those few, he assumed, had been compliant. Quiet. Forgettable.

He had learned long ago what it meant to be a Thorne in the shadow of the Greystone name. It was a role meant to be performed with grace, deference, and silence. He had watched it ruin men and women stronger than him. It had swallowed his mother whole. And still, the Greystones had watched with polite disinterest — curious, perhaps, but never intervening.

Winifred named none of the faces as they passed, instead motioning vaguely to the corridor with an outstretched hand.

"All the ancestors were guests here, once," she said. The line floated into the stale air like a riddle, its tone somewhere between invitation and warning.

They arrived before a familiar door, and something in Elias's chest ached. The study.

This room had belonged more to him than any room he'd ever had. It was their sanctuary once — his and Alaric's. They had sprawled across the floor with novels torn from library shelves, staging dramatic readings and inventing alternate endings. Alaric would voice Alice in a falsetto, Elias would counter as the Cheshire Cat, and together they would laugh until their stomachs hurt. Dinah, the cat, had always been Alaric's favorite. He'd claimed she was the only one who made any sense.

Now, as the door creaked open on stiff hinges, dust swirled in the golden shaft of afternoon light. The room was frozen in time, but colder somehow. Still touched by the remnants of boyhood, yet stripped of its warmth. Elias crossed the threshold slowly, his hand brushing the doorway like he was asking permission. The house allowed, and before him was the life he once held dear. Couches draped over with yellowing white cotton, sconces dripping with wax frozen in time, the rows and rows of books they'd once read together, it was all as if it were from a set on his stage where he performed for the ancestors. Frills and fabric swished from his costumed feet whenever he made any movement, a familiar lump growing in his throat.

"Curiouser and curiouser…" Alaric mused as he hesitantly stepped into the room, his fingers brushing the dust from a shelf beside the door. Was he taunting? Or merely uncomfortable? The question rolled around Elias' head as if it were a violin screech, painful and rattling. Instead of the outburst he wanted to unleash, Elias sighed and looked to the floor.

"Indeed," he managed, his voice low.

Alaric's' icy eyes shot to his uncertain frame as if sizing up prey. He couldn't tell if the blond was angry, equally rattled, or which was more likely. Offering no answer, he continued on to a soft chair by the fire, pulling off its covering sheet as if he'd left it there himself and plopped into its frame with deliberate ease. Elias lingered near the doorway, reluctant to step fully into the room, as if crossing it would make the past irrevocably real. His eyes roamed over the furniture, over the familiar chaos of books and trinkets, and finally rested on a small blue painted wooden horse.

Alaric's voice cut through the silence, soft but sharp. "Ah… claiming tokens already?" His eyes, those icy slits, didn't leave Elias.

Elias' throat tightened, a quiet storm of memory and guilt beginning to swirl within him as Eleanor remained blissfully unaware. He wanted to speak, to defend, accuse even — but the words wouldn't come, caught in the lattice of regret and fear. Instead, he stepped forward, hand hovering over the small object.

Alaric leaned back in the chair, fingers drumming lightly on the armrest. "Go on, take what isn't yours," he said, voice almost teasing. Words left unsaid lingered like cobwebs, heavy in the dust-choked air, as Elias' fingers closed around the small toy, lifting it toward his face for closer inspection.

The room seemed to shiver around him, the stale sunlight slanting across the floorboards and igniting motes of dust like trapped spirits. And then, a voice, no louder than a whisper — "happy birthday." Not Alaric. Older, warmer, and layered with a gentle authority that made Elias' chest tighten.

The memory surged within him, inexplicable and inaccessible: the year he'd been gifted this tiny object, the delight that had shone in that long-ago summer, the certainty that he would return to the study the next year to find it waiting. The ghost of that joy pressed against his frame now, mingling with the stalemate of time, and he realized how many summers had passed since with his small, blue horse waiting patiently for him on this shelf.

Elias held the toy closely, as if it were both a talisman and a burden. Elias' throat tightened. He made no reply, fingers tightening on it instead. His gaze drifted to the floor, to the dust, to the faint golden light spilling across the shelf where the little blue horse had waited, patient and unchanged.

"Along with your melancholy…" Alaric said after a long pause — almost a statement, almost a challenge. Alaric's fingers drummed again, deliberate and measured. "It survives," he finished, nodding toward the toy, voice soft, distant. "More than I might have expected."

Elias shifted slightly, glancing at the small toy again, as if the weight of it anchored him to some distant summer long gone. He sensed rather than saw Eleanor's eyes on him, curious, cautious, scanning the room, trying to read the undercurrents he would not speak aloud. She hovered near the doorway, hands clasped lightly in front of her, pretending casual interest while her sharp gaze flicked between him and Alaric.

Alaric paused for just a beat, eyes narrowing slightly, though his posture did not change. He leaned forward, resting his elbows on his knees, studying Elias with the same unreadable intensity in his gaze, as if measuring what was left of the boy he once knew here.

Eleanor cleared her throat softly, trying to intrude without appearing intrusive. "It's… a lovely toy," she said, voice light, careful. "Such delicate craftsmanship."

Alaric's lips curved faintly, almost imperceptibly, a shadow of amusement. "Indeed." He replied in a voice measured and even. "Some things endure better than others." His gaze flicked to her briefly before returning to Elias, and for a moment, the tension seemed to thicken, a subtle warning that he was aware of every movement in the room.

Elias' fingers lingered on the toy. He did not speak, though the pull of memory was strong— summer afternoons, laughter echoing through the study, the quiet certainty that some things would always remain. He shifted his weight, caught between the desire to retreat, to hide his thoughts, and just to fall into it all.

Eleanor's eyes narrowed slightly, sensing a history she could not yet decipher, a bond neither man would name. She took a cautious step closer, voice quieter now: "Were you… close, once?"

The question lingered in the air as if physically. While Eleanor knew their history to a certain extent, her distance became extremely apparent in moments like this, when Elias found himself stranded in his own universe of memory. When they had become betrothed, it was an arrangement made to establish her and her father, a foreign oil baron, in the upper society of England, and Thorne was secured to wealth that didn't associate with Greystone. Yet, here they both stood now, under Greystone's unmistakable roof.

Alaric's gaze flickered to her, then to Elias, and back again. "Close enough." He said softly, deliberately vague. "Perhaps more than we intended."

Elias' chest was caught in knots. He did not look at either of them. Instead, he traced the edge of the toy with his thumb, the quiet scrape against the surface almost a heartbeat in the room, carrying decades of memory, longing, and restraint that neither he nor Alaric would give voice to. Finally, he put it back on the shelf and stepped back fully, leaving the toy where it had waited all these years. He knew it was absurd for a man of his age to keep such a thing, but was unable to abandon the past entirely.

Eleanor shifted, stepping a little closer, the faint scrape of her shoe on the floor sounding unnaturally loud in the quiet room. Elias' hand twitched, as if aware of her curiosity but unwilling to engage. His eyes, however, betrayed nothing, scanning the room's shadows, the frozen wax of the sconces, the yellowed covers of the couches — a refuge from scrutiny.

The room seemed to hold its breath as all three scanned it in silence. Eleanor's heeled shoes made a sharp sound against the floor, unnatural, a reminder that she remained a spectator in this fragile, suspended conversation. Elias' eyes scanned the shadows, the shelves, the sconces, every detail a barrier against the quiet scrutiny of Alaric's unblinking gaze and Eleanor's quiet intrusion.

Alaric finally straightened in the chair, fingers still drumming lightly. His voice, low and even, cut through the quiet once more: "You never really left, did you?"

Elias' hand twitched but remained empty, and he allowed a long pause before speaking at all. "I didn't come here to stay."

"And yet… you did come here to take what's mine." Alaric uttered suddenly, his lips turning into a sinister smile. He was incapable of being civil during this stay, it seemed. The air in the room seemed to tighten, as though the house itself had leaned closer, listening. The monsters leaned into Elias, threatening to consume him in this very spot. Shadows seemed to lengthen in their pause, stretching illogically into Elias. Eleanor watched in careful, measured silence, heart quickening but refusing to move in the face of the beast.

"Alaric—" Elias tried, cut off by the eager man.

"No, you haven't changed at all, have you? I can forgive much… but you will always be a Thorne — chasing a Greystone as a hound might pursue its own shadow." He paused, rising from his chair with an uncharacteristic grace, every movement deliberate, measured. Alaric's fingers drummed lightly along the armrest before he released the rhythm entirely, letting them fall to his knees. His gaze, cold and precise, followed Elias' every move, catching the smallest flicker of reaction. There was a tension coiled in his shoulders, in the subtle tilt of his head, that suggested restraint as much as threat."I remember this place, Winifred. I'd like to go to my quarters and unpack, if that's alright."

Winifred stood near the door, hands folded in front of herself, unfazed by the sudden tension. She was almost unnervingly still, a fixture of the walls as they seemed to bend inwards on Elias. Shadows in the room seemed to bend with it, lengthening unnaturally towards him and making Elias feel ill. The air grew heavier, though no draft moved through the closed windows. A faint scent of old wood and candle wax hung in the space, grounding yet oddly oppressive. The dust motes in the slanting sunlight seemed to drift with purpose, swirling around Elias' feet as if nudged by invisible hands.

Winifred's gaze remained fixed on Elias, unwavering. There was no smile, no shift in posture, but the stillness carried a subtle weight—as if she were the only one capable of observing both him and the house without faltering, a sentinel of memory and circumstance.Suddenly, as if compelled by force, she bowed to Alaric and turned to lead him out of the room. Elias took a careful step back from the shelf, letting his fingers brush lightly over the edge of the couch as if testing the air. The small movement made the dust motes lift and swirl, catching the sunlight like tiny sparks suspended in amber. It was almost imperceptible, but he felt the room lean in more, as though noting the motion, cataloging it. Elias exhaled softly, steadying himself.

"I should.. Unpack too." He said quietly, lifting his head from the floorboards to give Eleanor a very rare smile —

one he only gave when trying to ease tension and keep her uninvolved in his own matters, especially any of the heart. She shifted uncomfortably, her shoes once again making soft scratches on the old wood. The manor responded with an almost imperceptible groan — so light they wondered if they'd imagined it.

"Right. As we're… unmarried, I'll need you to show me to my own quarters." She remarked softly, apologetic in her presence. Elias simply nodded, saying nothing more as the ravenous night began to consume Greystone Manor.

5

February (II)

The hush of the corridor pressed on Eleanor as she followed Elias down its narrow length. The sconces lining the walls gave off a pallid, uneven glow, so weak that the shadows seemed to stretch longer than the light itself. Every few steps, the floor groaned beneath her, a sound both intimate and accusatory, as though the house took note of her intrusion.

She kept her gaze steadily fixed on Elias' shoulders, the stiff line of his frame both a comfort and a reminder of her own displacement. Her hands brushed against the railing once, twice, as they drudged through the hallways, as if seeking a tether. A shiver traced her spine — a shadow not entirely of the cold. A strange, subtle awareness tickled the edges of her mind, as though the house observed not just her body, but her intent, her desires, and the small, unspoken complexities forming.

Elias paused outside a tall door, his hand hovering over the handle. "Your quarters," he said softly, his voice heavy and measured. She nodded, stepping forward, but the weight of the silence lingering between them, suddenly aware of the warmth of a glance that was not his — the flash of icy eyes — earlier in the day. Somehow it had been warmer than this moment alone with Elias.

The air seemed to thicken in anticipation as she crossed the threshold. Dust fluttered in the room, swirling around her skirts and the edge of the furniture as she moved further into the space, as though creating a space for her where there had not been before. The room was orderly, almost painfully so, yet a small envelope lay atop the writing desk, folded neatly and bearing no name. It waited expectantly as Elias closed the door behind her without so much as a goodnight." Today had sunk into the two of them like a broken promise, and as she turned back toward the door, she realized just how alone she was. However, she couldn't help but catch the sliver of a feeling of being watched — imperceptive, just out of the corner of her eye. Her mind must be playing tricks.

A soft draft lifted the corner of a curtain, and the room seemed to breathe with her, drawing her into its rhythm. Somewhere deep within the house, she thought she heard a faint sigh, almost like a voice guiding her towards something, someone. Disregarding her unease, she smoothed her skirts and moved towards the desk and unfolded the envelope. She couldn't shake the feeling of being watched, of being guided, as if the manor was aware of every thought. She opened the letter carefully, puzzled at the words inside.

Do not mistake stillness for absence.

Looking around her quarters now, she noticed that her clothing —her gloves, shawl, and even the small satchel she had carried — were neatly arranged atop a chair. Each fold was precise, deliberate, as though someone had taken an impossible amount of care to honor even the smallest crease. Crossing the room, her hand hovered over the garments. She had left them in a careless heap in the carriage when she arrived; she had not asked for this order. A quiet tug at her mind suggested it was meant to be seen, a subtle invitation: You are noticed. You are expected.

Her fingers grazed the glove. Beneath it, hidden like a secret between silk and wood, another slip of paper pressed against her hand. She drew it out slowly, her breath catching at the careful, deliberate penmanship.

Do not mistake presence for safety.

The words struck colder than the first, as though the second note had been waiting for her discovery, patient and certain, buried within the folds of her own belongings. The room no longer felt merely watchful; it felt complicit. On the card was no name, but the distinct flick of the pen in an ornate hand. Eleanor let the fabric of her shawl slip through her fingers, a little too quickly, as though afraid it might vanish under her touch. Her lips pressed into a thin line. There was only one man in this house, erratic and arrogant enough to orchestrate something so intrusive, with a wicked icy gaze.

Sleep that night did not come easily. Her ears strained with every creak of the floors, every sigh of the draft, every note of the foundation's settling. It was heavy and dreamless, as if caught underneath a vice, a pawn of the house itself. Eventually, sleep did overtake her, though mere hours later she stirred, blinking against the faint gray light that filtered through the heavy curtains.The room was still cloaked in shadow, the weak February dawn barely touching the edges of the floor, and a chill lingered in the air that made her shiver beneath the covers. Tomorrow did still come after all its teasing. Yet, tomorrow had come too soon. It was far too fruitless to attempt to sleep any longer, but not for the same effervescence of mid-morning light. Looking at the clock above her door, she managed to discern it to be hardly past six in the morning.

The manor was quieter at dawn;gone were the mysterious creaks, replaced by wind brushing the ivy off the windows. Eleanor's limbs were still heavy from sleep as she placed her bare feet on the cold floor, lumbering towards her skirts and beginning to dress herself. Thankfully, her level of attendance was nowhere near a Greystone, and the Lady Draven could do her own buttons, a fact for which she was grateful for as she slipped on her shawl and nervously exited the room.

The corridors were long and echoed her every step. Despite the carpet's attempts at muffling her, she felt simultaneously conspicuous and diminished. The old boards complained of her every move as she wandered past the library, a room smelling of dust and rot even from the threshold. She passed the ballroom, its mirrors reflecting the pale dawn and one remarkably loud grandfather clock. As she explored the depths of the beast, the sense of its never ending vastness crept in; she had never felt smaller. Finally, she wandered down the grand staircase and into the dining room, a room which looked out to the white of the icy gardens, as if eating alongside them were to ever be a comfort. Perhaps in the summer, she mused, as she ran a slender finger along the backs of the chairs, following the sudden scent of rosemary and wood smoke wafting through the room.

She paused outside the kitchen first, noticing the door open but admiring the glint of copper pans and dried herbs hanging from the pipes. A soft rustle caught her attention fully, and curiosity won over caution as she peered into the room from the doorway, observing. There, bent over a basket of fresh herbs, was a woman—slender, pale, hair pinned neatly. Her fingers moved deftly, separating rosemary and thyme with the ease of long practice. She looked up, meeting Eleanor's eyes with a calm, measured smile.

"Good morning, Miss Draven." The woman purred warmly, though was not overly familiar. "I must handle the herbs before they dry completely. If I leave them, even for a few hours, the fragrance fades, and the flavor is lost."

Eleanor hesitated, unsure whether to apologize for intruding or simply retreat. "Oh…thank you," she said. "I wasn't expecting anyone so early."

"It's quite alright," The woman said, turning her gaze back to her task with slow, practiced motions, "The house is quieter at these hours." Her words were casual, almost cryptic, but Eleanor didn't press.

"Do you… often start this early?" Eleanor asked, trying to shake off her nerves.

The woman looked up again, a smile tugging at the corners of her mouth. "Some things are best done before the day begins. The morning moves differently; The afternoon simply cannot keep pace." She gestured to the basket. "If you like, I can show you how to prepare these for the morning meal. It's easier than it seems."

Eleanor stepped closer, drawn by the simplicity of the task. "I'd like that," she admitted, trying to keep her voice steady.

"Good," the woman said, nodding. "Let's begin with the rosemary. One careful strip at a time. The rest will follow naturally."

Eleanor cautiously approached the basket alongside the

woman, who was pulling a stool out for her to sit on. The room was warming with the break of day, and the light began to seep through the windows as she handed her a sprig of fresh rosemary. Her smile was inviting, a stark contrast to how the rest of this manor had made her feel. She began to tear the springs from the thin stalks. Her shoulders relaxed, her shawl falling slightly as she realized her tremor had eased.

"Winifred, Miss." She said, answering a question Eleanor hadn't yet realized she had. "We met last night, but I understand that it may have been forgotten in the exhaustion." She exhaled, shaking her head in mock disappointment. It seemed to be more directed towards herself than Eleanor, however, as though Winifred herself were apologetic for the circumstances.

"I… do apologize." She confirmed, to a gentle nod from the other woman. Several moments passed in silence, though it grew more comfortable as the light crawled over the floor.

"You have a careful hand," Winifred remarked lightly, glancing up from the basket. "I imagine you were trained to do things just so."

Eleanor's lips pressed together, a faint smile tugging at the corners. "My father.. Insisted on perfection. In speech, in manners, even in small tasks. I suppose it comes naturally now." She paused, reaching for another spring of rosemary from the second, smaller basket at their feet.

"Your father must be prominent." Winnie commented, light.

Eleanor nodded. "He built his life on oil and enterprise. He often said China never afforded him the same wealth. America was too simple. But England has been… a mixture of duty and expectation. A place to continue my father's ambitions."

"Ah— That explains your cadence." She exclaimed, as

though piecing together a mystery. "You speak with a different rhythm than most who pass through here."

Eleanor tilted her head, brushing a stray curl from her face. "I suppose it marks me as American," she said, voice soft. "Old habits die hard." She paused, wondering if she should continue. Though nonsensical, she wondered if the house itself could hear her quiet admissions. "I've spent so many years here in England, I forget how noticeable it is sometimes."

"It marks you as memorable." Winifred added, so soft she was hard to hear over the gentle scraping of herbs.

Eleanor's fingers stilled over the rosemary, and she looked up, startled at the quiet weight of the words. "Memorable?" she echoed, voice barely above a whisper.

Winifred gave a faint, almost secretive smile. "Yes. Memorable." Her hands never stopped moving, avidly stripping the leaves, but there was a careful attentiveness in the motion, as though each sprig were once alive itself.

Eleanor felt an unexpected warmth at the comment, as though someone had noticed the parts of her she rarely let surface. "I… I suppose that is a comfort," she murmured, drawing another rosemary sprig from the basket.

* * *

Elias stirred from uneasy dreams with the pale light of morning filtering through the curtains. His body was heavy, but something, a presence or perhaps a restless curiosity, pulled him from bed. He dressed quickly and slipped into the corridor, his footsteps soft against the worn runner. Morning light was beginning to filter through the pale gray of the curtains, spilling onto the deep colors inside. The hour was so much kinder to him than the night, or perhaps the daylight only hid the fatigue of it. The way memory soaked into the floorboards didn't linger into the early morning air, lulling him into a false sense of security.

Descending the staircase, his fingers traced the mahogany railing with tender care. He caressed the manor as if being soft with it would set him apart, mark him as an ally. He made his way towards a faint clatter of platters and silverware coming from the downstairs kitchen, a curious sound when he knew that no servant had yet arrived by this morning. It was far too much commotion for just one set of hands, and far too loud to be graceful and practiced. His feet were slow underneath him, uncertainty caressing his form in the early morning light as he reached the kitchen and peered through a small opening in the door.

There in the lack of secrecy, he spotted his fiance and the maid from the night before, pressing it open only several inches more to drink it all in. Eleanor was dressed, though her hair was still unpinned and it fell gently down her back in onyx brush strokes. Her skin held just a touch of pearl, especially in this light, making her radiant in her least composed moments. Her slender fingers, which he'd only ever noticed before dancing along piano keys, were now knuckle-deep in a fragrant dough. She had nudged her sleeves, easily wrinkled and frivolous things they were, up to her elbows so she could work at the task and had spilled flour into her hair in the process — something he considered that pinning it back would've saved the trouble of.

However, despite all its difficulties and headaches, he couldn't deny that in moments like these, a less troubled man could fall absolutely in love with her. So sickeningly in love that these simple things could make him dizzy. But Elias couldn't figure out why what he felt instead was a deep-seated warmth. It crawled from his chest and radiated out, but lacked excitement — familiarity, perhaps. He knew where the scent of her hair mingled with the bread, knew the slight bend of her neck when she concentrated, the tilt of her shoulder when she laughed quietly to herself. Her soft movements made a small creak on the cutting board, a rhythm he could nearly hum along to. Her flour-stained apron hung loosely, quietly punctuating her movement. He'd never seen her so peaceful, and he just watched for a few moments that hung in the air as if they'd done this a thousand times before.

Like most peace, however, he couldn't linger in it forever. A glance up at the figure of another by the door caused her to jump up, only to laugh at her own start once she recognized the shadow.

"Elias! You scared me half to death!" She exclaimed, pushing a few floured strands from her face with her wrist and failing. Finally, the man stepped into the early morning light that washed over the entire kitchen. She was not alone, he noted, but accompanied by the vulpine maid from the night before — chopping up pork with precise, almost unnatural calm, without a sound that might betray her efforts. He gave her a quick, full, uninterrupted scan before allowing his attention to shift. Elias' gaze lingered on Eleanor a moment longer, tracing the curve of her shoulder as she bent over the dough, before he tore himself away.

"I hardly meant to," Elias said, smiling however warmly he was able. These moments felt safe enough for it. "Though I argue you deserved it, taking up these new… preoccupations before daylight."

Eleanor rolled her eyes, a light smirk tugging at the corner of her pink lips. "Preoccupations? I've been guided well, thank you." She retorted, gesturing to Winifred by the counter, now tossing pork fat into an unlabeled bin. Elias refused to look directly at it, or her. "Besides, it's not like anyone else would notice if I messed it up. Except you, apparently."

"Guilty." He said, leaning slightly against the door frame, hands folded behind his back. "And maybe a certain blond, who notices when his tea is cooler than he prefers. But," he continued, "I'd defend you."

Eleanor gave a soft laugh, shaking her head as she wiped her hands on her apron. "You watch me too closely, Elias. I'm beginning to think this is a form of surveillance."

"Merely observation." He said smoothly, a hint of teasing in his usually monotone voice. "I fear it borders on appreciation. Wouldn't that be indecent?"

She tilted her head, giving him a look that mixed exasperation and amusement. "Flattery will get you nowhere. Now, if you're finished staring, we could use a hand — or, at least promise not to tiptoe like a shadow all about the kitchen. It's creepy, Eli."

Elias grinned faintly, stepping back just enough to offer her more space, though his eyes lingered a moment longer on the flour dusted across her right cheek. "I make no promises," he said. "But I might consider helping if the offer of company is sufficient incentive."

Eleanor scoffed, a playful smile dancing on her lips. "Company? Not conversation? You'd rather dissect my kneading technique than offer a hand." She teased, turning back to her project with a childish vigor. "There's flour in the pantry. And if you're very careful, I may even trust you with the eggs."

Elias offered a soft laugh, the kind that said fine, you win. He crossed the kitchen, the floorboards groaning under his weight. The sound was almost instantly swallowed by the hush of the house and morning dew on the windows. He moved unfamiliarly in the kitchen, the discomfort palpable as he traded his ink pens and chess pieces for rosemary and feminine bonding.

"You know," he said, reaching for the bowl she indicated, "I'm not sure I've ever seen you like this. Covered in flour. Hair is a mess." He paused, smiling to himself, "Domestic."

"And you, willingly part of the laboring class." She quipped, witty. "Thorne, making bread early in the morning… The house seems to be inspiring a change in us all."

He smiled faintly, but his breath caught. It felt wrong to think that freedom was the thing awaiting either of them. He gazed towards the ceiling beams, admiring the old wood, the deep color of it. A moment passed, almost imperceptible, before he spoke again. "Does it feel… aware of us, perhaps?"

Eleanor looked up, pausing mid-fold, her fingers still deep in dough. "Aware?"

"As if… as if it remembers being lived in, once." He shook his head, laughing dryly to himself. He was prepared to write it off, but then Winifred reminded them both of her presence, her unbothered voice coming softly from the far counter.

"Old houses keep their memories, sir. That's all. Best not to think too hard on what they choose to keep."

Eleanor laughed lightly, her bell-high tone breaking the tension in an instant. "You see? Even Winnie thinks you're being morbid."

'Winnie,' she called her. Elias' gaze couldn't help but to

linger on the shadowed arch of the doorway. There was a faint outline of a hand print on the dust near the frame. It wasn't there when he entered, but it was there now. Unnoticed. 'Hardly morbid." He replied, his eyes fixed.

Eleanor, unaware, nudged the dough towards him. "Your turn, Eli. Let's see what those refined hands can do."

He tore his eyes from the frame, ripping his attention back to the moment and forcing another thin smile. "If it ends in disaster, you'll at least have something to blame me for."

"Perfect," She said, stepping to the side, "A failed catastrophe — isn't that what all successful marriages need?"

He didn't answer, just began to knead as the morning light shifted through the windowpanes. The flour drifted like faint dust in the air, mixing with the motes already within it. As the household woke, the house seemed to sigh under them, bracing for the impact they'd all make at once.

The three of them had gathered at the long oak table by eight o'clock in the morning. The dew was beginning to dry on the window overlooking the garden, and the ivy mixed with the primroses and the snowdrops on the windowsills in a haphazard sort of way. Equally haphazard was the way that Alaric's hair clung to his temples, the curls pressed to his ears in the way only sleep could manage. He sat a tad too far from the others to be natural about it, crossing his arms as Eleanor came around with a pot of tea that had gone slightly too strong. She poured, precise as always, despite her hair escaping the pins it had been tossed up in at the last minute. Elias sat across from her, polishing a smudge from his spectacles with his sleeve, though he wasn't wearing them.

"Good god," Alaric muttered, leaning forward to grab himself a slice of cooled, herby bread. On his plate, Winifred had served him a slice of ham and an egg — fried, of course. He was still in his robe from the night before — a silky, gaudy thing in a deep maroon with ornate details that reminded Elias of a curtain. His fingers curled around the slice of bread as if it were simultaneously foreign, exciting, and disgusting. He held it up to the light, turning it over in the air, his voice cutting through like shards of glass. "You've domesticated him."

Eleanor didn't look up, though an unbothered smile graced her features. "I'd hardly say that. He merely kneaded some dough."

"Progress," Alaric mused, placing the slice onto his plate without a single taste. His elegance made mockery seem effortless. "Next you know, he'll be scrubbing the floors, and where would his dignity be then?" Elias' eyes flickered up at his rival and quickly back down to his glasses, unperturbed outside of a slight arch tugging at his brow.

"Intact, I'd hope," He said, curt. Eleanor swallowed uncomfortably, setting down her pot of tea before seating herself beside him.

"In any case, let's all enjoy our first meal together, shall we?" She suggested, too light for the cool February morning. Unfortunately, Alaric's gaze fell on her next, having noticed that Elias was no longer taking his bait.

"I wouldn't dream of anything else." His grin flickered, an animal finding its next prey. "I didn't know you'd be taken to kitchen work. I thought heiresses left such things to the staff." Something in his tone was playful, but there was an undercurrent to it — something probing, almost suspicious. Eleanor met his eyes for a beat too long before answering.

"Some of us adapt, Lord Greystone. Even to a place like

this." She said simply, her poise a direct challenge. Alaric gave a sudden laugh, the kind that could be either mockery or agreement depending on who you ask.

"How very industrious of you."

Elias looked up then, meeting Alaric's gaze with a measured coolness as he placed his glasses back onto the bridge of his nose. "It would be far more industrious of you to find something to focus your time on that isn't irritating me."

The manor seemed to hold its breath. Eleanor picked up her fork and poked at her egg, the yolk spilling onto the white of the entire plate and encroaching on the rest of her food. Alaric offered a smile too sharp to be warm.

"Then I suppose I'd best stay busy. Wouldn't want to upset our gracious host." He mused, eyes narrowing slightly. Every sentence was a chess play. Eleanor cleared her throat between them.

"Please, Alaric. Eat something. We'll need all the civility we can manage before the day's out." She tried, her tone lighter than either of them had managed yet.

He fished for his fork, his expression unreadable. "Civility, yes," he said softly. "Though I find this house has a way of wearing it thin."

Elias glanced towards the high window, where the blooms of the early spring mixed with the remaining ice of the winter. What was morning light was now a grayish hue. Something cold passed between them, a breeze or a draft, but it felt heavier somehow. It felt like they were on display, characters in a Shakespearean play that everyone but the actors knew.

Elias took a sip of too strong cold tea from a chipped Greystone cup. He remained where he was for a long moment. The air was dimmed by a cloud passing over the window, his breakfast went cold and half-uneaten. Eleanor went to check the linens with her new friend, Alaric went to his quarters to dress. He rubbed at his temple, then stood, pressing a napkin to his mouth before disappearing down the hallway.

The library was cooler than the hall — quiet, save for the distant creak of the house settling. A faint smell of vellum and lamp oil lingered. Elias lit one of the sconces and began sorting through endless records, beginning his cataloging of financial comings and goings of the estate, though the words swam before him. It would be long, tedious work, though essential in closing its matters or with any luck, transferring them. His thoughts kept slipping, not to Alaric precisely, but to the strange, shapeless tension that had hung between them all morning.

* * *

Upstairs, Alaric's quarters were a study in faded luxury. The curtains were drawn halfway, clouded morning light spilling onto the floor and the carpet merely clinging to it. His coat hung where he'd left it the night before — draped unceremoniously over the back of his chair, the cuffs still wrinkled. His room was still partially chilled; the fire hadn't taken, and the windows glistened with condensation.

Before he could settle into the room's quiet, there was a sharp knock at the door. Winifred stepped inside, her presence as lilted as a breeze through autumn leaves. In her steady hands, she carried a cream-colored envelope

"This arrived this morning, sir." She said quietly, placing the sealed letter into his open palm with a nod before retreating into the shadows of the corridor. "I thought you'd prefer to have it before the day begins," she added softly.

There was nothing suspicious in her face. Only warmth, the kind found in old hearths and older kitchens.

"Thank you," he managed.

Alaric turned the letter over, the wax seal heavy on his fingers. A knot tightened in his chest as he caught the name — his mother. He paused before breaking the seal, letting the silence stretch thin. He sat on the edge of his bed, breaking the seal with his thumb, his breath short.

The letter was succinct:

Your presence at Greystone is not a choice. It is a duty.

Below that, in heavier, darker ink:

You know what is expected.

No signature. She didn't need one.

Alaric folded the paper once, twice, until it was small enough to pretend it weighed nothing. He slipped it into his coat lining, closed his eyes, and exhaled until the candle's flame wavered. By the time he stood, the words felt burned into his ribs.

He poured water from a cracked carafe into a generous basin at his dresser and splashed his face with it, flinching at the cold. The mirror above him caught his features as he glanced up, catching the fatigue in his expression. There was the faint bruise underneath his eyes, the faint tremor in his hands as he pulled his robe off his shoulders, the deep blue of his veins as his arms fell to his sides.

"Civility," he said under his breath, repeating Eleanor's words and crossing the room to unlatch a suitcase. It was an understated, mangled thing, its metal bits rusted and its edges bent. He'd chosen his worst luggage for this journey, expecting the manor to pry it open for its pound of flesh. That is to say, it felt like a situation lacking in fanfare. There was civility, and there was pretending. Eleanor wouldn't know either if it slapped her in her unmoved face. Present, perfect, polite, useful, worthy Eleanor.

He dressed, buttoning and unbuttoning his waistcoat until they lined up, internally bemoaning the lack of assistance. Thankfully, his own servants were scheduled to arrive the day after — delayed by Greystone affairs, but not delayed longer than his mother allowed. He thought of his maid, his cook, his butler and took one more look around his quarters, finding it nearly peaceful. He half-expected footsteps in the hallways — none came. It was just… so quiet. His reflection remained dim in the warped mirror, the collar of his shirt slightly askew until he tugged it straight.

From his luggage, he drew a small silver flask — not hidden, exactly, just kept out of sight of judging eyes. He took a measured sip, a gesture that demanded to be forgotten. The taste was sharp and familiar, drawing warmth down his body and waking him. It steadied him. He pocketed it and re-buttoned his waistcoat for one final time, listening to the eaves breathe around him. Somewhere down the hall, a door shut, the echo carrying down the corridor like a sigh.

When he exited the room, the hall felt emptier than before breakfast. He wandered without purpose, fingertips gracing the curved banisters as if tracing the rhythm of the wood. His footsteps felt as though they lingered as they carried him past room after room, eventually carrying him back into the ballroom. It was vast and half-lit, the curtains drawn so the light of the day filtered in gray and uncertain. The parquet floor bore years of dust, disturbed only by a few prints from their arrival the evening before.

He stepped inside. The silence here was thicker, indulgent even. Chandeliers hung like ghosts overhead, their crystal and chains dulled by age. Alaric exhaled softly, his breath fogging faintly in the draft. He closed his eyes, tuning into that which was and could be. In that blink, he caught a glimpse of another life. The chandeliers sparkled brighter, and he saw a smaller, grounded presence reaching towards him underneath them. They laughed, though the sound was muffled, as if he were underwater. A man in gold-tipped shoes twirled across the polished floor, palms brushing in a practiced step that felt both familiar and strange. They spoke. He couldn't understand. He blinked. The vision slipped. The laughter hung faintly in the air, untraceable, like an echo that belonged more to memory than reality.

He opened his eyes to cracked molding and faded murals. The dust in the air swirled around him like a bulletin, demanding to be seen. Already he was parsing the work in his mind—what could be saved or salvaged, what must be cleaned or destroyed in the process. The brandy's warmth moved through him as he twirled slowly, taking in everything around him as something to be rebuilt, and understood. It felt, oddly, like the manor had been waiting years for him to say its name again.

"We'll start here," He murmured, almost as if to the air. Then he set about finding where the light fell best, pulling back one of the enormous curtains to let the gray spill onto the mirrors like a tide. The ballroom, awash in February light, had never looked more beautiful than when it held him within it.

* * *

Elias ran his finger down the spine of the thick ledger, its gold-plated letters faded to time. His eyes wandered to the higher shelves, the rows of books curling toward the ceiling, endlessly. For the first time that morning, he felt a sense of steadiness; numbers, unlike people, behaved predictably. They never concealed their meaning behind tone or motive. There were no hidden meanings, no surprise emotional shifts; they simply revealed, if you knew how to read them.

With his back pressed to a rather large desk chair, he adjusted the lamp beside him and the light pooled over the pages once he opened them. The ledger was part of the formal process — inventory, assessment, a clean record before the estate's transfer could be finalized. There was a certain comfort in the bureaucracy of it all: lists, appraisals, valuations. Everything was reduced to its worth on paper.

He turned the page, careful not to tear the edge, and began to total the figures in the margins. The ink smudged lightly where his thumb brushed it, then frowned as the error drew his eye to the line it accented. An inconsistency, in a previous steward's notation — small, but irksome. He made a correction in neat script, the act steadying his breath.

He flipped another page. The ink on this one bled unevenly, as though written in haste. The entries here were different. They were less careful, less symmetrical, and messier. Columns of numbers that should balance cleanly did not. He checked the sums more than once, expecting them to line up, as they continued not to. A transfer noted in the margin — to "private holdings." No location given. No date.

Elias leaned back, frowning faintly as his gaze drifted to the shelves towering around him. How many others had noticed similar peculiarities, gone unnoticed for decades? He tapped his pen against the mahogany desk, the sounds sharply echoing in the stillness.

There was a pattern here. He could almost see it, just beyond the edges of understanding. His fingers tightened around the pen, poised to trace it further when—

"Elias."

He startled slightly. Eleanor stood in the doorway, her coat draped over her arm and his own over the other. The fading light caught the faint gloss of her hair. How was it already late afternoon? He could've sworn—

"You've been shut in here all day," she said, her tone light but careful. "Come walk with me. It's near sunset, and you'll ruin your eyes in this light."

He hesitated, glancing once more at the ledger as if it might vanish the moment he left. How had he lost so many hours? Then, with visible effort, he closed it, the soft thud echoing in the still room.

"Very well," he said. His voice sounded distant to his own ears. "Just a moment."

She smiled faintly, polite and almost grateful, and waited as he straightened his collar and snatched his coat from her arm.

They stepped into the courtyard just as the sun dipped below the hills. The sunset was painted rose this evening along the dark gray of the oncoming clouds. The air was sharp, almost metallic, carrying the smell of damp earth and the faint smoke of the chimneys. The manor's shadow stretched long across the frost-dusted grass. Eleanor drew her shawl tight around her shoulders.

"You'll turn to stone if you keep yourself in there all year," she said softly. She looked up at him hopefully, with the innocence of a kitten.

Elias sighed, looking past her to the moors, though offered a small smile of amusement. "Maybe, but someone needs to balance our books and we both know it won't be him."

"No," she replied. "But I'd imagine the math would allow you at least a few moments of fresh air every now and then."

They walked in silence a while, their footsteps faintly crunching the frozen path beneath them. The garden was long overgrown — Thorn bushes crawling across gravel, broken ivy still crawling in the remains of a trellis. A few withered roses clung desperately to their stems, blackened by the frost. Eleanor stopped beside one, brushing it with a gloved hand along its petals as even the soft silk couldn't keep them together and they disintegrated at her feet.

"There's something sad about it," she noted. "Still hanging on."

Elias' eyes found hers slowly, his gaze moving from the petals on the ground to her rich umber eyes, finding her fixed on him in the same moment. "It's not sadness," He said after a moment passed between them. It still held in the air as he spoke. "Just persistence. It doesn't know it's dying."

Her hand fell from the branch. "You sound like you admire that."

"Perhaps I do."

The wind came stronger the further they moved into the garden. Eleanor held her shawl close to her body, eyes half-shut as her face turned into the icy blasts. It tugged at their coats as they stopped on the edge of the garden, Eleanor turning to her betrothed.

"When you're finished with all this bookkeeping and the will," She said, "what will you do? Stay here?"

He hesitated, unsure. "Until it's all settled and transferred.

After that, I suppose—"

"You don't suppose anything—" she said with a gentle, yet pointed smile. "You plan. You always plan."

Eleanor glanced sideways at him, her voice quieter now. "You don't have to keep proving you can make sense of it all, you know. You just need to prove you're trustworthy."

His eyes stayed on the horizon. "It's not about proof," he said. "It's about order."

"Is there a difference?"

They walked until the overgrown path gave way to the moors, the silence between them stretching long moments but comfortable. The grasses here rose in pale, brittle waves and the light had gone thin — that fragile moment before dusk when the world drains itself unceremoniously of color. Elias slowed, his eyes catching on a dip in the field ahead, where frost had gathered like lace upon the wildflowers. Eleanor slowed as well, her soft smile returning. She had been leading him here the entire evening; the manor had been leading him here his entire life.

"There," She said quietly.

Elias' eyes followed her gaze. "What is it?" More accurately, he wondered how much she knew and how much she pretended not to. Beneath the frost, the land opened into a hollow — a small, forgotten meadow, ringed by skeletal birches. The air was still here, unnervingly still, as if the wind dared not cross its boundary. Long gone were the rays of sun that bathed this clearing in the summers, replaced by snapped twigs and drips of almost—ice. Arcadia was gone.

Eleanor tilted her head. "It's beautiful," she said, unaware, "isn't it?"

Elias didn't answer. He knew this place. It graced no map,

and remained uncounted in ledgers. The air around him seemed to shift, the present slipping at the edges. He could almost feel the sunlight on his skin, hear the golden laughter among the twigs, light and reckless. The shimmer of water caught his eye nearby, where they had once thrown stones to watch the ripples catch in the light. Alice's Wonderland.

He turned — his gaze settling on a much smaller Alaric. He was younger, brighter, and his eyes held a vibrancy that had dulled years ago. They stood only feet apart, the air between them trembling with everything unspoken. Elias wanted to warn him, to speak with him, to just ask why. No noise came from his lips before the apparition spoke.

"You're staring again." Alaric said, though smiling.

"Am I?" Elias' voice sounded lighter, carried by the warmth of the sun.

"Alaric stepped closer. "If you keep looking at me like that, someone will start to wonder."

Elias, younger now himself as memory buzzed around him, almost laughed. "There's no one here to wonder."

Silence. The meadow hummed with the quiet of insects, the far-off murmur of the stream. Alaric's expression softened, something raw and human slipping through.

"Then why do you stop yourself?"

Elias opened his mouth to answer —

"Elias?"

The cold returned like shattering glass. The meadow of summer was gone, left dead in front of him once more. Eleanor's hand was on his sleeve, her brows knitted together with concern.

"You looked ill," she said with concern. "You just stopped."

He blinked, disoriented, his breath fogging in the persistent cold. "It's nothing," he said, his voice trembling slightly. "Just the air."

Eleanor looked back toward the hollow. "Let's go," she murmured. "It's colder here than it should be."

He nodded, but his eyes lingered on the birches, the faint impression of a shape in the frost that might have been two figures standing side by side, or perhaps merely the play of the wind on the grass.

By the time they reached the manor once more, the lamps had been lit and a fire roared in the hearth. Though the air had grown cold enough to sting the skin outside, the interior was at least warm enough for the two of them to remove their overcoats, shaking the frost from the sleeves. The warmth of the entrance hall hit him all at once as he followed Eleanor inside — too warm, and too alive. Somewhere deeper in the house, faint music drifted through the halls, the hesitant notes of piano searching for a melody. Eleanor paused, placing her own coat on a hook by the door, eyes following the sound as she tried to place it.

Elias frowned, "No one's supposed to—" But then he recognized the uneven rhythm, the touch that leaned too heavily on certain keys, as if testing them for sound.

"Alaric," he murmured.

They found him in the ballroom, sitting at the grand piano at the far end of the wall. His sleeves were rolled up to his elbows, his collar loosened. The fire in the hearth burned low and steady, throwing long and distorted shadows across the parquet. He looked up as they entered, his expression forming into a bitter smile.

"You've taken to walking at dusk, then. Romantic."

Eleanor hesitated by the door, a polite half-smile forming

on the corners of her mouth. "We thought the air might help. It's—"

"Damp." He finished, curt. He turned back to the piano, letting his fingers drift over the keys in an idle, discordant run. "Still, one must make one's own company."

There was a faint sweetness to his breath when he spoke — nothing so strong as to offend, but something he'd recognized in his tone a few times before. Brandy. The edge of it hung in the air between them. Elias crossed the room, eyeing the scattered papers on a nearby table. There were rough sketches of the ballroom's layout, pencil lines circling damaged corners and drafty eaves.

"You've been busy," Elias said, voice quiet but taut.

Alaric shrugged, still not meeting his gaze. "Idle hands are the devil's plaything."

"I wasn't aware you'd taken an interest in renovation."

"I take an interest in things that are falling apart," Alaric replied evenly. His tone was almost offhand, yet the words lingered longer than they should have like thick molasses.

Eleanor shifted slightly, reminding both of her presence as the atmosphere thickened in the room. "Dinner," she offered, simply. "If we mean to eat before it gets cold."

Alaric rose, pulling the cover back over the keys with a deliberate click. His movements were measured, graceful even, but something about them felt delayed, as if he were moving through water. "Of course," he said. "We wouldn't want to keep the ghosts waiting."

Eleanor nodded, offering a polite smile. Elias didn't speak, turning his lips into a thin line and placing the sketches back onto the table before following the two down the hall.

* * *

The dining room had been set with more elegance than sense. A decanter of Cabernet sauvignon sat open beside three polished glasses. The silver was impeccably chosen, the candles fit snugly in their holders. Alaric had insisted on lighting them himself, though his hand trembled slightly as he did so.

They ate slowly and silently, the scrape of metal against porcelain carrying down the hallways. Elias barely touched his food, the whole affair feeling somehow wrong and distilled. Eleanor spoke first, in that deliberate, composed tone she often managed.

"I saw the east wing on our walk," she said. "It's in dreadful shape. I imagine most of it would have to be torn down."

Alaric didn't look up from his plate, stirring some of his pork in its sauce. "Most of it will hold, if it's seen to soon enough."

"Seen to?" Elias said, the corners of his mouth twitching into a grimace. "Are you still seriously suggesting—"

"Whether there's conflict or not, it's part of the estate," Eleanor cut in, dabbing the corner of her mouth with a napkin. "You'll need to account for it, Elias."

"I have," he replied. "There's nothing of real value in the east wing. The ceilings are compromised, and the windows—"

"Windows can be replaced," Alaric interrupted. "History can't."

Elias gaze flickered to him, setting down his silverware with a careful clink. "I thought you hated this place."

"I do," Alaric said laconically, pouring himself more wine.

"But that doesn't mean it ought to rot. A ballroom like that—" he gestured vaguely toward the adjacent doors, "—deserves a second life."

Eleanor looked between them, sensing a spark catching in the still air. "You truly intend to restore the manor?"

"Eventually," Alaric said. "When the papers are settled, and Elias finishes playing mathematical historian."

Elias' gaze stilled, locking on the blond with something between annoyance and loathing. "The ledgers ensure that your flights of nostalgia don't bankrupt us before the year's end."

A faint smile touched Alaric's lips, dangerous in its restraint. "Ah, there it is. The financier's poetry. Please, romance me more aggressively."

Eleanor's eyes narrowed slightly. "We could at least consider what guests might think, if we mean to entertain again."

Elias turned to her, something sharp in his expression. "You think this place will ever host polite company again?"

She froze, though only for a breath. "I think it must, if it's to live. Otherwise it's just another mausoleum."

That word, mausoleum, hung heavy in the air between them. It was pregnant with malice, though Eleanor could never mean it to be. It was a word of damning, a word that marked them as mangled, long-dead things in the will of Greystone. Across the table, Alaric's fingers traced the edge of his glass. "Then let it be a beautiful one," he said softly.

Eleanor set her utensils down, too carefully. "If you'll excuse me," she said, rising. "I'll have Winnie bring us tea."

Her footsteps disappeared down the corridor, her skirts swishing along the carpet. The two men were left alone then, Alaric's half-lidded gaze meeting Elias' edged one. The candlelight flickered between them, a faint smell of wax burning filling the room as they locked in place. After a long, tense moment, Elias leaned back, staring at the red in his silver glass. She could see them in the mirror above the fireplace still, even from the kitchen, no true separation managed. "You're drunk."

"Not yet," Alaric murmured. "But I'm working towards it." He added, lifting his own wine glass in a mock toast before unenthusiastically bringing it to his lips.

"You shouldn't be," Elias said, though there was something almost tender in the words.

Alaric gave a short laugh. "And deprive you of your evening's martyrdom?"

Elias looked at him for a long time — too long. The candlelight danced on his rivals' features, highlighting every pore of his skin, the stubble at his lip, the light amount of sweat at his collar. In this light, he almost looked human. Long gone was the man of bravado in every ballroom over all the years, every party they'd ruined with their bickering, the way he could let it slide off his shoulders. But so long gone was his friend — the bright, enthusiastic brat prince who once pulled him by his hand through every hall of this once living manor as they ran from their lives outside of it. Instead, what sat in front of him was nothing more than a young man — slightly drunk and incredibly tired. Elias stood abruptly, pushing his chair back with a muted scrape.

"Do as you'd like," he said. "You always have." The door shut behind Elias with more force than he likely intended. The echo of it traveled the length of the dining room, stirring the candles on the table. Eleanor returned with a pot of tea, her eyes following him a moment after his departure before a sigh pushed out her lungs.

Across from her, Alaric also exhaled, long and low, and tipped the last of his wine into his glass. "I forget," he said, swirling it idly, "how much he hates to be wrong."

She looked at him sharply. "He wasn't wrong."

He raised a brow. "About which part?"

"The one where you treat money as if it grows from the ground."

"I'm not running an estate." He took a small sip, eyes drifting toward the darkened hall where Elias had gone. "I'm trying to keep it alive."

Eleanor's voice softened. "By drinking it back into its youth?"

Alaric's smile faltered, though his tone stayed light. "By remembering it as something worth saving."

They fell quiet once more, Eleanor lowering her head as she sat across from the man. She lifted the pot, pouring herself a steaming cup of tea and holding the cup between her palms to warm herself. The candlelight flickered, casting shadows on her cheek. Eleanor set down her teacup back onto the saucer not having ten a single sip.

"Has he always been like this?" She asked, staring into her own face reflected in oolong and honey.

Alaric's gaze returned to her slowly, the edge of a smirk pulling at one corner of his mouth. "Mathematical? Unbearably proud? Yes." He hesitated, then added more softly, "But not cruel. Not once."

Something in his expression — tender, too human — made her look away again. She rose, gathering her shawl and her teacup, pressing her lips together in thought for just a moment. "You should rest, Lord Greystone."

"Rest is for men with peace of mind." He retorted, examining his wine in the light of the candles.

She paused at the threshold, her fingers caressing the side of the door frame. She did not turn. "And what do you have?"

"Debt," He said, watching the light bend through his glass.

Eleanor almost smiled, despite herself. The moment caught her as quite silly, given the weight of it. "You speak like a poet," She said, light.

"Only when I've had too much to drink." But he didn't sound drunk. Only tired, the edges of his charm fraying with the wind outside.

The manor's shadows deepened as the candlelight waned, settling into a silence thick with things unsaid. After some time, Eleanor too said goodnight and drifted into the halls.

* * *

Alone now, Alaric's eyes drifted to a small, worn object half-hidden beneath the edge of the rug — a tarnished key, its metal dulled by time. He bent to retrieve it, fingers brushing the cold surface as a memory stirred.

That forgotten chamber behind the east wing, a silent refuge and a shared burden. They had found it one evening while searching for quiet, reckless children unknowing of the weight it would carry. He traced the faint etchings of the key's surface, the patterns nearly lost to misuse and time. How strange, he thought, that such a small thing could hold so much. The manor had always been a cage, but that room was the heart of it, the place where secrets whispered louder than voices, where promises were made in shadows.

He remembered the hush as they slipped inside, candlelight bouncing off the walls as if it were an accusation. The cold stone walls, the faint smell of dust and disuse, the heavy stillness pressing close. They had sworn never to speak of it again, a pact forged in fear and something unspoken, something that had begun to unravel the tender bond between them.

Alaric pressed the key into his palm, a slow, bitter ache settling beneath his ribs. The manor's unrest was no stranger to him, but tonight it felt closer, more urgent, as if the house itself demanded the secrets buried within that room be unearthed once more.

He glanced toward the door, half-expecting Elias to appear, to challenge or to retreat, but the room remained empty.

Alaric remained coldly, and terribly, alone.

II

Part Two

6

March, 1880

The thaw came reluctantly to Greystone manor. Snow still clung to the edges of the courtyard where the sun refused to mingle, and the air inside the manor had taken on that damp, heavy chill that seemed to come from the cracks of the stone. Elias had made the library his refuge, spilling documents across every desk within it and only drawing the curtains open in the mornings to cast light on the ledgers and correspondences he'd uncovered. The estate's accounts spread like veins across parchment, each column of numbers pulling him deeper into the rhythm of calculations. He barely looked up when anyone passed the threshold, a world outside of his own.

They'd settled into a pattern that one could hardly call peace — Alaric in the east wing at all hours, taking measurements, logging damage, tallying rot. Elias remained in the library, turning figures across centuries into order. They spoke only at meals and when necessary as Eleanor, caught between them, had grown pale from the strain of their civility.

By mid-month, Alaric had the ballroom half gutted. The

tarps over the furniture looked like funeral shrouds. Dust rose in gentle plumes whenever someone crossed the floor. He'd pulled down the curtains recently, his flask always at his hip, his hands restless when there was nothing left to move and he was compelled to call in a crew to begin his watch over.

"You'll drain the accounts before it's even started," Elias said one afternoon, leaning tiredly against the doorway.

Alaric didn't turn, a slender finger at his lips in thought. "Then I'll sell something else. Like your sense of proportion."

Elias' lips tightened. "It's not the proportion I mind, nor manage. It's a waste."

"I prefer repair."

The exchange ended as most of theirs did— not with resolution, but with silence, Elias turning on his heel and withdrawing, the sound of his steps swallowed by the corridor.

Eleanor, who had taken to taking walks on the grounds alone, watched the two of them from a distance. The manor seemed livelier, but its floor creaked more every night, its walls whispering faintly in the wind. It kept her awake, but she had been keeping track of it in a journal, as though it might chase away the ghosts.

That was the month Winifred began to linger longer in the morning, perhaps in pity, or perhaps in concern. She'd appear with bread or with tea, speaking softly with Eleanor of trivial things — the weather, old Greystone gossip, the strain of work — and somehow, those conversations began to fill the emptiness Elias had left. Once, Eleanor had asked, "why do you stay here, when it's all so cold?"

Winifred smiled faintly, her eyes lowered. "Someone must remember the warmth, ma'am. Otherwise, the house forgets it ever had any."

She stayed mostly in the drawing rooms that month, the corners of the manor that still felt lived-in. The others were too cold, too heavy in their grandeur. Every morning, she began to wake to the sounds of hammers in the west wing — Alaric's workmen, scraping plaster and demolishing old brick. It was a comfort at first, that distant noise of labor, but by the third week, it began to feel intrusive. Winifred came and went as she pleased, never announcing her presence, but appearing with the soft authority of someone who had always belonged there.

They took tea by the hearth when the afternoon turned gray, the sound of rain on the glass almost pleasant. Winifred had a way of coaxing her to speak— not of present, but of before. Of America, of her father's company, of the long months she spent after his remarriage to some Englishwoman in mink, pretending to fit in in rooms she didn't belong in. How Elias made her feel at least somewhat comfortable in those rooms, and the long months spent alone after their engagement was announced. How she missed her mother in San Francisco, and how illness should have spared her… Elias, again.

"You must have been proud," Winifred said once, handing her a slice of bread. "To marry into an English line so storied."

Eleanor smiled faintly, "pride isn't the word."

"What, then?"

"Obligation, perhaps," She paused, pressing her lips together. "Inevitability."

Winifred tilted her head. "That's not the same as a choice."

No," Eleanor admitted. "It isn't."

The maid only nodded, as if she already knew the answer.

For a while they said nothing, listening to the rain outside on the camellias. It came down harder now, tracing faint silver paths along the windowpane. Somewhere in the house, a clock struck the hour, the sound lingering longer than it should have. Eleanor rose to fill the teapot, and when she turned, Winifred was watching the window with a faraway expression — almost reverent.

"Do you ever think," The maid muttered, "that the house knows when someone doesn't belong?"

Eleanor's brows furrowed, unsure she'd heard correctly. "Knows?"

Winifred smiled, the expression soft rather than mocking. "It has its ways of keeping balance. Every house does."

Before Eleanor could respond, a scuffle of hurried feet sounded in the corridor beyond the parlor. Voices—two of the maids, speaking in hushed tones. Then, a name. Martha. When Eleanor stepped into the hall, they fell silent. Only Winifred remained seated, pouring herself another cup with unshaken calm.

* * *

As the rain thinned and the daylight shadow crawled across the floors of the manor, Eleanor pulled her shawl tight around her shoulders and left the parlor. The remainder of her morning tea was cut short by the commotion, and she found herself restless. The house felt heavier in these moments, it's hush intent rather than comforting.

As she meandered, her gaze caught a glimpse of Elias through the half—open door to the library. He was bent over his papers, his hand moving feverishly across a page. He didn't look up. She could hear the forceful sound of a book cover snapping shut as she walked away, and the following sound of a spine from another cracking open.

In the corridor ahead, she spotted two maids stood whispering, their faces pale as they turned towards her. One of them curtsied too quickly, the other muttering something about, "not since breakfast," and fell silent. Eleanor hesitated, then nodded politely and carried past them, her footsteps echoing through the long gallery into the adjacent wing until she reached the ballroom doors.

Alaric stood near the windows, a pen tucked between his middle and forefingers, caught in thought. Afternoon light spilled across the parquet, catching in the fractals of his glass. The brown liquor caught and rippled light onto the stool behind him as he spoke quietly to himself — numbers, proportions, textures. His voice broke the silence in a way that felt almost defiant.

When he heard her approach, he straightened, turning on his heel. "Lady Draven," he purred.

She lingered near the threshold, watching the pale light play games with his curves and in the gold of his hair. "I… I didn't mean to interrupt," she said softly, crossing into the room. It was as if she were pulled in, her curiosity leading her.

"You didn't," he replied, lifting his crystal glass from its clashing resting place of an uneven stool and taking a single, quick swig. "There isn't much to interrupt."

For a moment, neither party spoke. The air was still except for the faint groan of the old windows, a protest against the pervicacious cold. She looked past him as she joined his side, eyes scanning the state of the room since she'd seen it last. The mirrors were dull, the parquet scuffed, and the chandeliers hung like cobwebs, but there was indeed a sliver of life within it these days.

"Does it start here?" She asked at last. "The work, I mean. Beyond simple repair."

He followed her gaze, then nodded. "It has to start somewhere. And this—" He gestured broadly at the room before them, "—was meant for dances, laughter, all the illusions that make this life tolerable."

She almost smiled. "You sound like a poet."

He gave a short, mirthless laugh. "Elias said the same once. Though, I think he meant it as an insult."

Eleanor smiled once more, stepping into the room further to brush her hand against one of the mirrors. "The air is colder here than anywhere else in the house," she noted, almost absentmindedly.

Alaric followed her lead, standing close enough for her to smell the starch of his collar and the sharpness on his breath. "The air gets trapped in rooms like this," he said, eyes focused on the far wall, as though a memory had unfolded there. "No one opens them up long enough to let it out."

She found herself gazing over at him in the reflection, finding something wistful and almost gentle in his tone. In this golden light, he was almost real. The way the light danced on his skin, the slight smell of some sweet cologne mixed with brandy, She found herself wondering how someone like Elias would wish to spar with this man so much; Alaric seemed to her in some moments like some misunderstood child. Much as he'd said about Elias only a month before, both could be stubborn, but not cruel. Never once cruel. Upon finding herself staring, she dropped her gaze from the mirror's cold truth to the safety of her own hands.

"And you intend to change that?" She asked.

"Perhaps," He smiled faintly, tilting his head. "If the manor will allow it."

She studied him for another long moment. He looked different in the gray afternoon light — less flippant, and so normal. She wanted to say something kind, something that might tether the moment before it slipped back into silence, but he was already turning toward the center of the room again, lost in thought.

"Tea is in an hour or so." She said, politely nodding once more.

"I'll be down shortly, Miss Draven." He said absentmindedly, his glass back to his lips and his eyes scanning the window-panes.

* * *

As she left, the silence settled back in like dust. Alaric remained by the window, listening to her steps fade into the creak of the floorboards. He caught himself glancing toward the door, listening for her voice, her laugh, some small proof of her life. When he heard her footsteps pause in the corridor, he spoke before he could reconsider.

"Lady Draven," He called, his voice light but uncertain.

She turned, framed by the door, pulling her shawl closer to her core.

"Stay a moment," he said, nodding toward the decanter at the far end of the room. "There's still a little wine left. It'd be a shame to waste it."

For a moment, she seemed poised to refuse. Then she smiled, polite and restrained, and crossed back into the ballroom. The

101

light had begun to fade now, dimming into the pale gold of the late afternoon. He crossed the room, fetching the decanter and a glass which did not match his own. While his own glass of brandy remained abandoned on its podium, he poured one glass of the Cabernet into a silver chalice and the other into a porcelain teacup, offering her the proper vessel in a show of politeness.

"How is the mathematician these days anyhow?" Alaric asked, his tone gentle and fragile. His companion sighed, taking a sip from her glass that seemed too long.

"Elias works himself to the bone," she answered after a while. "I can scarcely get him out of that chair, let alone out of the room."

Alaric gave a small laugh, though it didn't sound amused. "He's been like that since boyhood. Numbers, measurements, figures— all that order to keep from thinking too much."

"About what, exactly?" She pried, her eyes wide with concern. Alaric looked down into his cup.

"The rest of it."

They fell silent again. She sipped from her stemmed glass, and he couldn't help but to watch the faint color return to her cheeks as she did so, the way her eyes softened when she gazed at the floor. Her dark hair fell in loose strands around her face, the rest pinned tightly in an intricately braided style. He noticed the soft curve of her fingers as she smoothed them over the sides of her cup nervously, her mind miles away. Her eyes were deep and longing, as if simply looking into them could transport others far away with her.

"I do wonder," she said, "if he even notices how alone he's become."

Alaric hesitated, then met her gaze. "I think he does. That's the cruel part."

She nodded softly, and for just a moment — just long enough for him to feel it — they understood one another. Distantly, both heard the faint snap of a heavy book closing.

* * *

Elias had placed himself in the library before noon, but now the gold of the late afternoon began to touch every item on the worn desk. Strewn across it were ledgers in no particular order, heavy with dust and their columns fading into sepia. He had begun transcribing figures hours ago, but the rhythm of it had dissolved into something else entirely.

He traced fingertips along the margin of a page, notes in another hand entirely scrawled beside the figures and fortunes. *Lord Edwin Greystone, 1829.* The name appeared again and again as though insisting on being remembered. He could almost imagine the man in this very room, poised above these very same pages, thinking the same thoughts or perhaps none at all.

He leaned back in his chair, pressing his fingers to his temples and closing his eyes. Edwin Greystone had been a distant man in his later years, yes, but he had still raised the boys in his own way, a handful of summers and a sliver of hope stretched across their youth. Elias's own father had been a ghost long before his death, muttering to walls, empty pockets jangling where affection should've been, though technically living. His mother, proud and threadbare, had followed him into that same quiet madness, clinging to the estate with only enough sense left to keep it standing.

He could not remember a single smile between them. But through a generations-old partnership, he'd been sent to the Greystone estate each summer, the lone bright thing in an otherwise colorless childhood. Even now, that memory carried a strange tenderness, a reminder that hope, however meager, had once existed.

He exhaled, slow and unsteady. The study smelled of dust and old leather, and he could almost hear Edwin's voice somewhere between the pages, that calm, exacting tone that had once steadied him. It was Edwin who taught him to balance a ledger, to watch the margins, to notice when something didn't add up. Edwin who'd said that a house could only stand as long as its keeper remained attentive.

What had become of Edwin was no cleaner than what had become of his golden boys. Between them lingered only broken promises and the aftertaste of words said in anger. Laughter had long since fled these halls; nearly a decade had passed since it last echoed against the marble. Its absence felt as tangible as the sinking of the east wing— undeniable, but heavy. Once, they had torn through these corridors hand in hand, whispering secrets beneath chandeliers. Now, that joy had gone the way of the summer sunsets, swallowed by years they could not reclaim.

The quiet loomed around him, its silence more accusing than kind. He wondered if Edwin would recognize what had become of his home. When the letter had come, he'd been too in shock to let the full weight of it hit him; those summers had been gone for years, but now too was the guiding presence he'd relied on for so long. It settled beneath his ribs and stayed there, a dull companion, whispering of debts unpaid and promises unmet.

Then, through the stillness, a faint warmth stirred like sunlight slipping through a cracked window. It carried with it the scent of earth and blossoming trees, and for a moment, the heavy silence cracked. The orchard wall rose before him, bathed in the soft gold of late afternoon, rough stones cool beneath small, eager hands.

Elias could almost feel the roughness of the stone beneath his palms, cool and uneven, a tactile certainty against the rot of a faded memory. He and Alaric had been reckless then — two boys chasing freedom in the edges of the estate. Their laughter had threaded through the tree branches and halls like birdsong. The orchard was a secret world, a paradise of Victoria plums and sunlight, a pocket suspended in time.

He remembered the warmth of Alaric's hand as it brushed his own in its clumsy hurriedness. His touch was quick, but electric, and left a lasting heat behind. They whispered secrets beneath the heavy boughs, voices low and urgent, making promises they did not yet understand. Every glance held the tremor of things left unspoken, and the excitement of what they could mean.

The sky was a furnace of gold and pink, and the sun slipped low, gilding the leaves in fire. Even then, their laughter lingered on something fragile, as if the coming dusk and the loom of the manor may swallow it whole. Elias' chest tightened with the ache of knowing, but lightened with the softness of Alaric's gaze. The orchard wall was a threshold. Between the stones and the sky, between who they were and what they could never return to.

As the sun dipped behind the distant hills, the orchard's golden light faded, and the boys' laughter was swallowed by the growing dusk. The secret world had folded closed, leaving only echoes that shimmered faintly beneath the surface of memory. Elias' breath hitched in his throat. The weight beneath his ribs pressed harder, a dull ache whispering of debts unpaid, of promises broken long ago.

Elias blinked, and the vision slipped away. The room was empty again. His fingers curled tightly around the ledger's worn edge, seeking something steady amid the rot. The orchard lingered, a flicker of light in the gathering shadows — a reminder that once, beneath these broken halls, there had been something worth holding onto.

He opened the ledger again, though the figures swam before his eyes. Elias blinked hard, though it did little good. A few tears had gathered at the corner of his eyes despite himself, as he thumbed the page. It was foolish to mourn all this rot, but as he pressed his thumb to the page, he felt himself using it to steady his body.

He drew a shallow breath and lowered his gaze to the ledger once more. The ink had bled faintly in places, curling into veins along the paper as if the damp had gotten to it. He traced a column of figures down the page, routine and familiar, until one caught his attention. The ink here curled unnaturally and branched out into the crevices of the paper as if it were still wet. The entry bore his own signature, dated months before he'd even arrived.

Elias frowned, leaning closer. The handwriting was unmistakably his, right down to the way he looped his E. Yet, he had no recollection of ever signing this book, let alone seeing it before now. He turned the page, finding another entry, and another— all in his hand, all impossible.

He exhaled, pushing back in his chair. "Ridiculous," he muttered to no one. A trick of fatigue, of memory. He shut the ledger, pressing his palm to its cover, and sat in silence. The room seemed to settle around him. The whisper of the fire, the faint creak of wood, were all too alive for his liking.

He gathered the ledger under one arm and made for the door, intending to take a walk through the corridors and clear his head. The air outside the library was cooler, thinner somehow, touched with the faint echo of voices from the servants' quarters. He paused on the landing, listening.

"…Since dawn, they said. No one has 'een her since went for the linens."

"Not a word? Not even her apron?"

"Nothin' but the bucket by the scullery. And Martha's rosary."

Elias hesitated mid-step. The name was one he recognized, though not a servant he had much interaction with. Yet the note of fear in their voices gave him pause. He leaned lightly on the banister, as if listening from a dream. For a moment, he considered investigating himself, tossing on his coat and embarking on a hero's mission, but the impulse refused to release. It would be handled, he told himself. These things happened in large estates; servants would go missing for a day or two and turn up in the opposite wing with a basket of new laundry no one had thought to mention.

Still, as he turned away, he couldn't seem to shake the thought of her things in her room— her rosary, placed in the center of her bed, as though left as an offering. The sound lingered like a drought behind him as he climbed the stairs, the ledger pressed close to his chest.

He walked instead. Down the hall, past rooms that had been left unopened since their arrival. The silence deepened there — the kind that makes its own presence known, pulsing faintly in the walls.

He stopped outside Edwin's old study. The door was shut, though he could have sworn he left it ajar earlier that day. He opened the door again, stepping inside hesitantly but curious. The air inside was stale, heavy with pipe smoke that could not possibly linger still but must have bled into the wallpaper. Edwin's desk stood as it had been left. Papers were stacked neatly, and the old clock had frozen beside the window. A layer of dust graced the desk, undisturbed. Elias touched the edge of the desk, tracing a finger through it. There was a faint indentation near the blotter, as if someone had once rested their hand there for too long, accompanied by a half-smoked cigarette put out in an ashtray. His throat tightened unexpectedly.

He sat. Edwin's chair creaked underneath him, and for a while he did not move. It felt as though the house were listening expectantly, waiting for him to say something, anything. He tried to speak — apologies on his tongue for Alaric's distance, for Edwin's solitude, for his own melancholy as of late— but the words all died in his throat. Before he could find better words, easier ones perhaps, a faint sound drew him back.

He tilted his head towards its source. A slow drip from the corner of the ceiling had begun to form. The plaster there was stained, faintly darker than the rest, as though damp from the spring rain during the week. It should have unsettled him less than it did. He rose, stepping closer. The droplets hit the floorboards one by one, darkening the grain. The smell that accompanied it was not of water. Metallic. Sharp.

He exhaled, shakily. "You're losing it, Thorne," he muttered, adjusting his cuffs as if to restore some dignity. As he left the room, he did not feel alone. While he passed the cavernous windows leading towards the dining room, he could have sworn he caught the faintest reflection of a figure beside him. He could not shake the feeling that something in the house had just turned its gaze upon him.

* * *

Elias followed the long corridor to the dining room, where the table had already been set in meticulous symmetry. Candlelight flickered along the polished silver and fine china, casting wavering shadows across the walls. The house was too quiet and the occasional groan of settling wood reminded him how ancient the place had become. Alaric sat already at one end of the table, his posture loose as he twirled a half-drained glass of wine slowly between his fingers.

Eleanor occupied the head seat of the table. She looked up when he entered, a faint flush lingering on her cheeks. For a moment, his eyes flickered to his rival and back to hers, convinced they had been speaking but finding only silence now. Only the faint sound of the clock ticking and the low hum of the fire filled the room, the faint scrape of his chair on the floor breaking the pressing stillness.

"So you do live," Alaric said, his tone light but carrying a familiar edge of mockery. "You've hardly left the library in days."

Elias took his place across from him, a maid rushing to hand him a glass of red wine. She seemed unfamiliar, inexperienced and nervous even. His thoughts wandered to the talk he'd overheard earlier, trying to remember if Martha was the one who normally attended them for dinner under Winnie's cold, careful direction. He cleared his throat, placing a napkin in his lap and smoothing it.

"There is much to be done, Alaric. That is all," Elias remarked, refusing to meet his gaze.

"Always is," Alaric murmured, leaning back. The candlelight caught the curve of his smile. "Though I doubt the dead keep such long hours."

Eleanor glanced between them, her brow slightly furrowed. "The dead?" She repeated, a small polite question in a restrained tone. Elias' eyes glanced up to meet hers for the first time in weeks. Her piercing gaze suddenly sent a wave of guilt through him as he picked up his fork and managed a bite of roast chicken, feeling defeated.

"An old family joke," Alaric answered before Elias could shift the spotlight off himself. "The manor has a way of keeping its ghosts busy."

A flicker of irritation crossed Elias' face. "If we must personify it, I'd prefer to think it simply drafty."

He reached for his wine, finding it stronger than he remembered. His hand trembled slightly, enough to make the glass ring faintly against the table. The sound lingered, unnervingly sharp. For a moment, no one spoke. Eleanor's eyes were downcast, her fork idle against her plate. Alaric looked elsewhere — the hearth, the plate — his usual confidence tempered by something unseen.

"You've been unwell," Eleanor finally said softly. "You look pale."

Elias forced a thin smile. "Merely tired. The damp has been worse than usual. I promise, once the warmth returns—"

"The damp," Alaric repeated, almost amused. "Yes, that

explains everything."

Their eyes met across the table, a spark catching between them as Eleanor watched both carefully. She managed a few more bites of her food before being interrupted by a cautious Winifred, who leaned down to whisper something into the lady's ear. She excused herself with a soft, polite "if you'll excuse me," flashing one more pitiful glance in Elias' direction before disappearing down the corridor. The food had gone cold. The candle nearest him flickered, guttered low, and steadied again.

Elias stared after her for a moment longer than was proper. The echo of her footsteps retreated into the corridor, leaving only the tick of the clock and the faint pop of fat in the candlesticks. When he finally looked back across the table, Alaric was watching him. His gaze was not too cruel, but not kind either, with the faintest trace of a smirk that never reached his eyes.

"Seems the lady's grown weary of our company," Alaric said, reaching for his glass. The wine trembled faintly against the rim before he steadied it. "Pity she's wasted here."

Wasted. Elias' appetite was gone as he turned, gazing into his dinner as if it would save him from this interaction. His jaw tightened.

"And yet you thrive."

A faint smile touched the corner of Alaric's mouth, bordering mischievous. "Oh, I make do," he responded, bringing his glass to his lips. "Adaptation is a virtue, wouldn't you say?"

"Or opportunism," Elias said, more sharply than he'd intended.

Alaric tilted his head. "Is there a difference?"

For a moment, the tension hung thick in the air between

them. The air felt oppressive, leaning in to watch as the two argued, encouraging it. Elias reached for his wine, the movement deliberate as if reaching through honey,

"You always did have a talent for comfort, no matter whose table you sit at."

"And you," Alaric returned smoothly, "always mistake solitude for dignity."

Their eyes locked, and the silence that followed carried with it something familiar. When Alaric finally rose, it was with the careless grace that Elias had always despised. The blond collected his empty glass, walking towards the decanter by the hearth.

"Do try to take better care of yourself, Thorne. Before you start conversing with the wallpaper."

Elias frowned, caught in his charisma like a fly in a web once more. "I'd expect better conversation than this."

That earned him the faintest laugh — low, genuine, and infuriatingly soft. Alaric turned then, refilling his glass to the rim once more, a single drop of the liquid rolling down the side of the thick glass bottle. Elias remained at the table for a moment more, his eyes wandering again to the corridor where Eleanor had gone, and rose without a word.

The warmth of the dining room fell away behind him as he stepped into the darkness of the hall. The house had settled into its nightly silence, the dark pressing in as if to listen closer. Somewhere above, a beam groaned and a draft wandered the hall like a living thing. He pulled his dressing coat closer to his body, feeling rather small, like a prey animal in an unkind forest. He told himself it was the wine, or the fatigue, or the creeping damp that found itself into the walls, the paper, lungs.

He paused at the base of the stairs. Eleanor's room was just at the far end of the upper corridor, where the candle sconces burned low. For a moment, he considered the following: He could knock on her door, ask if she was unwell, offer some apology he could not name. He could offer her companionship and warmth in this situation he felt he'd placed her in, despite her choice to join. Instead, he turned toward the library.

The door resisted him slightly, as if swollen by the rain settling over the moors. Inside, the air was heavy and stale with the same metallic tang he'd noticed in Edwin's office. He lit only one candle; the room seemed to prefer the half-dark. He sank into a worn armchair, the leather cool beneath him, and wrapped his coat tighter. The storm's voice grew louder— a low, rolling growl. For all his anger and hurt, the loneliness clawed with equal ferocity.

A quiet step approached. Alaric appeared in the doorway, his face softened by the flickering candlelight, eyes steady and concerned without a word. He carried a folded blanket, which he draped gently over Elias's shoulders before settling into the chair beside him. From the far younger appearance of the boy and his own closed eyes, he could recognize this as a vivid memory, tinged with the wine from dinner.

The distant rumble of thunder drifted through the manor like a restless whisper, barely disturbing the fragile quiet between them. Elias' eyes stayed fixed on the rain sliding down the windowpane, tracing lazy rivers through the glass. Outside, the world folded into shadow and water, but here in the dim candlelight, time felt suspended. It was fragile, like a breath held too long.

"You know," young Alaric said softly, voice careful, as if afraid to disturb the silence, "I keep thinking about the White Rabbit."

Elias glanced over at the boy beside him, wary and curious. "The one who's always running?"

"Yeah," Alaric said, a small, bittersweet smile tugging at his lips. "Always rushing, like he's chasing something he can't quite catch… always a little frantic, like he's scared of being left behind."

Elias' eyes slipped back to the windowpane, the incessant battering of the rain against the glass.

Alaric shifted closer, the candlelight playing shadows across his freckled face. "And Alice— she's the one who follows, even when the path's confusing. Even when she's scared."

Elias swallowed hard, the tightness in his chest twisting. He felt raw and fragile, but Alaric felt so warm beside him that it almost didn't matter. "I'm no Alice," he said quietly, almost bitterly. "I'm the rabbit. Always running. Always afraid."

Alaric's hand moved slowly, settling on Elias' shoulder with a warmth that felt unearned. "Maybe," he whispered, "even the White Rabbit needs someone to slow the chase. Someone to remind him it's okay to stop, even if just for a moment."

The thunder cracked and the candle flickered then, earning a wince from Elias. His fingers curled around the lapels of his coat, knuckles white as the shadows danced on the walls like ghosts. His voice cracked as he finally let a piece of the truth slip free. "The thunder… it's always been louder for me. Like the sky's trying to find me, no matter where I run."

Alaric's thumb smoothed over Elias' shoulder, a quiet promise. "I know." After a long pause, Alaric's voice came again, fragile and full of hope. "Sometimes, I think Alice was brave because she wasn't alone. Because someone was beside her, even when the way was dark."

The thunder rolled again, softer this time, like a distant

memory fading at the edges. Elias's breath slowed, the chill inside him loosening, letting a fragile warmth seep in. "Thank you," he whispered.

"Always," Alaric replied, hand lingering for a heartbeat longer before retreating.

Always.

In the current hour, the ledger still lay open where he'd left it. While the ink had dried into dull strokes, the words seemed to lurch out at him, as confronting as they'd been before. His own handwriting — confident, diligent— swam across the page, recording transitions that could not exist. Figures that made no sense. Names of men long-dead and men half-alive. He'd scrawled his own father's name with a chilling aggression. He brushed his fingers along the margin. The paper was cold.

He had wanted to laugh at it earlier. He had wanted to dismiss it for exhaustion, or an idle mistake of the imagination. But now, alone in the dimness, the thought of his hand as it clutched the pen now poised in its holder, moving across the page without memory… it filled him with something quieter than fear.

He thought of Eleanor again, her expression at the table: patient, worried, almost loving. Her brows knitted together with that same faint crease she wore only at her most unsettled. He should have said something — anything. He should have given her less reason to worry. Instead, he'd let Alaric's words curdle the air and he'd only upset her for it.

He closed the ledger, carefully as if it might protest, and pressed a hand to his temple. "You're fine," he whispered to no one. "You're fine…"

The candle flickered low, its light catching a brass latch on the door. For a moment, something seemed to shift —

as though something behind it had exhaled. Elias looked up sharply, but there was nothing. Only the stillness of the shelves and the light tick of the rain at the windows remained. He exhaled, long and unsteady, and remained there — a solitary figure in the half light, burying his face into his palms— while the manor listened.

* * *

The corridor upstairs was dim and narrow, lit only by the weak light of a single candle Winifred carried. Eleanor followed, her steps soft against the runner, her pulse still quick from the tension downstairs. Eleanor was frayed, her eyes betraying a slight panic to them. If it weren't for her companion, she would feel completely engulfed by the dramatics of these so-called gentlemen.

"I hope you'll forgive me, miss," Winifred said, her voice low but not unkind. She closed the door behind them, pausing to place her candle in a nearby bronze stand. With her own hands free, she followed Eleanor to her dressing table, standing dutifully by her side as the lady removed her earrings in haste. "I thought you looked in need of a breath."

Eleanor pressed both hands on the furniture, sighing to steady herself. "I daresay that was a mercy. The air down there could be cut with a knife."

Winifred gave a quiet laugh, though it didn't reach her eyes. "You've not eaten much," she said softly. "It isn't wise to sit through these dinners on an empty stomach. The gentlemen forget, but you mustn't."

"I wasn't hungry." Eleanor untied the ribbons at her wrists,

116

her movements distracted. "It's only that the room felt…" She paused, searching for the word. "Close."

Winifred smiled faintly. "This house does press upon the nerves, if you let it. It's best to keep the mind elsewhere."

Eleanor sat, her body growing weary with the tension it had held throughout the entire month. Would that interaction be the only time she'd see her fiance all month? The thought hitched in her throat, swallowed, unaccepted. She leaned lazily on her palm and her elbow as she spoke, her eyes finding Winifred's in the reflection. "He's been working himself thin again," she finally said, met by concern rising to Winnie's face. "Elias, that is."

Winifred hesitated, her hands joining in front of her. "I'd noticed," she said, almost mournful. "It's not good for a man to be left alone so long with his thoughts. Or with this house."

Eleanor's eyes found her own reflection, pale and tired, shadowed by the candle's glow. She reached up to unpin her hair, met by Winifred making quick work of unbraiding and brushing the rest of it. She sat in a chair beside her, caressing her locks as if they were something precious, which was more concern than Eleanor often had for herself. For a few beats, they sat in silence, letting the night ease them into their safe solitude once more.

Then, as if it were the crash of a wave, "And what of Mr. Greystone? He doesn't strike me as the sort to suffer solitude."

Winifred's expression shifted, the faintest crease of disapproval. "That one makes company of anything that flatters him. You'd do well to mind that."

"I intend to," She said, quiet.

Winifred came closer, placing a strand of hair behind Eleanor's ear. It reminded her of a mother's touch; there was a certain warmth to it that felt like the draw of a venus flytrap. Her descent into its confines would be molasses—sweet and safe. She cast her eyes down to her own hands in her lap.

"You've a kind heart, miss. Too kind, perhaps. Be wary where you place your sympathy. Men like them…" Winnie paused, her gaze momentarily distant. "They draw the warmth out of a room and call it affection."

Eleanor turned slightly, meeting her eyes in the mirror. "You speak as if from experience."

The candle guttered once, throwing their reflections into brief disarray. When the flame steadied again, Winifred's face seemed softer than before. It was almost motherly as she twisted her lips into a faint, thin smile. "You should rest," She said. "Dream something kinder than this place."

It was then that Winifred placed a soft kiss on her forehead and stood, her footsteps echoing in the room as she made her way to the door. She gave Eleanor one last dutiful nod before sealing her in entirely, leaving her to her own reflection. The candlelight seemed to recede from her face, as if ashamed of its own brightness. She removed her jewelry piece by piece, each small sound amplified in the stillness.

She could not recall the last time Elias had looked at her and truly seen. Not through her, not past her, but at her. His eyes were always somewhere else: fixed on the ledgers, on the cracked ceilings, on some private torment she was not invited to share. There had been a time when she pitied him for it. Lately, the pity had thinned into something like impatience. Her gaze analyzed the woman sat before her in the glass, faintly doubling in the warped surface. For an instant she imagined another face behind her own — not a ghost, but a shadow of who she had been before entering this world.

Lively, certain, still in possession of a future. A shiver crawled down her arms. She pulled her shawl closer and turned toward the window. Below, the courtyard lamps burned low, and she thought she saw movement — someone passing by, quick, golden-haired. A rosary catching the moonlight.

She blew out her candle. The room darkened, and the rain's rhythm filled it entirely.

7

The Lost April, 1880

The rain had stopped without anyone noticing.

For weeks, it had been their constant. The subtle tapping of droplets on glass fell into a sort of rhythm that none of them found abrasive. Now, the silence it left behind felt unnatural. Even the house seemed to hesitate, still holding on to words unsaid. April had come, or so Elias believed. The almanac said so, though the pages were warped and spotted from damp. He could not remember turning them.

The mornings had grown brighter, the light spilling into the entire west wing, but the halls remained gray and oppressive and the air thick with dust no one could seem to clear. Somewhere in the east wing, Alaric had begun tearing at the walls, the plaster a mess on the floors and the boards exposed to the elements and his audacity. Elias could hear the crew hammering at odd hours — morning, noon, midnight, he could no longer tell. The rhythm slipped into his thoughts until he swam in it.

In the late evenings, when the fire settled and burnt its last embers, he would find his writing again in the ledgers. These were entries he did not recall making, though they were neat as if written by his steadier self. April 9th, one of them read. *The work continues. Progress immeasurable.* A sum. An impossibility. He had not written it. But there it was.

The clock struck once, twice, and faltered on its third attempt. Elias straightened, waiting for the sound to repeat. It did not. For a long moment, he simply sat, listening to the hush that followed, and wondered whether this was how the month had been lost: not vanished, but quietly replaced. Perhaps it was 3pm.

A folded slip of paper slipped from between the ledger's worn pages, fluttering to the floor. Elias bent down, fingers trembling as he unfolded it. The paper was thin, edges frayed, and the ink faded but unmistakably Alaric's handwriting — precise, deliberate, but hesitant.

Elias,

I don't know what to do anymore. It's getting worse. Your father's eyes aren't the same. He talks to shadows no one else can see, and sometimes he looks right through me, like I'm not even there.

I'm scared. I don't want you to be here when it gets bad. Please don't come back. Stay at school. Stay away from all this. I wish I could fix it. I wish I could make it stop. But I can't. Not anymore.

I'm sorry.

The edges of the letter trembled in his grasp, the room suddenly colder, heavier. How long had this been hidden? How many nights had passed without either of them speaking a single word of it? The weight of silence pressed against him, the ache of a secret kept too long burning beneath his skin.

Elias folded the letter carefully, fingers lingering on the fragile edges as if the paper might dissolve beneath his touch.

He pressed it to his chest, a silent plea for understanding he wasn't sure he deserved anymore.

Outside the library, Eleanor's laughter echoed faintly. She moved with Alaric these days, teasing and light, brushing his hair from his eyes as he adjusted a new scaffold. Their interactions had grown bolder, threading the air with tension, but Alaric barely noticed—his mind was elsewhere, in the rhythm of renovation, in the compulsion to uncover, fix, and preserve. Elias was thankful for this latest feverish obsession of his companion's. It kept him out of trouble.

In the corner of the library, the painting of them lay propped at an angle on the floorboards. The frame had been removed during renovations, but its presence was still felt. He'd tossed a drop-cloth over it to avoid his own sad, pitiful eyes boring into his skin while he worked. He remembered the meadow—the golden sunlight, Alaric's crooked daisy chains, the confessions he'd made too freely. He remembered the tightening in his chest, the fear in his eyes, and the death of his childhood. He sensed the weight of it still, unceremoniously crumpled onto the library floor.

It hadn't kept his eyes from tracing those familiar shapes. How suddenly, when he looked at it directly, the meadow returned. The sun slanted golden across the grass, warm and lazy. Alaric's laughter threaded the air. Elias stretched out on the grass, watching, heart tight with something he didn't fully understand.

"Why not?" he had asked, reaching across clumsily, hand brushing against Alaric's. "I don't care about the rooms, the roses... I care about you. I always have."

Alaric had pulled back so fast that the touch left a hollow ache. "Don't," he muttered, chest tight, pulse quick. "Don't say that again. You don't know what you're binding yourself to." Elias had blinked, staring at his empty hand, a whisper of hurt and confusion curling in his chest. The memory hovered now: warmth and fear, love and a sudden, unnameable fracture.

The memory clung to him, bittersweet and sharp. Warmth and fear, hope and fracture, past and present — tangled. Elias pressed his hand to the ledger, the words swimming beneath his eyes. Elias blinked, forcing himself back to the present moment. The ledger waited, blank where it shouldn't have been. His pen hung loosely between his fingers, a drop of ink trembling on its tip but refusing to fall.

Outside, the laughter had gone quiet. He could hear the faint thud of Alaric's hammer somewhere above, but it came irregularly, like a heartbeat that had forgotten its rhythm. Eleanor's voice crawled through the hall, low and strange. When he blinked, the light from the window had nearly faded. Eleanor stood in the doorway with a tray of tea, her face concerned as it often had been lately. The clock read 8pm. Impossible.

The fire had gone down to coals and the room smelled faintly of smoke and damp paper. On the tray was some lukewarm tea, a single cup, and a single slice of bread. He suspected it was simply leftover from her own dinner, a meal he hadn't joined in weeks.

"I thought you might need a break," she said. Her tone was soft, but not tentative. Familiar, almost practiced.

He closed the ledger slowly. "You've been busy," he commented, bitter.

Her lips curved, faintly defensive. She crossed the room to place the tray on his desk, on top of some of his books. "The west wing is nearly clear. Alaric thinks the beams can be salvaged."

"Of course he does."

She hesitated, folding her hands in front of her. "He's been working without rest. You should be pleased; he's doing good work, Eli."

Elias leaned back in his chair, studying her. "I'm always pleased when Alaric throws himself into something. It keeps him occupied."

The words landed colder than he meant them to. This was apparent in the way Eleanor shifted, suddenly glancing down to the desk. "You speak of him like he's a child."

"And you defend him like one."

Her eyes flicked up, startled. For a moment he thought she might leave, but she stood still. Those dark umber eyes searched his face briefly, watching every micro-expression. "You're tired," she said quietly. "You've been shut in this room for days. He worries about you." Elias wondered why she did not speak of herself anymore. She used to speak about her own worries far more frequently. It was as if she'd begun to be erased before him.

"I'm sure he does," Elias murmured, though his pulse gave him away. "Tell me, Nora — do you spend all day in the east wing now?"

Her shoulders straightened, a trace of indignation surfacing through her composure. He hadn't used that nickname since their first months together, when the sunlight still made sense and the bricks still stuck to mortar. "Someone has to make sure we don't all go mad."

"And does he thank you for it?"

Silence followed. The clock ticked unevenly behind them. The sound seemed to fill every hollow space between their words. When she finally spoke, her voice was mournful and a touch angry.

"Do you?" She retorted, her voice shaky and brash. "You think I don't see what is happening, but I do. You're fading, Elias. You're going to rot in here and it will be all your doing."

He finally looked at her—really looked. Dust smudged her sleeve, a smear of grease darkened her wrist. A flush lingered high on her cheeks from work or anger, he couldn't tell. Her chest rose and fell too fast. The firelight caught in her hair, haloing her like something untouchable.

"I'm not fading," he snapped, met by a flinch and a furrowed brow from the other. "I am only keeping records, while *you* enjoy your holiday."

Eleanor ended the conversation abruptly, turning on her heel and gliding towards the door in haste, as if one more moment in the library would eat her wit. She paused at the door. "You keep records of everything except for what matters."

Then, she was gone. She shut the door hard behind her, and Elias reached out for the teapot she'd left, holding the sides with both hands. It burned him slightly the longer he held, and he continued feeling it, waiting for the moment he recoiled in instinct. When he did, he could confirm once and for all that he was still, in fact, alive.

✳ ✳ ✳

Her heeled shoes struck the floor harder than she'd intended, the sound too loud in the corridor as she sped her way down it. Her skirts fluttered all around her, the draft picking pieces of her hair from her braid, her appearance just as insane as she felt. Who did she think she was anyways? She spoke so freely with the men, and yet she felt everything she wanted could be tied to them, but then what did that make her?

The corridor's chill met her all at once. Steadying herself, she brought both her gloved hands to her chest and drew one, long breath. Her eyes scanned the space for any sense of presence, but thankfully she was finally alone. She closed her eyes, and the light of the sconces flickered against her lids — deep reds and whites — when the scent of lilac began to fill the air. Memory rose with it.

It had been a wet afternoon in late spring, just like this one, the kind that blurred garden and sky into the same dull gray. The Thorne estate had been smaller than she'd expected, modest, and well-kept. She remembered thinking it smelled faintly of starch and old roses. As her carriage pulled up in the front, she noticed a small orange cat dip over the hedge.

They'd arranged an afternoon tea in the drawing room. Her own family had been called away on business — that is, her father made a real excuse to do with "business" and her stepmother feigned a headache. This, of course, left her to perform her part entirely on her own. She'd been sure to bring an attendant and wear a high collar, both things that at least felt high society, however silly they were.

Elias Thorne had entered quietly, every inch the proper English heir. His gloves were off but folded in his hand, posture faultless, expression measured to the point of being devoid. He couldn't have been older than twenty-two, though there was already something weary in his eyes.

"Miss Liang?" He asked uncertainly, standing at the threshold.

"Draven," she corrected before she could stop herself. The word tasted wrong.

He blinked, then nodded, recovering his composure. "Miss Draven, forgive me. I wasn't informed of the change."

"It's a recent improvement," she said lightly, though her smile didn't reach her eyes. Her stepmother had insisted upon it in immigration, and her father was merely too eager to refuse. That Englishwoman effectively had begun to mold them into the perfect English socialites, and while she protested, the security of the status was highly attractive. It warmed her heart, however, to hear Liang on his tongue.

He crossed to the table, the silver tray between them catching the weak light. "My mother thought it best we meet privately," he said. "Without… expectations."

"Ah. So I may disappoint you in peace."

That startled a small laugh from him, cracking him open an ounce. "I doubt you'll manage that."

Eleanor sat and lifted a small porcelain cup for Elias to fill it on the other side of the chipped oak coffee table. The couches were soft, but almost too soft, as if they were far older than they presented themselves as. The room was decorated in old paintings of still lifes, the unwavering baskets of fruit and bread oddly comforting. In the corner of the room, the orange cat had reappeared, licking mud from its paws. It almost felt homey.

"You sound very sure of a woman you've only just met."

"I'm sure only of first impressions," he replied. "And mine is that you'd rather be anywhere else."

Her hands stilled. "How very perceptive." Though she could admit, Thorne estate wasn't the most unsettling of places either.

"I mean no insult," he said quickly. "Only that I might understand it. I didn't have a choice either."

Something in his tone—flat, almost ashamed—made her lower the cup. The rain outside had softened to a whisper, and for a moment, she saw him not as the stranger across the table but as someone else caught in the same net.

"My father says it will be good for me," she murmured. "England, I mean. A chance to belong."

"Do you want to?"

The question was so simple it disarmed her. "Want to?"

"To belong."

She hesitated, then smiled faintly. "I think I'd rather remember who I was."

A moment passed between them in silence. Something resembling warmth crossed Elias' face then, or perhaps simply recognition. He continued to study her for a moment — gently, curiously, as if the answer moved him in some way — then, he brought his cup to his lips to take a sip. He placed it softly between them, the soft clink resonating as more routine than clinical. For a moment, the arrangement almost felt like a choice.

"You must find England dreary after America," he said, a flicker of interest in his tone.

"I find it quiet," she murmured, studying him as much as he was her. "It's the kind of quiet that listens to you."

"And does it listen kindly?"

She'd thought then that he meant himself, and her heart ached with the wish to answer honestly. "I suppose we'll see."

He smiled then — awkward, sincere, and entirely human. The memory dissolved as quickly as it had come, leaving her disoriented. The scent of lilac had passed, leaving only the choking taste of dust. The silence in the hall felt like a pulse, pressing on her ears and drawing her gaze to the east wing. Somewhere beyond the dark came a soft sound — like something dragging across stone. Slowly, intentionally. She told herself it was Alaric. She told herself a great many things. Still, she didn't move.

The clock struck twelve. She'd only just left the library minutes ago.

* * *

Alaric slumped against the cool wall of the ballroom, glass in hand, the deep red wine catching the moonlight like spilled rubies. The plans for the renovation lay around him in disorder: sketches, notes, measuring lines. He barely looked at them, instead tracing the rim of the glass with a finger, letting the warmth from the drink settle in his chest. All these deep reds were proving too smooth of a vice, he thought, as the clock struck twelve.

He tilted his head back, watching the moonlight trace the contours of the ceiling. He'd taken off his overcoat hours before, tossing it absentmindedly on the stool across the room. He'd been in this room the entire day, and the day before that and so on, since the start of their stay. Drunkenly, he pulled at the bottom of the bow tied at his neck, letting the silk deflate into a pool of red beside his leg. He closed his eyes, allowing the mirror at his back to chill him to his bones. The polished parquet beneath him felt alien and unwelcoming, cold and hard.

The wine burned pleasantly down to his stomach, a temporary balm to unpleasant tightening in his chest. He rubbed his eyes, fingers leaving streaks on his temple, letting himself lean just a little further into the wall, slumping into the cool embrace of the ballroom floor. He let his glass droop to his side, swirling it absentmindedly in the dark in lazy circles. As he watched the color deepen, his thoughts wandered — the manor's empty grandeur, the men and women he had left behind, the laughter of summers long vanished, all for this. He swayed slightly, imagining a better day with a better waltz. Each shadow twitched with life.

Then, it came — a low, deliberate sound from just behind his shoulder. It was measured, as though following a pattern, and sounded identical to the dragging of something large. At first, he assumed a curtain or perhaps a servant moving furniture late at night, but no.. this was too deliberate. It was deeper, even and purposeful, and was coming from inside the wall itself. Alaric froze, pulse quickening. The wine had dulled his caution, yet he felt it now like a sudden jolt.

He placed a trembling hand on the wall. Cool, solid, ordinary. And yet the dragging persisted, slow, insistent, impossible to ignore. He could hear the drag pause, then resume, as though whatever caused it needed to stop and gather its strength before moving on. He could almost follow its progress by ear: the weight shifting, the faint hitch every few seconds, like a shoulder striking stone. Pressing his ear to the cold glass of the mirror, he could hear it stop until the quiet began to hum in his ears, then start again — returning, retracing its path, slower.

His pulse beat in his throat as he listened. He told himself it was everything else — a shifting beam, or the wind under the foundation somewhere. As his throat went dry, he listened for anything else it could be, any evidence that made just enough sense. He turned towards the hall, dark and empty at this hour. The blueprints came to mind, the corridors he'd memorized in the renovations, and his stomach twisted as he realized there should be no passage there at all. The ballroom's outer wall bordered the open air.

Alaric's mouth went dry.

The drag wasn't coming from the ballroom or the hall. It was coming from behind it.

Suddenly, the dragging stopped, right on the other side of the mirrored wall. For a heartbeat, he thought he could hear breathing. The silence pressed in, suffocating him in the dark. Then, a knock.

Alaric stepped back, his heart immediately rising thick into his throat. His glass slipped from his hand, shattering on the parquet, the sound too loud and sudden. When it died, the dragging was gone.

He stood there for a long time, waiting for the sound to return. It never did.

He could taste iron in his mouth.

By morning, the manor had settled into its usual hush, but the memory of the night before had not. It clung to him like dust — dry, metallic, refusing to shake loose. His hands still trembled when he went to button his shirt, though he pretended not to notice. He found his way to the library before acknowledging his steps, the morning light flooding the corridor. It felt imposing, crushing him under its weight, instead of welcome and comforting. Blossoms outside the windows had come in violently, spreading the windowsills with their thoughtless crimsons and lilacs.

The library smelled of wax and ink and the faint sourness

of sleeplessness. He lingered by the door, peering into the room through a crack in the door in a form of almost fear. For almost two months, this had become Elias' space, and every passing of the room was met with the sound of a page turning or the crack of a book. It had slowly become more and more of a forbidden space — Elias' lair, and it held an energy neither he or Eleanor wished to mingle with. But Alaric needed the maps of the architecture; he must breach the threshold to continue his own descent.

Elias was there in careful disarray. His collar hung open; his expression was distant, dull, and faintly fevered. The ledgers were spread about on the desk in front of him, some open and others closed and bookmarked with loose scraps of paper marking the pages. He was hunched, scribbling in a notebook with a book in front of him in those familiar yellowed pages. Alaric pushed the door open, met by an uncharacteristic lack of reaction.

"You've been up all night," Alaric said from the doorway.

Elias still didn't look up. "Is it morning already?"

Alaric crossed the room. "Either that, or I've gone mad."

"I'd hardly notice the difference," Elias muttered, scribbling something in the margins. He'd made his way back towards 1600AD already.

Alaric gave a thin, crooked smile. "Then we're both doing splendidly." He moved towards the shelves, the boards of the library creaking underfoot. "I came for the maps," he said. "The old ones. Of the east wing."

"Why?" Elias pressed, his tone soft but edged. He still did not look up.

"For the renovations," Alaric suggested, a touch unsure of himself. "Something in the measurements isn't right."

Elias finally looked up at him. His eyes were alert, but hollow. Deep purple bags had formed under his eyes, and they were puffy, as if he'd been crying. Alaric couldn't picture it. "Something in this house never is." He said, something ominous hiding behind his expression.

"That's comforting," Alaric said dryly, offering a nervous laugh. He avoided eye contact, eyes instead flickering to the shelves again. "I'll print it on our invitations, once the ballroom is complete."

The corner of Elias' mouth twitched, not quite amusement but not disdain either. He bent back down, over his books, as Alaric began to search the tall bookcases for anything useful. Then, suddenly, "You've been spending a great deal of time with Eleanor."

Alaric's body tensed, looking over his shoulder at his companion. "Someone has to make sure she remembers to eat," He said casually, despite the acid rising to his throat. He thought of her image in the dining room every evening — her lips red with wine, her hair coming undone from its pinning, her cheeks drunkenly flushed as she'd excuse herself for bed. She was remarkably lively in an environment that paled Elias before his own eyes.

"Or perhaps someone enjoys being noticed."

Alaric's tone cooled. "I might say the same of you once."

That landed. Elias' gaze faltered before he turned a new page. "You've grown cruel."

"You've taught me how," Alaric said, barely more than breath.

Silence stretched unevenly between them, the clock attempting desperately to fill it. Elias ripped his gaze from the other, standing finally and walking not more than three strides to a case behind the desk. The morning air held the bookcase here in contempt, blocking all the light from reaching the stately mahogany. From this, Elias plucked a box made of cherry wood. Its lock was warped from time, one strap ripped from damage and the other barely hanging on. The box itself was merely a nondescript chest, and it must have brought a visible look of confusion to Alaric's face, given the man added, "I've been cross-referencing."

"Right," Alaric muttered, taking it in his lightly shaking hands.

"I shouldn't have said that. About you. About her," Elias admitted. Another moment of silence passed.

Alaric's first impulse was to dismiss this with a joke, but the words didn't come.

"You didn't mean it," he said instead. "That's worse."

Elias looked smaller somehow, folded in on himself, so much like the boy he remembered that it made his heart tense in his chest. The ledgers laid open before him, like a confession he couldn't read. Elias reached for his wineglass, though it was empty, and set it back down without drinking. "Take the maps and go. I've got work to finish."

Alaric offered a smile, too human for animosity to fester. It felt unusual. "I suppose I'll see you in the early hours soon," he mused. "Won't I?"

Elias didn't answer. His eyes dropped to the ledger instead, as though the page might absolve him of the silence between them. A faint smile ghosted across his lips—fragile, uncertain, already fading. For an instant, the air between them warmed with something almost familiar, a cruel echo of the men they had been.

Then it was gone.

Alaric gathered the map box to his chest and slipped from the room. The door shut with a sound like a sigh, sealing Elias in the weighted hush that followed. The silence pressed close, intimate as breath.

The corridor beyond the library seemed to hum faintly, a soft violence felt rather than heard. Alaric moved through it with the map box clutched tight to his chest, the weight of it strangely alive in his hands. The latch trembled when he set it down on a table in the ballroom in the east wing, as though eager to be opened. He unfastened it, the room filling with the scent of parchment and dust. For a moment, he could almost pretend this was an ordinary morning — simply work, paper and ink, clean lines and reason. Things stayed where you left them.

He unrolled the first map. The ballroom unfolded in obedient geometry; every angle and curve was diligently recorded. He traced the east wing with his fingertip, following the edge where the drafter's pen had stopped. The line here didn't end — it simply refused to continue. A blankness remained there— white, deliberate, whole.

He frowned, pulling out the next map. Older, brittle. Same omission. Another, and another. Every map — the same silence. It was impossible. And yet, the longer Alaric stared, the more he felt the presence of the missing space. It existed not as a space, but as a presence. It bled on every copy of the map, pretending not to exist.

The table beneath his palms felt uneven, sloping very slightly downward. The room tilted with it. He muttered something — words meant to steady him, though they sounded foreign in his mouth. "Old ink. Inaccurate drafts. Nothing more…"

But the air had changed. It felt charged and oppressive,

pressing on his head with an incessant ringing. He shuffled the papers, faster now. Ink bled faintly where his fingers touched, pressing into the cracks of the parchment like skin. The ballroom lines darkened until they were under his fingers like a bruise.

He stepped back. "It's not there," he said aloud. "It's not there." He stared at the rolled maps, heart hammering, then snatched them up and forced them back into their case. The clasp resisted him once before snapping shut.

In the silence that followed, he could hear it again: that dragging, deliberate sound. The bones crashing haphazardly into stone. The pausing. The breathing. Not beneath him now, but behind. He turned slowly towards the wall from the night before, finding it perfectly smooth. The only irregularity was his own gaunt, pale expression gazing back at him, slowly losing its glow. Still, he saw the faintest ripple beyond the glass, like breath under skin.

He wandered toward it absentmindedly, drawn in like a magnet. He pressed his palm to the cold chill of the glass, gently at first, then harder. The surface was cold, solid, reassuringly real.

The wall's chill crept up his arm. He didn't move. For a moment, it felt as though something on the other side had pressed its hand to his, matching the shape exactly. Then, it was gone.

He felt it long after.

* * *

For a long time, Elias didn't move.

The latch closed behind Alaric with a finality. He stared at the space Alaric had just vacated, the dust swirls still rising in the light, and felt a sort of bleak sickness rising in his throat. He felt something twist inside him — a pang of guilt so brief he nearly mistook it for hunger. The quiet seemed to consume every corner of the room, expanding until it pressed violently against his ribs.

He crossed his desk, slumping into his chair. The half-finished ledger lay open before him, the ink drying unevenly where he'd pressed too hard. He rubbed at the stain on his thumb, trying to ground himself in the small, practical fact of it. The morning light had begun to creep through the curtains, pale and cool. It spilled across the desk, catching on the ridges of the books and glinting on the neck of the empty wineglass. The library smelled of wax, ink, and the faint sourness of ancient vellum.

As a boy, this library seemed so vast and welcoming. It was a cathedral of dust and quiet, where the dog days of summer passed by in a haze.

He could still see it: Alaric, no more than thirteen, splayed on the carpet with his collar undone and a book balanced and open on his chest. Elias sat dutifully beside him, his posture immaculate and his pen hovering with the reverence of a sermon. It was late afternoon, and while their summer lessons had concluded for the day, their tutor still wandered the halls in an effort to prevent them from running to the moors without a single word in their notebooks again.

"Say it properly," Elias ordered. "Je suis. *Suis.*"

Alaric's lips quivered with mischief. "Je suis… ennui incarnate."

"That isn't real French."

"It's real, though." Alaric said, grinning now. "One must feel the language, Thorne. That's what I'm doing." He propped himself up on his elbows, the book falling from his chest and clattering to the floor, discarded. "I'm *feeling* it."

Elias pursed his lips, scribbling in his notes. "You're butchering it."

"Same thing."

Elias had rolled his eyes, trying to hide the tug of a smile. Alaric always did this — found the softer spots beneath his statuesque exterior.

"Then you'll fail." He said, turning a page.

"Then I'll fail in style."

He'd said it with such infuriating ease that Elias laughed before he could stop himself. The sound of it rang against the room — the walls, the books, the shelves, all held the warmth of it in its clasp, desperate for the heat. Just then, their tutor appeared in the doorway, peering in with a disapproval that would've made God Himself ashamed.

Alaric waited before she left to lean over slightly, whispering "She'll forgive us. I'm her favorite."

"She isn't fond of you," Elias said.

"She will be," Alaric said lazily, laying back down on the carpet with satisfying ease and his ridiculous, sun-drunk grin. "They all are, eventually."

Elias had pretended to scoff, but the truth was simpler than he'd wanted to believe then. Some people were just loved by nature, despite others' efforts, without trying. The world bent for them.

The same sunlight reached across the same shelves now, grasping for a glimmer of that boyhood joy that had long since evaporated. Elias looked at the space where they'd once sat with an ache in his chest. It was the ache of something that never truly died, just became mangled over time, writhing on the floor in the waves of gold. He could almost hear Alaric's laugh again — bright, free, impossibly young.

It was easier to remember him that way in his solitude. Easier than attempting to speak to the cruel, brash boy downstairs — half a stranger, half a shadow. Elias leaned back, staring into the sunlight until it stung. The ledgers lay open in front of him, expectant and scribbled with notes he didn't pretend to be able to decipher for now.

Repairs deferred. inventory incomplete. structural irregularities noted. — Aubrey Thorne. His father.

He didn't pick up the pen that morning.

* * *

Eleanor hesitated at the door, poised to knock. No sound came from within — no turning of pages, no cracks of book spines, no murmur of Elias' voice as he read passages to himself as he sometimes did when he forgot she was near. That comforting ease of domesticity faded with the gold of the daylight on the latch. She let her hand fall. The silence felt too complete, as though the afternoon air around it resisted intrusion.

"Best leave him," came a voice beside her.

Eleanor turned. Winifred stood several feet behind and to her right, hands clasped in front of her. The woman's presence still comforted her, but lately she had seemed almost spectral in her calm. While Eleanor was prone to reaction, Winifred had kept her kind but precise smile placed on her lips — a

139

thousand reassurances, but not one spoken.

"He hasn't eaten," Eleanor said. "Not since yesterday." I gave stale bread, at that, she thought. She didn't wish to kick herself for that so brazenly.

"Then he must be very busy," Winifred said, in an unnervingly even tone. She approached with slow, careful steps. "Men do take comfort in their work. It spares them from the weight of other thoughts."

Eleanor glanced back towards the door. "It's not comfort I'm worried about, Winnie. He's… slipping."

Winifred's gaze softened. "You can't reach a man who's already gone inward. You'll only follow him into the dark."

Eleanor's brow furrowed at that. She wanted to argue, but the words refused to form. Instead, she looked down at her hands, at the faint line of dust at her sleeve from where she'd leaned against the scaffolding that morning. "I just thought— … perhaps if I sat with him—"

"He wouldn't thank you for it." Winifred's tone was not cruel, merely certain. "Let him have his silence. There are other souls in this house who still see you."

Eleanor's head lifted. She still had some sense to be offended. "You mean Alaric."

"I mean whatever keeps you from fading," Winifred said with a barely audible sigh. "You've been kind to them both, Lady Draven. But kindness can curdle into sorrow if it's left unaccepted."

Eleanor exhaled slowly, feeling the truth settle uncomfortably in her chest with an alien warmth. "And if I've already begun to sour?"

Winifred's expression flickered —sympathy, perhaps, or something close to recognition. "Then find warmth where you can, before they take that, too."

Eleanor eyed her a moment longer, eyes scanning her frame for any trace of a lie. Her gaze dropped to the floor finally, and wordlessly she turned on her heel and continued down the hallway towards the staircase. The house felt vast around her, the air weighted and still. Somewhere in the distance, she thought she heard the faint scrape of metal. Alaric, perhaps, starting his work. She straightened her shoulders, gathering the composure she had left, and descended toward the sound.

Behind her, the corridor remained hushed. Winifred watched her go, eyes unreadable in the half-light.

The soft scrape of Alaric's tools led her through shadowed halls, winding toward the heart of the house where the long-forgotten ballroom waited. The heavy double doors remained closed as she approached, dulled by dust and age. She hesitated, her fingers brushing the cool brass handles before forcing them open. She wandered inside, the room expanding before her.

The room was still, but buzzed with the excitement of the blond in the center. He was applying thin plaster to a far point of the floor, the motion somehow both messy and calculated. Her skirts tossed dust motes into the air, catching the moonlight as she stopped before him. She clasped her hands in front of her, waiting for him to look up at her, but he remained focused in an unnatural trance.

"Good afternoon," She greeted, neglecting the light already fading into the evening.

Alaric looked up at her finally, a smile breaking onto his face as he set down the trowel in his hand haphazardly. It clattered against the parquet in a symphony of noises. "Nora! Always a pleasure."

She gave a small, tired smile. "You're still working at this, are you?"

He shrugged, eyes glinting with mischief. "The floors don't repair themselves. Besides, someone's got to make sure they're good for dancing."

Eleanor's gaze drifted over the vast room, shadows pooling in the corners, the air thick with dust and silence. "Dancing, huh?"

He stood and gestured down at the floor beneath them. "Think of it as testing their patience," he said thoughtfully. Then, without breaking eye contact, he reached out one slender, practiced hand toward her. A warmth crossed his gaze—something unfamiliar, unsettling, electric.

"Might as well make sure they can hold us without complaint."

She hesitated, the weight of silence pressing down like a shroud. This felt like a reckless impulse. And yet, she couldn't explain the way her body warmed, her eyes searching his face for any flicker of doubt. Her breath caught as their fingers lingered just an inch apart, the space between them humming with unspoken promises and dangers. For a heartbeat, neither moved. The quiet thrum of the house seemed to pulse in time, quickening with her heart. She took his hand, and he pulled her gently towards himself.

"I don't remember how," she protested.

Alaric offered a soft smile, a trace of vulnerability seeping through it. "See? The floor holds."

She flushed then, eyes casting to the floor. She wasn't sure if she felt embarrassment, shame, or warmth too bright to look at. "There's no music."

He stepped closer, the warmth of his presence wrapping

around her like a fragile shield against the chill. "No need."

Eleanor's eyes searched his when she met his gaze once more, an unspoken question hovering between them. He nodded, an invitation without words. Then, their bodies moved together. Their waltz was slow and uncertain at first, each step testing the floor of the old room, the space, and each other. The vast room seemed to shrink around them, folding, cocooning them in their shared revelry.

Alaric's hand was warm against hers, sudden heat in the everlasting chill of the manor. His fingers curled loosely around hers, pulling her with confidence across the corners of the room. She felt the roughness of his palm, calloused from work and his dedication to it. There was a slight tremor in the wrist, betraying a sliver of the vulnerability that lay just below the skin. Her breath mingled with his, the faintest catch as their bodies hesitated, inches apart. The cold air brushed against exposed skin where her sleeves had slipped back, sending a shiver that mingled with the ache in her chest. Their shadows flickered and spun on the high walls, elongating their silhouettes. Their feet moved together, slow and deliberate, the rhythm unsteady but real as it bound them in emptiness. As their steps slowly found a fragile rhythm, Alaric's hand tightened gently around hers. With a careful grace, he dipped her — just slightly, just for a moment— and Eleanor's breath caught in her throat.

His voice was low, teasing. "Well, I suppose if the floor is good enough for us, it's safe."

She didn't answer; her eyes instead focused on the subtle ripple around her own form in the mirror. The room felt impossibly still and time seemed to wash past them with intention. Slowly, she released his hand and stepped back, a quiet weight settling over her. Then, she let out a quiet breath, somewhere between unease and warmth.

"I haven't seen you all day," Alaric said suddenly, his tone a touch gentler than usual. His voice was low, as if afraid to disturb the fragile stillness.

She didn't answer immediately. "It's harder to breathe here than I thought it would be."

Alaric stepped back from her, the cold seeping back into her chest as he wandered to the window looking out onto the courtyard. The fog there threatened to consume the house, but just an hour ago it had been so bright.

"I tried walking the east gate earlier," he admitted softly, as if revealing something far more private. "Didn't get far."

Eleanor felt something tense in her throat as she observed him. She'd always felt he knew more about this house than he let on, but the tinge of confusion and worry in his voice unsettled her more than she expected it to. "I thought I saw the gate closed... but it must have been my imagination. And I heard the men complaining of a fog heavier than usual for this time of year."

She saw the shadow flicker in Alaric's eyes, the hesitation beneath his calm. His voice dropped low, almost a confession. "Sometimes the hallways... they don't lead where I expect."

She finally met his eyes, searching for something solid, and finding nothing but her own concern mirrored back at her. It threatened to consume them both. "We should be able to leave," she whispered, "but it doesn't feel that way."

Alaric's smile was thin, a flicker of something restless beneath it. "Sometimes, it feels like the house doesn't want us to."

Eleanor stilled, her brow knitting in quiet confusion. It

struck her as odd how, despite everything, no family had come calling, and only a handful of servants lingered beyond brief stints. She had told herself it was the remoteness, the relentless weather, the way the manor seemed to press against the windowpanes like a living thing when challenged.

But beneath that, a colder thought took root: perhaps everyone was exactly where the house wanted them to be.

8

May, or Something Like It

From the journal of Eleanor Draven, a recovered excerpt:

May 17th.

Alaric found a passage behind the east wall in the ballroom this morning. The men said the panel sounded hollow, so he struck through it himself. The opening sloped downward, narrow as a throat. None of us wanted to go far, but the light reached just far enough to show the floor curling away into the dark. Then we heard something... a dragging, slow and wet, as though cloth being pulled across stone. No one spoke. Alaric told them to seal it again.

They boarded it up before the day was done.

The sound hasn't stopped.

* * *

Extract from the recovered ledger of E. Thorne, same date:

The east wing opened today. We are not certain what was inside. The workmen declined further excavation. Three planks and one length of timber were replaced, 1 shilling 8 pence paid. Expense noted as "maintenance of structure."

No further accounts to be made in that corridor.

* * *

Elias remembered his father best in these months, when the sunlight crept up the ivy and the nights weren't quite as long. These warmer months had once been a reprieve — by May, he'd be packing up his dorm at the boys' school, and by mid June his mother would send him north with a valet and far too many books, perfumed and precise in their organization. He'd stack them in his room in the west wing and read only a few all summer, preferring the excitement of the manor.

Aubrey Throne had been lucid, then. He had been a thin, elegant, a man whose intellect was spoken of in church pews and banking halls alike. He worked tirelessly, spending each summer since Elias' childhood with their family friends, the Greystones themselves. His voice would carry faintly through the halls, reciting figures like prayers, keeping the house in perfect order alongside Edwin Greystone, his confidante. Elias had admired him for his pragmatism.

But something in the manor shifted the summer he turned nine. He found his father sitting in the study at dawn, counting out the same ledger line over and over again, followed by a soft, broken "no…" each time. The ink had blotted in places, dried into small constellations of error.

"Father?" he'd asked, voice small.

Aubrey had smiled then, though it was not quite a smile. "Every number tells the truth, Elias. If you listen closely enough, you can hear the house speaking."

He'd returned to school in September and tried to forget.

The next summer, his father barely spoke. By the time they'd reached the manor, he'd begun to take his meals in the study and leave the windows open at night, even in the rain. Elias spent those days mostly with Alaric, who lived in the east wing and seemed unbothered by the strangeness growing around them. They would race through the corridors, speaking in mock—French and stealing apples from the kitchen, pretending not to hear the slow, rhythmic counting that rose from the hall below.

By the time Elias had turned ten, the ledgers multiplied. His father's handwriting had thinned to a whisper, looping and frantic. His mother warned him in writing all year while at school that his condition had not improved, that he'd been having night terrors that left him practically stiff. He no longer came down for breakfast. The staff avoided the study. Once, his father rushed into the night only to be found hours later, eyes wide and shivering. Edwin had mournfully slid a blanket over his shoulders and sent him home. It was the last summer his father had said anything intelligible at all.

"Balance. It's all about balance."

After that year, Elias came alone to Greystone for the summers — and always with the creeping sense that a similar fate awaited him. Alaric's letters during the school year, bright and infrequent, were the only reminder of warmth those halls had ever held.

His father never did shake that bewildered, horrified look from his eyes.

* * *

The east wing smelled of plaster, dust, and wet oak. Alaric stood before the boarded wall, sleeves rolled and palms raw from that morning's work. The new wood gleamed pale against the old of the ballroom — fresh, clean, and frankly ghastly against centuries of rot. The men had left early again, muttering about light and air and noises, scared off by ghosts. Alaric hadn't bothered to stop them.

The corridor held its breath as Alaric ran a finger along the seams where plaster met oak. It wasn't long before a thud answered back — resonant, deep, and familiar. He frowned, leaning in. The sound that followed was thick and wet, broken only by the familiar pause that may follow something gathering its strength, and followed by more wet dragging.

A familiar sickness stirred in his stomach. "Still at it?" he muttered. "Persistent little bastard."

The sound never changed, only grew louder or softer and took breaks throughout the day, as if taunting him.

He stood, brushing the dust from his hands. The ballroom often was quiet enough to hear the slightest change, and the sounds that were made reverberated off the mirrors like playground taunts. While progress had been made, significant steps had been taken backwards too, namely these boards blocking whatever mystery he knew he should not pursue. Whatever was down there felt raw and dark, and he wanted no party of the household to investigate it, himself included.

Still, it had been a month since he'd last spoken to Elias. He knew the man was alive, given away only by furious pen scratching and worse still, the muttering of numbers coming from the library. He could not be sure his companion had eaten nor slept, but he could not be sure if his concern was warranted. When he'd last seen him, his eyes were dull, distracted, glazed over. He could no longer be sure if Elias had been looking at him or through him. He told himself it didn't matter. He told himself many things that weren't true.

Eleanor had started keeping him company in the evenings—an accident, at first. She'd brought tea to the drawing room one night when he was sketching floor plans and stayed to talk. The next evening she'd come again, and again after that. She'd begun teasing him, lightly at first, about the dust in his hair or the way he forgot to eat. The laughter felt good. Dangerous, maybe, but good. Now, she lingered in his thoughts the way old music did — pleasant, unwanted, unshakable.

He crouched again beside the wall, laying his palm flat and leaning in to hear the manor speak once more. It was cool, but not still. Something beneath his hand pulsed — slight, but wrong. He pressed harder.

"You can stop now," he said quietly. "I'm not impressed."

When he drew his hand back, his fingertips were faintly damp. He wiped them on his trousers quickly, despite himself. He felt faintly ill.

He straightened, half—expecting someone behind him. But when he turned, it was still. He'd half—hoped for Eleanor, her bright but uneasy smile, chiding him for working late again, for ruining another pair of trousers with dust. Instead, there was only the faint glimmer of dust and his own, small, gaunt reflection on the other end of the room. From here, he could see the rain streaking silver as it raced down the giant windows, blurring the courtyard below. He could just make out the faint glow of the library across — the same lamp that had burned for weeks without rest.

He stared at that too long, his jaw tightening.

"Enjoy your solitude," He muttered, though whether to Elias or the manor, he couldn't say.

The rain didn't stop all evening.

Alaric had stayed in the east wing until the last of the lanterns burned low, measuring, marking, pretending at progress. He'd told himself he was waiting for the boards to dry, for the sound to return— anything but the truth, which was that he didn't want to go back upstairs. When the knock came, he nearly laughed from relief.

"Come in," Alaric called.

Eleanor stepped through the ballroom door, a shawl pulled close to her shoulders. Her hair was slightly undone, an imperfection she normally would have corrected during the day, but instead made her face appear younger. Her dark eyes held concern.

"You're still here." She said, half-accusation.

"I suppose someone has to be." He gestured to the boarded wall. "The ghosts are excellent at conversation, less so at renovation."

Eleanor stepped closer, inspecting the timber. "You should rest." She chided. Alaric paused, giving her a half-smile. She sounded just like him sometimes. The air between them held heavy with a question neither of them dared to ask aloud. Despite that, Eleanor still answered, her tone wistful.

"I keep thinking I'll walk in to see him at dinner one of these nights. That's why I keep coming."

"He's still here," Alaric answered too quickly, betraying perhaps too much of his fondness. For Eleanor or Elias, he couldn't tell. "He's only hiding behind ink."

She looked up, her eyes meeting his. Her expression was worn, her distance carefully crafted in an act of loyalty. But what was loyalty when it was given to a traitor? As quickly as her gaze met his, it dropped to her hands, refusing to break open.

"He's been gone for weeks," she said quietly.

When he looked at her again, her expression had softened. It wasn't pity, exactly, but something near it. For the first time in a long time, he had nothing to say.

"So," she continued, in her soft beckoning, "you don't have to stay in here all alone. You could come to the drawing room. I kept the fire lit."

"Did you?" He prodded with a lightly teasing raise of his brow. She caught it, face turning peony pink.

"For myself," she replied, too quickly.

He almost smiled. "Then I'd hate to intrude."

"You'd hate not to."

She hadn't meant those words to sound like that — or perhaps she had. Even through all their dinners or late evening teas together, this had been the first time anyone had been so raw. A drop of water fell from the ceiling between them, as if punctuating the moment. Alaric had recoiled and realized this only now, laughing once and pushing the hand grabbing his vest through his hair. It was streaked with dust.

"I've been in worse company."

"I'll believe it when I see it." she replied, and smiled again—soft this time, a siren. "Come upstairs, Alaric."

He looked once more at the boarded wall. The sound had stopped, or perhaps it was only quieter now.

"Just for a little while, Alaric," She coaxed. Her voice sounded like the call of a fae. He nodded, finally, and followed her out of the room. The ballroom doors closed behind them with a heavy, wooden sigh.

For the first time all night, the manor was finally silent.

* * *

The fire had burned low by the time they reached the drawing room. The last of the embers glowed a deep, sullen red, like a wound refusing to close. Eleanor crossed the room urgently, her skirts trailing behind her as she knelt to tend to it. Her shawl slipped from her shoulder as she stepped forward, the lamplight highlighting the curve of her neck and shoulder.

Alaric could recognize that she was a beautiful woman, as he leaned on the door frame. Many of his high society friends had told him as such — the way she glided around parties as though she'd been there all her life. She was confusing to many of them — a foreign girl on multiple accounts, shy but brash when pressed, her refusal to take on English customs but her ease within them. Many men found her intimidating for these reasons, and he could see why Elias would not have.

"You'll catch your death," Alaric teased, a half-smile coming to his lips.

"Better that than die of boredom." She looked back at him, smiling. "Besides, I had the impression you were already planning the funeral."

He stepped inside, removing his overcoat and hanging it

by the door. The upstairs drawing room was a smaller one, wedged between studies and bathrooms, meant for business dealings held in private. It smelled of wood smoke and cigars, the fire outlined by a mantle dressed in some very tacky lions. Atop the mantle were precious family heirlooms — photos of Alaric as a child, a palm—sized painting of Edwin and his father, a taxidermied butterfly in a frame.

"I thought about it, yes. Something tasteful, minimal. I'd give a short speech about your virtue."

Eleanor turned over her shoulder, giving Alaric a small glare. "Liar."

He grinned faintly. "You'd hate it if I told the truth."

"I'd hate it if you didn't."

Her laughter was softer than before — real, unforced, almost shy. He sank into the armchair across from her, stretching his legs toward the fire. The heat prickled his shins through the fabric of his trousers. Eleanor began to pour them both glasses of red wine from a carafe on the hearth, one she'd prepared earlier in the evening and poured half-hollow. She handed him one of the understated glasses, sinking into her skirts on the chaise beside him. It was striking how little of the version of her that he'd met remained, and how much of real Eleanor had clawed her way back to the surface. Of the three of them, she looked the most alive.

They sat like this for a while in silence, inhaling wood smoke and painting their lips red with the wine. Rain tossed itself violently at the windows, racing down the panels, demanding to be experienced. The glow of the fire lit her hair like a spotlight, drawing the walls in towards her as she relaxed. She reminded Alaric of a luxurious ancient queen, and were she one, how men would lay swords at her feet to devote their lives, and how the man who should be doing just that for her was instead not even two rooms away losing his grip on reality. How if this all meant anything, the only thing that could mean anything was warmth—

Then, suddenly, "Elias hasn't left that room in weeks."

Alaric shifted his gaze to the fire, realizing he had been staring for a while now. "As I've gathered."

"What if you went to him?"

He gave a short, sharp laugh. "And say what? Tell him the walls are humming at night? That the floors are bleeding numbers?"

Her expression faltered. "I didn't mean—"

"I know," he exhaled, pinching the bridge of his nose. "I know."

Eleanor swirled her wine and took a cautious sip, eyes falling to the ornate rug between them, tracing the patterns. "I think, on some level, you miss him." She said quietly. "And I think… I think he'd benefit."

Alaric pursed his lips, eyes wandering to the silver trails on the window. It was dark out, but the light of the moon caught each trail as if accosting them. He sipped his wine before responding, gathering strength. "That's the trouble, isn't it? Missing people who aren't worth the trouble."

"Is he not?"

He swirled the wine, watching the light catch the surface. "He used to be."

Eleanor hesitated. "What was he like — when you were boys?"

A heavy pause stilled between them. Alaric's eyes found hers once more, which were hungry for understanding. He had always assumed that she must have known something more than she let on, but in this moment it was abundantly clear that this was one thing Elias also kept close to his chest. It made his own chest feel warmer, as though Elias may still want to keep the mangled mess of them as close as Alaric had. As though it were holy enough to. He let out a small breath, his smile too brief to be convincing.

"Smaller. Too clever for his own good. Always trying to make sense of things that… weren't meant for him."

"Like what?"

He took his time answering, watching the liquid dance around the reflection of the moon. "The manor. His father. Me."

Her brow creased. "You?"

The air felt like it was pressing on his shoulders. He felt a choking heaviness in his throat as he spoke. He realized she was the first to hear this story in a decade. He realized he needed to tell it so badly that it bled out of him unwillingly, like an infection.

"I wasn't the kind of friend you trusted, not really," he admitted with a bitter laugh. "I used to tease him until he blushed, goading him into breaking rules he'd written for himself. He thought I did it to amuse myself."

"And didn't you?"

He looked at her properly then, and the air tightened between them. The rain fell quieter. "No. No, I did it because I thought I could save him from it. From this." He gestured vaguely at the room. Eleanor watched him carefully.

"Save him from what?"

He gave a small, uneven smile. "Duty. Obsession. Legacy. It's all the same, isn't it?"

She didn't answer, but she didn't drink and she didn't break her stare.

"I thought if I could turn him against it….make him angry, make him reckless…he'd stop listening to whatever called him here." His voice faltered. "But he didn't. He listened harder."

Eleanor set her glass down slowly onto the low coffee table in front of them in stunned quiet. "So… what did you do?" Her voice carried a tone of slight fear, the kind a prey animal might have when faced with a sleeping bear. Alaric's gaze flickered. He couldn't stop talking.

"Something unforgivable. And very stupid." The fire cracked, making a sound like a bone splitting. "I made him believe," Alaric said, the words quiet but steady, "that he'd done something wrong. That what he'd found here wasn't real, only the madness he feared becoming. I told him it was his own fault. That he'd imagined it." He paused, letting the words linger. "I framed him to Edwin. Edwin was heartbroken. For us both, I think."

Eleanor's breath caught. "…Why?"

"To free him," he said simply. "I thought if he hated me enough, he'd leave."

Eleanor's breath caught. "Did he? Then, I mean?"

Alaric looked away. "He tried. The legacy — it took his father's mind, it took my freedom, and I thought I could give his back, and now…"

Silence fell again — thick, unbearable. The rain outside pressed harder and Alaric could feel something pressing on his throat. Whatever compelled him to tell the entire tale now compelled him to wire his jaw shut. The wine could only do so much to soothe him, and it failed. Everything had failed.

Eleanor sat beside him as the firelight played in her eyes, unsure if she'd just heard a confession or a curse.

"You should stay away from me, Eleanor." He mumbled into his wine. It came out like a plea.

"Should I?" She replied, colored with shock. Her umber eyes searched his face for a hint of resignation, a touch of panic behind her own. It was unclear if it came from self-preservation or desperation.

"You won't," he said, certain. A touch of despair colored his tone. The fire popped again once, loud in the silence.

He reached out, not quite touching her, his hand hovering over her wrist. "Do you ever feel it? The house breathing through us?"

Her breath caught. "You're tired, Alaric."

"Always," he said, and leaned back.

The distance between them remained, but the echo of closeness played in the walls around them. The air felt charged for the rest of the night. Somewhere in the east wing, the sound began again, as both fell into the lull of wine and weariness.

* * *

In the haze of a dream, Greystone manor was windless and still. Elias and Alaric were still fourteen. The world felt still, as if the air had agreed to hold its breath. The two of them sat on the stone steps of the now decrepit entry, half in sun and half in shade. Somewhere in his stupor, he recognized this as a recolored memory, an idealized pact.

Alaric had a pocket knife open, the blade catching invisible stripes of light as it twisted and turned shapes into the stone. No words — just lines, loops that seemed full of meaning.

Whatever it meant to the blond, it made a small smile dance on his lips as he worked. Elias watched in admiration with his chin on his knees, uncertain and nervous.

"You'll dull the blade," he murmured.

Alaric didn't look up. "Worth it," he replied, pride oozing into his tone like honey.

A curl of stone dust fell between them. It caught in his golden locks, and without thinking, Elias reached out to brush it from his mess of curls. For a moment, the dream memory faltered, the colors all fading red before returning. He drew his hand back awkwardly, pressing it into his stomach and clasping it with the other.

"You'll ruin the steps," he said, a little too quickly.

"Then they'll remember us like this." There was no laughter this time, only the soft rhythm of the knife scoring stone. Elias found himself watching Alaric's profile: the faint curve of a smile that wasn't for him, the way sunlight tangled in his hair. He'd never noticed the soft flex of his hand before, the focus he had while he worked on something for himself. Elias swallowed.

"Here," Alaric said suddenly, offering the knife. "If I ruin them, you should too."

Elias hesitated, searching his companion's face for permission. Elias had never done anything this bold before, this permanent. "And what shall I carve?" *What do I have to add?*

Alaric tilted his head, as though the question were foolish. "Anything you'll regret."

The words caught him off guard. The handle of the knife was still warm, still alive as he held it. He pressed it softly to the stone beside Alaric's crude AG, worried he'd remove it in his hesitancy. When he briefly looked up, Alaric was already watching him. Their eyes met, and for an instant, Elias felt a strange certainty that he'd carry this moment with him, that some moments held more weight than others. The wind stilled, faint and cool, as he scratched a rough ET close enough to the existing tag that they nearly crunched together in one racy initial.

The spell broke as another gust of wind rattled through the dream. Alaric froze beside him, as though held by magic. Elias still sat on the steps, the knife replaced by his open palm. Half-manic, he looked down to the step, pressing his thumb to the spot he'd just carved and found nothing there. Then harder. Rougher. Harder still, until his thumb bled.

And suddenly, the dream shifted. The stone steps dissolved into the gentle lapping of water against the shore. The world grew quieter still, save for the faint whisper of breeze through reeds. Suddenly, across the manor, Alaric began to feel his breath color this space, soon filling the dream instead. Alaric's gaze snapped towards Elias — pale and silent, crimson slowly creeping down his sleeve, staining his cuff a deep, unforgiving red. Horror flickered in his eyes as he reached out, snatching Elias' wrist. He was unable to stop the spreading stain while the stone steps dissolved into the gentle lapping of water against the shore. Its placid surface rippled beneath an unseen wind, and somewhere in the manor, the walls seemed to breathe in tandem.

The lake was still, its surface holding the pale shape of the moon like a secret. They'd snuck out past curfew again, boots damp with dew and trousers streaked in mud. Alaric sat on the crooked dock, Elias now tossing pebbles into the black water and watching the ripples swallow the light. Cautiously, he dropped the boy's hand, disappearing in the memory. He looked out past the banks, watching the small stones sink.

"Bet it's bottomless," he said after a while. "Swallow you whole before you even scream."

Elias huffed, the sound too tired to be amused. The blood had dried, flecks still dotting his thumb. "You're morbid."

Alaric grinned faintly. "You like that about me."

"Do I?"

"Mm. Keeps you from thinking too hard."

Elias didn't respond at first. His gaze drifted out toward the opposite bank, where reeds bent in the faint wind. "He used to bring me here," he said finally.

"Who did?" Alaric asked, his gaze following his companions' eyes.

"My father." Elias' voice thinned, uncertain. Alaric's throat tightened. "Before… everything."

The water lapped gently against the dock. Alaric wanted to say something clever, but the words didn't come. The look in Elias' eyes was too far away, too still for boys their age. His gaze dropped to the surface of the water.

After a while, he nudged his boot gently against Elias', which earned him a sniffle. "You'll worry yourself sick one day, Eli," he said, trying for lightness. "Maybe I'll toss you in. Cool off that head of yours."

Finally, Elias looked at him, his eyes focusing on Alaric's soft stare. "You wouldn't."

Alaric's grin returned, faltering at the edges. "Wouldn't I? It's not like you'd scold me too hard."

The corner of Elias' mouth twitched, almost a smile. "Maybe."

A faint breeze shivered across the lake. The moonlight caught the edge of Alaric's hair, turning it pale silver. For a moment, the distance between them vanished. They'd been close like this before, but something about this time felt more final and dangerous. The air buzzed with an unspoken tension, their eyes finding one another's as though it were their natural resting place. Alaric's heartbeat fluttered in his chest and his eyebrows pulled together in confusion, his ears ringing and hot.

"Promise me something," Elias said suddenly, his voice low.

"What is it?" Alaric asked, swallowing. He'd never been more thankful for the sound of his voice.

"Don't—" He hesitated, swallowing. "Don't end up like them."

Alaric blinked. "Like who?"

Elias shook his head, refusing to answer, his eyes finding the water once more. The moonlight bounced off the surface of the ripples, playing in shapes on his face. He glowed in the moonlight, as if under a spotlight. Alaric wanted to ask again, but the words died in his throat. This was their first summer without Elias' father and Edwin's light banter filling the halls. What remained was cold stone and Edwin's melancholic watchful eye. He could hazard a guess.

"Fine. But only if you don't either."

It earned a quiet breath of laughter from Elias — small, but real.

For a little while, they stayed like that, side by side, their reflections rippling and breaking against each other. Behind them, the manor loomed unseen, patient as the tide.

Alaric opened his eyes.

The fire had gone to faint orange embers in the grate. The room was still, and Eleanor's shawl was gone from the chaise beside him; she must have gone down the hall to her quarters.

He rubbed his eyes and sat up. It was the pale gray of morning, light bleeding through the windows, struggling through early morning fog. The taste of the lake air lingered in his throat, cold and metallic.

Crossing to the window, he pushed the heavy curtain aside. The glass was misted, but he could still peer through it. The faint outline of the grounds lay faint and colorless. In the distance, too far to see clearly but too close to forget, he caught the gleam of water. The lake, or what remained of it.

He rested his forehead against the pane. Much like back then, no one was there to witness it but the creaking, groaning house.

* * *

Elias woke before sunrise, groggy and unsure of what month it was. He'd made a habit of this; he'd wake in a daze, at this mahogany desk, his wax candle having burnt out while he rested into a pool of wax. It had sealed his notes to the wood. He peeled them loose, reading the half-finished line written in his own hand: *water rising in the east passage.* He had no memory of writing it.

He looked down at his hands. Under his nails, the skin was stained gray, as if by silt or stone. A headache pulled beneath his eyes. It was too still. He wandered to the window, hoping to let in some fresh air.

In the courtyard below, Alaric's voice called to the workmen, barking various orders to his skeleton crew. Elias froze, not from surprise, but from the peculiar feeling that the sound of his voice had become commonplace and familiar again, and yet he was a stranger. The morning fog rose thick over the grounds, swallowing the shapes of men and scaffolding alike. Only Alaric's outline moved clearly, the easy, familiar tilt of his shoulders.

Elias watched him for longer than he intended to. When he turned away, the silence felt heavier.

There was a knock at the door. Winifred pretended to wait for only a moment before entering without an answer.

"Mr. Thorne," came Winifred's gentle voice. "Forgive me, sir. I thought you might want something warm." She shuffled into the library as though it were just as comfortable for her as her own bed, a tray lightly clattering in her hands as she approached the desk. She slid it in front of him, careful to avoid his mess of wax and papers, and turned to fuss with a throw blanket atop a lounge chair nearby. "You've been shut up here all night."

Elias blinked, looking at the silver tray on his desk. It displayed a porcelain teapot and a matching cup, both adorned with tiny blue flowers and stripes painted by patient hands. The handle of the cup was a pure, crisp white and thin enough to snap if grabbed by unsteady hands, requiring poise to handle. It was the kind of set only the wealthy would own, and a stark reminder of the household he inhabited. If he could just pull through this year, it was wealth that could be his family's, but for now it was teased in his face whenever the walls let him breathe. His eyes did not return to Winifred's angular face.

"Thank you," He said, sitting and returning to his writing.

"Mr. Greystone was much the same earlier," she said, voice light, conversational. She folded and refolded the same throw blanket over the back of the chaise. "Out before dawn again, I think. Miss Draven passed him in the hall and said he looked half-frozen. Poor man never could rest easily."

Elias' quill stilled for a beat. "They seem to find much to discuss lately."

"Oh, don't think too much of it. Souls here find anything to fill the corners." She laughed lightly, crossing the room to adjust a few books on the shelf closest to her. "Anyways, he said he'd dreamt of water. Of all things, a lake, right in the foyer. Isn't that strange?"

The quill in his hand snapped with a faint crack. Ink bled up between his fingers. "He told you that?"

"Oh, not told me," she said airily, brushing the sound aside. "He mentioned it to Miss Draven at breakfast. She laughed, said it sounded peaceful. He didn't look peaceful, though. He said it was so still it frightened him."

Elias wiped his hand with a handkerchief nearby, though the ink only smeared darker. "He's prone to dramatics. He probably dreamed of the rain and decided it was a revelation."

Winifred smiled faintly. "Perhaps. But he said you were there."

He froze, pulse audible in his ears. "I beg your pardon?"

"Oh, yes. Said he saw you as a child with him by the water. You two skipped stones. Isn't that funny?" Her tone was all curiosity — unhurried, even fond. "Dreams can be so cruel that way…showing us what we've lost and making us reach for it again."

The air between them thickened. Winifred crossed behind him, adjusting the curtains. Suddenly, her presence brought Elias a heavy sort of dread he couldn't describe. "Dreams have such odd ways of traveling in this place. One might think they whisper through the walls. Why, I half expect I'll be dreaming of that lake myself tonight."

He looked up sharply, but she was already striding to the door frame, her hand resting lightly on the frame. "Do have your tea, Mr. Thorne," she said, tone bright again. "It's gone cold, but it might still do you good."

When she left, the quiet swelled back. Elias sat very still, listening to it settle. It sat heavy on his bones, dripped into his marrow, rotted his skin. From the pot before him, he could hear the faint lapping of liquids, though no movement accompanied it. It sounded just like the shore from his memory.

9

June (Revised)

The heat had been building for days, swelling in the corridors like breath trapped under glass. By noon the air had thickened into something almost visible— a shimmer that blurred the light in the long gallery and drew sweat from the servants' necks as they worked. Eleanor had rolled her sleeves to the elbow and tied her hair with a strip of linen she'd found in the laundry. Her hands ached faintly from polishing, but she found the repetition steadying, almost reverent.

Each careful stroke felt like reclaiming a small corner of this vast, restless house— her own quiet act of defiance. She placed the pot she had been polishing on the island in the center of the kitchen atop a cotton tea towel, reaching for her hair. She tightened the linen there, a flimsy thing that scratched her skin, and exhaled. A quiet smile tugged at the corner of her mouth — the comfort in smaller things like this kept her moving these days. She told herself that there was strength in knowing where to look for it.

The heavy stillness was broken then by the soft, deliberate

click of footsteps on the polished floor. Eleanor turned as the kitchen door swung open, revealing Winifred's serene, familiar form in the corridor beyond. Her clothes and hair were effortlessly maintained, not a strand out of place. In the crook of her elbow was a basket overflowing with herbs, the scent of lavender and sage spilling into the room with her entry.

"Still at it, are you?" She said, voice low and soft as the glow of a fire. She set the basket gently on the counter, a soft smile on her lips.

Eleanor offered a tired one in response. "It's all I can do to keep from being swallowed whole at times."

Winifred nodded, pulling the springs from their nest. "This place has its ways, doesn't it? It feeds on what it can, and demands more." She hardly reacted, as if speaking with a certainty beyond her years. Turning around to walk towards the island, a flicker of discontentment crossed her face. She reached out, brushing a stray lock of hair from Eleanor's face with a tenderness that felt both comforting and unsettling.

The gesture caught her by surprise, though it wouldn't have been the first show of intimacy between them. They'd become nearly inseparable, and Eleanor had never had a female friend so close before. In a way, she felt thankful for the dreadful situation, if only for that. "You sound like you know."

"Oh, I've been around long enough to learn its language," Winifred murmured. "But sometimes, it's not what the house says, but what it doesn't, that tells you the most."

Eleanor leaned against the counter, studying her. "And what is it saying now?"

Winifred smiled faintly, eyes lowered to the polished copper pot between them. "That depends on who's listening." She traced a finger along its rim, leaving a pale line in the condensation. "Most people only ever hear their own echoes."

Eleanor's eyes dropped. "I try not to," She said, her voice coming out softer than she'd intended. That much was true; when she paused too long, she could hear it all, especially in the dark of the night or in moments of solitude. It disturbed her more than it seemed to bother the men — the creaking, the breathing, the cracks and scrapes. They were progressively more unnatural the longer she paid attention. "Sometimes it's just... too quiet here."

"That's when it's the loudest," Winifred replied. "When you start to wonder what's in that silence."

Eleanor hesitated. "You make it sound alive."

Winifred looked up then, her face suddenly excited, bright. "Don't you feel it? The house always seems to breathe when no one's looking. It sighs when you open the windows, hums when you close them. It likes to be remembered."

Eleanor's throat felt suddenly dry. "You pity it."

"Perhaps I do." Winifred's tone softened, drifting back to her basket behind her, relaxed once more. "Places like this— forgotten, misused...they collect what people leave behind. Grief, longing, pride. All those little ghosts that never had names." She grabbed a thick spool of twine from the back of the counter, tying bunches of lavender together in domestic bouquets. She set them aside, stacking them to be hung later in the day, a task too peaceful.

Eleanor folded the cloth in her hands, her voice low. "That's why I like helping so much. If I can contribute... maybe it won't haunt me so much."

Winifred nodded, working quietly. "Or," she said gently, "you like your ghosts polished."

Eleanor laughed quietly, but there was a tremor beneath it. "That's unkind."

"True things often are."

For a long moment, the two remained silent, the only sound the soft rustle of herbs brushing against one another. Eleanor's eyes lingered on her quick hands — precise, unfaltering, composed. Silently, she wondered if Winfred had a past outside of Greystone — did she have a family? A husband? A reason to remain so tethered to the location? They talked about much in their days together, but so little personal chatter that it bordered on unnatural. It was kept to moments like this, Eleanor revealing her discomfort and Winifred at least pretending she saw her.

Then, Winifred reached into her basket, pulling out a sprig of sage. "Burn this tonight," Winifred offered, holding it out to her. "It keeps the air honest."

Eleanor hesitated. "Do you really believe that?"

Winifred tilted her head. "Belief isn't the point, my dear. Habit is." She smiled again, serene, unreadable. "You keep the house busy, and it keeps you company. That's the bargain most of us strike with it, whether we know it or not."

Eleanor lingered a moment longer, twirling the sage between her fingers before slipping it into her pocket. She gathered her towel and the pot, tucking both neatly away underneath the island. It had become a habit — leaving no trace, as though the house could be coaxed into believing she belonged within its walls.

By late afternoon, she had joined the others in the scullery. The air was thick with heat and vinegar, the dominating sound the light scraping of knives against a wooden block. She sat with a group of the Greystone maids, all of them in pristine matching uniforms and hair tied with ribbons. Her sleeves were pushed up to her elbows, sharpening some of the kitchen knives to precision at the discovery that some no longer cut the chicken for dinner.

"Ms. Vane said the west end gallery's gone damp again," one of the maids muttered.

"Always does when it storms," another replied, rinsing her hands.

"You could seal it with pitch." Eleanor kept working, but looked up at them. Both women paused, exchanging a look. Eleanor felt the prickle of their silence and hurried to explain. "My father's men used to do that when the mine walls began to sweat. Keeps the damp from spreading."

For a moment, only the sound of water dripping from the basin filled the space. Then one of them let out a low, surprised laugh. "Well, imagine that. Mrs. Thorne teaching us tradesman's tricks."

"I'm not Mrs. Thorne," Eleanor corrected softly. "Not yet."

The maid by the sink nodded, offering a smile. Eleanor offered a nervous one in return. She crossed, sitting beside her companion. Comfortably, she crossed one ankle over the other and drew a box of cutlery to her hip, the pieces clinking softly. From her apron she produced a scrap of cloth, nudging the other maid with a small, conspiratorial grin. The girl hesitated, then passed her a bowl of baking soda and water. She set it between them, dipping the cloth and working the silver in slow, patient circles. The air filled with the quiet rhythm of their labor — a small, human sound against the heavy stillness of the house.

"So then, not Mrs. Thorne—" She began.

"Eleanor." She answered, excitedly cutting off the other

woman. The maid smiled, a bright flash that softened her features, and nodded without another word, turning back to her task.

"Eleanor," she repeated, this time slower, tasting the name. There was a quiet strangeness in hearing her own name repeated in that way, without duty or expectation. Just Eleanor. She felt a light warmth settle in her chest.

* * *

The day dragged thick and airless, the kind of heat that made thought itself feel sluggish. The maids had drifted off to cooler corners of the house, leaving Eleanor alone with her work. She crouched beside the block, the whetstone rough and unyielding beneath her fingers. She moved the knife's edge carefully, the scrape steady and precise, her breath measured.

All around her, the house exhaled faint noises — a cacophony of sighs, floorboards creaking, whispers of wood settling into things amorphous. She didn't flinch, or lean into the strange symphony. She instead focused on the cool of the blade, the rhythm of stone against steel, the soft drip to the floor. This was work she understood, and as she set down a larger knife to pick up a small paring knife, she refused to let the moment pass in stillness.

But the sounds persisted, shifting in volume and cadence, weaving through the halls and the still air. Eleanor didn't hear them as warnings or calls the way she once had; she heard them as a conversation she wasn't invited to join. A soft scratch from the hallway. Footsteps that stopped just beyond hearing. A breath caught somewhere in the manor's spine, as if choked on. Finally, she paused.

She let the paring knife rest on the whetstone, closing her eyes. She recalled Winifred's words from earlier that morning — that the house collected the things that people left behind. She listened for the first time since she'd arrived, not sure what she hoped to find, but listening for people. For what might be said between the walls in hushed tones, for human moments hidden beneath the house's groans.

Her fingers tensed on the knife's blade as she leaned in. She'd spent years learning to sharpen her blades, learning what had dulled them, learning to place them in the hands of men who could polish them for her. Months of solitude and a drifting fiance had sharpened her senses; it was her turn to cut through the home's silence to the truth beneath.

But for all that, Eleanor kept her voice low and dry when she finally spoke, more to herself than anything else: "Not yet. Not mine to hear."

She bent to the whetstone, steadying the blade. Just as she did so, something caught her eye — a faint glimmer nestled between the floorboards, half-hidden beneath dust and shadow. Curiosity pulled her close, forcing her to set the blade down on her bench and abandon her task. Kneeling, she pulled up a delicate silver chain, cradling a tarnished, but intact, oval locket. Worn yet evidently cared for, it bore the unmistakable imprint of a crest on its face — Greystone family property. Her thumb traced the softened edges, feeling the weight of secrets pressed tight within the cold metal. Still, she refused to open it.

She hesitated, the locket heavy in her palm, its silence louder than any whisper. The house around her seemed to pause, breath hitching in the walls. Eleanor slipped the chain carefully into her pocket, folding the moment away like a secret too fragile to reveal. A distant rumble echoed through the walls. It sounded like a growl.

* * *

The heat hung thick and heavy in the air, pressing against the walls like a living thing. The storm-blackened afternoon stretched before her like a bear, hibernating and conserving its energy for its first hunt. Eleanor kept her hands busy folding laundry in the servant's quarters, the steady rhythm a balm against the restless house. The maze of hallways stretched just beyond the room, consuming light.

She glanced up, her eyes drifting toward the dim corridor beyond the laundry room. It was unsettling just how dark the forgotten corners of this manor could get. They mangled light at times, the warped wood and blackened stone cracked with age and revealing themselves bare. Her hands stilled as she fixed her gaze on the end of the corridor; a door she had never noticed before had become ajar — framed in shadow, narrow. It hadn't been there before, she thought, or she'd just never noticed it. A faint chill seemed to whisper from it, carrying a chill that tugged underneath her skin.

Without realizing she'd been walking towards it, she became aware of her fingers lightly tracing the brass doorknob and the deep wood of the frame. Before she could press on further, a familiar voice broke the trance.

"Making friends with forgotten corners, I see," chided Winifred from behind her. Her fingers snatched closed into a close fist, pulling her hand into her chest and clasping the other over it. Eleanor turned only her head, catching a suggestion of a smile. "Only a storage closet. Moths and dust. Best left alone, if you ask my advice."

Her gaze flickered briefly to Eleanor's hand, then her face. "This house has a way of watching, especially those who poke where they shouldn't. Curiosity can be a dangerous companion here."

Eleanor turned, meeting her steady look and giving a soft nod. Her mind still churned, however. The house was whispering to her, though she chose to stay silent. She would have noticed a storage closet here before, especially one with such an odd door.

It appeared to be of an older style; in fact, the entire corridor was styled in this way. While the rest of the west wing had been retrofitted with experimental electric lighting in public rooms and redecorated at least thirty years ago, this corridor remained ancient, as if from hundreds of years ago and unceremoniously forgotten. It was a mangy beast, untamed and anxious under her hand.

Eleanor glanced back at the door, then met Winifred's steady gaze. "Have you ever—?"

Winifred smiled, but it did not reach her eyes. "Oh, I've seen plenty in my time." She paused, linking her arm with Eleanor's and walking back down the corridor. Eleanor's eyes looked back once more, then found Winifred's face with a touch of brand new fear. "Tell me, have you noticed how the maids are beginning to speak more freely? There's a rhythm here, if you know how to listen."

Her voice softened, drawing Eleanor's focus inexplicably. "If you want to understand this house, sometimes it's the living voices you must follow. Not the ghosts behind closed doors."

Eleanor nodded slowly, her curiosity briefly sedated. She felt colder somehow.

* * *

The corridor's shadows deepened as Eleanor moved away from the ancient door, her fingers lingering briefly on the worn wood before she turned. Winifred's steady presence beside her was a quiet anchor. As they walked down the hall, the fading pale light cast their shadows onto the weathered carpets lining every corridor. By the time they reached the laundry room, the sun had dipped low, its light dim and silver—gray through the grimy panes.

The air here felt close — too many whispered words and shifting drafts that did not belong to wind. Winifred attempted a few subjects, but Eleanor couldn't listen, her mind drifting back to the oddities of the house and the small silver locket on her hip. The heat compressed her, molasses—thick and smelling of damp wood and that metallic scent she'd become too familiar with.

Eleanor's breath caught in her throat. "I think I need some air," she murmured, excusing herself before Winifred could respond.

She slipped into the west corridor, aiming for the parlor downstairs. Her unease clung to her like static as she passed room upon room of dust and despair. There were entire rooms for things like suitcases, others for people who hadn't so much as breathed in the manor since before the Gold Rush. The manor moaned slightly as she passed — old pipes, settling beams, or perhaps something else entirely. The heat clung to the walls and the windowpanes, the patter of rain beginning to beat them relentlessly as she neared the grand staircase of the entry. She began to step past the library when she heard the jarring thunk of a book larger than average snapping closed. She hesitated mid-step, noticing how the light poured from a crack in the doorway.

It illuminated a man she once knew, or the form of him rather. What she could see of him was hunched over a desk, candlelight stuttering over him in wild disarray. His hand moved, writing or circling something, movements too quick, too precise. The air near the doorway was warm with the smell of burnt wick and sleepless hours.

He didn't look up.

In fact, he didn't seem to notice anything at all.

Eleanor pressed her lips together, guilt prickling her spine. She reached for something she could say to him now — anything at all. That was when she heard the faint mumble of numbers under his breath.

"Ten thousand… no— it's four thousand in 1455 but it's eight thousand units in 1456, that's—…. No… no, it's…"

His voice splintered, folding in on itself. His fingers shook against the ledger. The lamplight made his face look hollow, almost fevered.

She felt rooted in place, watching his lips turn numbers into soft curses. There wasn't a thing she could do to reach him now. Maybe never again. And she was too afraid to try. She finally pried her eyes from the man she once found so much warmth in, a glimmer of humanity in this oppression, this devastation, and forced her weakened legs down the stairs. The air felt colder with every step, heavy with the damp pressure of the storm gathering outside.

At the foot of the stairs, a blast of frigid air rushed in, carrying the scent of icy rain and wet earth. Eleanor's eyes looked up just in time to meet the shadowed figure creeping in, emerging from the gloom.

Water cascaded from Alaric's usually immaculate waves, soaking his coat and dribbling down the sides of his face. As he peeled his overcoat off, a small puddle accumulated on the worn floorboards, his boots whispering wet against the wood. The storm clung to him like a second skin, droplets trembling on his skin and the fabric of his once white sleeves. His top button was unmatched to its hole, his tie missing, and all that would be acceptable were it not for the distant, glazed look in his eyes.

She paused mid-step, surprise flickering through her chest. "Alaric," she said softly, her voice carrying down the stairwell.

Alaric stood dripping in the foyer, eyes finding her descending each stair and coming alight. "You should see it out there," he said, voice lifted. "Biblical."

She stopped a foot from him, taking in his form with an anxious disquietude. "Or idiotic," she replied, a hand on her chest. The skin there had gone cold. "You'll catch your death."

He grinned, easing her ever so slightly as he shook the water from his hair like an unruly hound. "If that happens, tell Elias I went heroically, defending the rose bushes." A wild look lingered in his eyes. She inhaled deeply before speaking, a faint pout at her lips.

"I'll tell him you drowned in the fountain."

"Better. A touch of scandal." He mused, passing her into the parlor, his footsteps leaving damp prints as they walked. She followed at first, crossing him to the fireplace and fetching a towel from the sideboard. She held it out to him. When he took it, his fingers brushed hers — light, deliberate, electric. It might not have meant a thing if only she weren't so aware of it. They stood like that for a moment, the thunder growling overhead like a beast.

"Do you ever miss summer storms?" He asked rather suddenly, pressing the towel to the side of his jaw. "When they meant something?"

She blinked. "Miss them?"

Her mind drifted to the storms of her own childhood— when her mother was still alive, before the steady drum of rain had become just noise. California's rare magnanimity had wrapped around their modest home near the harbor like a fragile promise. She remembered the soft, firm presence of her mother, gathering her close by the fireplace, murmuring prayers in their ancestral tongue as the scent of damp earth and incense wove through the heavy air.

Outside, city streets clattered with shutters slamming and sandwich boards pulled in tight, the world pausing beneath the storm's wash. But not long after, the storms had grown colder, quieter. So had her mother.

"You sound nostalgic," She continued, her voice sounding more like an accusation than an observation.

"I'm damp," He said flatly. "It brings out my melancholy."

"You say that as if you don't already bring it out just fine without the help," she teased.

He laughed, a quick, warm sound. Then, without a word, he gestured toward the lounge chairs nearby, and they both settled down. Eleanor rested her elbow on the arm of hers while Alaric absently tried to dry his golden locks. They stayed like this for a while, listening to the thunder crack above them with revelry, the lightning silvering his profile in beats. Finally, she said carefully, "I found something of yours today."

"Should I be alarmed?"He mused, raising a brow.

She pulled the locket from the pocket resting at her hip, dangling it loosely from its chain. The surface glistened in the firelight as it absently twirled towards and away from her. "This," she said, "downstairs."

For a fraction of a second, something in his expression faltered, as if she'd pressed a bruise.

"Ah," he said, moving to reach for the small locket. "You've a talent for unearthing things best left buried."

"I only wanted to return it."

When he took it from her, his hands were uncharacteristically careful and his expression was far away. His thumb smoothed over the silver clasp and the slight warp of the hinge at the side, exploring something remembered closely like one would a wedding band. Finally, he latched it open, revealing a lock of dark hair and the small but unmistakable portrait of a woman she didn't recognize. He gazed at it warmly, swallowing. His gaze lifted for a moment to meet hers.

"My mother," he answered, anticipating her question. "A token of protection, I suppose."

"She must care for you very much," Eleanor said softly, unfamiliar with this softer shell the man inhabited now.

Alaric smiled faintly, running a thumb over the silk ribbon tying the hair together. "Not in the ordinary sense. Her affection comes pressed and folded… To be admired and never used."

"That sounds lonely," Eleanor breathed, searching him with her eyes, uncertain.

"She'd call it refinement." He turned the locket over in his hand, sealing it in the process. "She told me this would remind me of where I came from, and what I owed her." His tone was bordering on tender, but something threaded beneath. "I don't know what she meant. I suspect neither did she."

Eleanor studied him, watching the shadows play on his face like old friends. "You don't speak of her often."

"There's little to say." He smiled again, wryly. "She made me clever enough to survive her. That's love of a sort."

She hesitated. "And your father? I speak of mine—"

He looked up sharply then, cutting her short as if the question felt too bare. "I don't know him." He said, too quickly. His gaze returned to the small metal clasp of the jewelry, examining it absently. "Never did. There were rumors, of course. There are always rumors. All that mattered to us was that Edwin agreed to take me on despite how much he hated the man. But my mother never confirmed anything. I think she liked it better that way. The mystery suited her."

A beat passed between them, the air heavy with storm light and unspoken things. There were rumors Alaric was nothing more than a servant's son, conceived out of wedlock and hurried away under some other nobleman's conveniently timed death. She thought them cruel and unnecessary. She never thought any of them could be accurate. But now, watching this much clumsier boy twirl the trinket in between his forefinger and thumb, she saw something much less refined in him too. Hearing it spoken aloud, the edges softened into something painfully human.

He turned the locket once more, then held it out to her, offering. "Keep it."

She blinked. "Don't be ridiculous, Alaric."

He smiled feebly, his mind elsewhere. "I mean it. I'll forget about it by morning." He took her hand in his, pulling it from her lap and caressing it as he pressed the necklace into it. "But you'll keep it safe."

She stared at him, unsure if he was mocking her. "You can't mean that."

"I can." His smile softened into something softer still, disarming. "You still remember how to treasure things."

Outside, the thunder rumbled deeper, and Eleanor felt the hair rise on her arms. When lightning struck again, she looked down at the locket, seeing both their reflections shimmer in the metal: his blurred by the heat of the fire, hers too sharp and small beside it.

She clasped her hand around it, a silent vow. "Then I'll keep it safe," she whispered.

Alaric's expression shifted, unreadable—halfway between gratitude and regret. The storm groaned across the roof, and for a moment it seemed the whole house leaned in to listen.

Rising slowly, Alaric gave her one last glance—fleeting, electric—before slipping toward the staircase.

He paused briefly at the landing, catching sight of Elias seated in shadow. The tension in his shoulders tightened, and with a steadying breath, he ascended quietly and then, suddenly, stopped at the threshold.

* * *

Elias sat hunched over the cluttered desk, the candlelight flickering like it was struggling against the dark. His fingers trembled as they traced the chaotic maps and frayed letters sprawled before him, the names and dates swimming like

182

phantoms just beyond reach.

Numbers twisted and subsequently unraveled in his mind like threads pulled too tight. Four thousand in 1455… no, eight thousand in '56… but the ledger said otherwise, and his pulse quickened with the maddening uncertainty.

Outside, the storm clawed at the ancient walls, a ragged breath that bled through his ribs and under his skin with fervor. His vision blurred, the edges of the room shifting and pulsing in menacing shadow.

He caught himself murmuring fragments of sentences—"Lineage… betrayal… it repeats…" The words repeated with less and less sense by the minute, but they felt vital, as if the key unlocking a door he dared not open.

He rubbed his face with shaking hands, but the madness had already begun to bloom inside him. It was a feverish root taking hold, twisting his thoughts into a tangled maze with no exit.

A single tear slid down his cheek, unnoticed, as he whispered, "What have we done?"

A faint sound—a scrape, a creak—pulled his gaze to the crack of the door. There, framed in the threshold, stood Alaric. His eyes were sharp, the storm still clinging to his shirt like a second skin.

For a heartbeat, the madness retreated, and the fragile tether of reality snapped between them. Then the weight returned, as the house seemed to watch and wait. Alaric stepped inside, wind-wild.

* * *

Alaric's voice was low but cut like a blade. "Hiding? That's all you do now? Locking yourself away in this room, shutting me out… and you expect empathy?"

Elias snapped back, voice harsh and uneven as he adjusted the candlestick. "I'm working—while the two of you laugh loud enough to wake this cursed house."

Alaric's brow furrowed, tension coiling in his jaw. "What are you talking about?"

Elias's words sharpened, cracking on Eleanor's name. "I hear you. You and Eleanor. From the hall. You talk… laugh…I'm glad you can make her smile," Elias whispered, voice fragile now, trembling with a slight quiver. "She hasn't come to see me in a month."

Alaric stepped forward, cautious but firm. "She's worried about you. We both are."

Elias let out a bitter, hollow laugh. "You're worried, so you keep each other company? How noble."

"That's not fair," Alaric said, voice thick with frustration.

"No," Elias shot back, voice rising, eyes wild. "What's not fair is that I'm the only one who remembers why we're here! While you—both of you—pretend the house isn't rotting around us!"

Alaric's patience snapped. "You think I don't see it too? You think you're the only one who hears things at night?"

Elias spun, eyes blazing. "Then do something! Stop skulking around looking sorry for yourself! I'm trying to make sense of it and you stand there like it's some joke!"

Alaric's jaw clenched, voice low, sharp. "You sound like your father."

The words landed like a blow.

Elias froze, a shadow darkening his eyes. "Don't you dare," he whispered, voice shaking but deadly still. "Don't ever compare me to him."

Alaric looked away, regret hovering at his lips. Elias gripped the desk edge so tightly his knuckles blanched.

"Get out," Elias breathed.

"Elias—"

"Get. Out."

Alaric froze, the oppressive weight of the manor pinning him to the floorboards before he wrenched himself free. He spun sharply, his footsteps quick and uneven as he stormed from the room, the sting of his own words echoing behind him. The door slammed hard in his wake. In the dim corridor, he caught sight of Eleanor—her eyes wide, caught between fear and something else—while the locket at her throat caught the pale moonlight, shimmering like a fragile secret.

10

July Never Came

The manor was thick with heat, the kind that clung to skin and pooled in lungs like a second, suffocating breath. The heavy summer air hung almost viscous, sticky with humidity and seeping through the cracked windowpanes and pooling in corners where shadows seemed to settle deeper. It pressed against the walls like a living thing, whispering its slow, relentless weight through every hall and empty room, as if the house itself were breathing—slow and shallow.

Eleanor moved through the dim corridors, her footsteps muted against the worn, faded carpets, threadbare from years of neglect. Each step felt leaden, the exhaustion buried beneath her skin making her limbs feel heavier than they ought to. Yet the restless ache in her chest tugged her onward, a silent summons she couldn't resist. Her hand drifted instinctively to the locket nestled beneath her dress, fingers curling around its cool metal as if it could anchor her to something real. She had kept it close ever since that night, though why, she wasn't sure. It felt like the last fragile fragment of humanity she clung to in this house of ghosts.

Even she could see the way she moved, slow and cautious, like a spirit drifting through these endless, omnipresent halls. The manor wrapped around her like a shroud, its silence thick and watchful, and Eleanor wondered if she too was becoming just another shadow here caught between past and present, between memory and forgetting.

The night air here was often cooler than many other corners of the monolith. The breezes in the east wing caressed her as an old friend, whispering sweetness in her ears. She often found herself in them late at night, idling until the house would finally hush enough to let her rest. It was something about the concentrated energy in the library that made everything else feel much safer, though she still heard it moan and creak with increasing urgency. Still drawn to that quiet comfort, she continued down the halls to the small flight of stone steps that led to the polished parquet of the ballroom.

She spotted Alaric there that night, shoulders hunched against the weight of the summer night. He seemed distant, lost in that darkened space, his eyes fixed somewhere beyond the glittering chandelier above. The steady sound of her footsteps on the worn carpet stirred him. He glanced up to look at her, a small and tired smile finding its way to his mouth. Something about it made her heart wrench.

The air between them was thick. The manor creaked around them, moaning softly like it waited with bated breath.

It was Alaric's voice that broke the quiet first.

"He missed dinner again." He said, a tone of mourning seeping through his words as his smile dropped.

Eleanor's eyes refused to meet him. She gazed to the floor, feeling suddenly very guilty. "Long nights. The records date back to the 1400s. I'm sure—"

"Don't." Alaric interrupted. She swallowed. "Don't make excuses for him. Not this time."

A pause stretched between them, filled only by the faint creak of the house settling. The flicker of candles in the ballroom was the only illumination, playing on his cheek as he sank from his argument. She couldn't help but notice the freckles there, the faintest sign of life in his skin.

"Does he even remember what it's like," Alaric muttered, almost to himself, "to want anything more than… this?"

Eleanor swallowed hard. "I hope so. I think part of him must."

"But it doesn't show." His voice tightened, like a thread stretched thin. "Not anymore."

Her throat went dry. "Maybe he's protecting himself in his own way."

Their eyes met then—a quiet fire lurking just beneath the surface of Alaric's bitterness. Before either of them could name it, the sudden clatter of something falling in the ballroom broke the stillness, sharp and unexpected. Eleanor startled, the spell between them broken. Her bare hand shot to her mouth, covering her breath in shock, but Alaric smiled, making her uneasy. He rose first, brushing off the wrinkles at his pantlegs and reaching out for her other hand, which she hesitantly offered in return.

"Probably just the wind," Alaric said, though his voice held a note of doubt.

Together, they moved towards the grand doors, the heavy silence following like a shadow. The chill of the night seeped through the cracks, drawing them into the vast, empty room. They were adrift in the dark, guiding one another, however loosely. Alaric had left the candlelight in the room lit for god knows how long, the scent of several sources burning out filling her nose with the distinct smell of burnt cotton.

By the edge of the far wall, a heavy brass candlestick had wrenched itself free from its sconce and now unceremoniously rolled to and fro on the polished floor, dripping a confetti of wax and fat as it did so. A hollow silence filled the room after the moment passed, leaving them once more in the uncomfortable pauses between reality.

Alaric dropped her hand, striding to the pillar and scooping it up. He placed it on its side on a windowsill there, gazing at the floor a moment longer before turning and pressing his back against the wall. He slid down it, placing his forehead on his knees. He seemed so much smaller now, and she couldn't help but wander his direction as if pulled by an unseen rope. She sat beside him, hesitant and curious.

When they were this close, she could get a good look at him finally. His hair was beautiful, true, but it was also lightly frizzed from the humidity inside the manor. While his skin was soft and bright, it was also lightly pockmarked in some places and redder in others. A small scar rested on one of his forearms, a mark just the right positioning for something caught on a careless nail or a shard of glass, likely a careless youth's reckless accident. He was poised and well-dressed, but his clothes hung loosely in places and were too tight in others, a small ring of sweat at his collar.

This was not his home, and it never had been, but the weight of it clung to him all the same. She saw, in that unguarded moment, how the place had been eating him hollow from the inside out. How everything he'd tried to hold at arm's length had crept back and taken root like a witch elm.

The performance he wore—careless, sharp, untouchable—had begun to crack, its purpose long since slipping from his grasp. And beneath it, she glimpsed the truth he would never speak aloud: that all his efforts to keep Elias from this fate had only tightened the snare around them both.

He had not saved Elias.

He had only damned him to suffer alone.

And somehow, she understood that he would never forgive himself for it.

The chandelier flickered above them, dripping wax onto the floor from inappropriate heights. The echo of it felt uninvited.

* * *

Late into the night, the library's heavy silence pressed down on Elias. The familiar scent of leather and parchment was tinged now with secrets long buried, brought into the open.

He had moved the ledgers from Edwin's private study—those hidden books Edwin never intended anyone to see—stacking them on the desk beneath the oil lamp's flickering glow. He had discovered them one feverish night, pressing on a false bottom located in the old man's desk and lugged them back one by one. The pages were brittle, the ink faded but the numbers were still stark.

As he explored the ledgers, Elias took meticulous notes. Grain shipments detailed with relentless precision. Tithes logged in cold, looping letters. Villages listed, then crossed off like bad debts. These books were older, dating to the birth of the manor itself. There, his own ancestors recorded the comings and goings of Greystone finances, ever the dutiful accountants with far less of the glory. His fingers would smooth over the faded script of Thornes long passed, chronicling the orders of Greystones long since dishonored—the swirling ouroboros of legacy.

The notes he made found their way to the walls and shelves, arrows and reference numbers tangled in a rat's nest of breadcrumbs. Indecipherable to anyone but him, they painted the furniture and tables in fevered obsession. Sweat slicked his brow as he added one piece after another, certain that beneath the surface, something was wrong. Dates that didn't belong. Entries that vanished without explanation. And then: *"lost mouths."*

The phrase was clinical, detached. Human beings counted as nothing more than inventory, crossed out and erased with a pen. Silence and disappearance, losses to shipments, a history of erasure stretching back generations.

His lips moved in near silence, muttering calculations and connections no one else dared see. "It's all here. They wrote it all down. They always wrote it down."

Then his eye caught something else, an entry half-hidden, folded into a note between columns as if added later. Written in a smaller, more careful hand, almost as an afterthought: *"Maintenance paid discreetly for the heir, debt owed for blood unacknowledged."*

Elias paused, fingers trembling as he traced the words. The phrase unsettled him, stirring questions he wasn't ready to ask. He refolded the page carefully, eyes flickering toward the door as if expecting a ghost to appear.

But there was only silence.

His mind was a storm, chaos swirling so fiercely there was no space for clarity or shock. The cryptic words became just another number, another code to decipher, another piece in a puzzle consuming every waking thought.

A soft footfall startled him. The door creaked open, and Eleanor stepped inside hesitantly, her eyes wide as they took in the sea of scattered papers and the fevered look on Elias's face. She held a hand to her chest, and the other clasped a small bowl of soup. Their eyes locked for a moment and in that stretched silence, he could almost hear her fear.

"I—" She started, but the room pressed in, suffocating her. She placed the bowl quickly on the side table by the door, slipping into the hallway and shutting the door behind her.

Elias remained frozen, the words she didn't say echoing in silence.

* * *

Eleanor tore down the corridor, her blood running cold from what she'd just seen. Elias no longer looked like the man she knew. He seemed almost unmoored from humanity. His body was brittle, gaunt from the meals he'd forsaken. His hair hung wild and tangled, dust clinging to strands as if the shadows themselves had settled there. But it was his eyes—God, his eyes—that shattered her. Vacant and wild, burning with a fire that told no stories, held no warmth. The safety she once found in him had vanished, leaving behind only a hollow, flickering shadow of the man she remembered.

Suddenly, as she ran, Alaric caught her by the shoulders, steadying her as she pitched forward. His grip was firm, grounding, utterly unlike the frantic shudder running through her. She'd parted from him not long ago, but seeing him again now, someone still whole, still warm, made a tremor of relief break across her face.

"Eleanor?" His voice was barely a breath. "What happened?"

She didn't answer. Couldn't. Her voice had abandoned her, locked somewhere in her chest with the terror she'd fled. All she could do was look at him with wide, pleading eyes, desperate for something solid to cling to. Alaric's expression shifted to concern. Regular, human concern. It felt like rain in the desert.

She took a step towards him. Then another.

He didn't move as she reached him, didn't question the way she folded herself against him, sinking into his chest as they slid down to the cold marble floor. Her body trembled violently, breath hitching, seeking refuge anywhere she could find it. His hands settled on her instinctively: one warm at the small of her back, the other rising gently to cradle her cheek.

His hand lingered there, thumb tracing the fragile line of her jaw. They stayed like this for a long moment, just breathing while the walls groaned softly around them. Slowly, deliberately, he tilted her face toward his. Their breaths mingled, tense and shallow, the world narrowing until nothing existed but the space between them. Not desire, but something else, something more primal in the desperate need to just feel alive.

When their lips met, it was soft and uncertain, and it was the first flicker of warmth the manor had seen all year.

They broke apart as quickly, Eleanor's breath catching in her throat.

"I shouldn't have—" She started.

"You didn't—" Alaric fumbled equally.

"Forget it, please, I—"

"I will," he promised. She knew he wouldn't.

They held each other's gaze for one long moment, sinking in words and sentiments unsaid. Eleanor stood first, smoothing her skirts and swallowing hard before she spoke at all. She nodded to bid him goodnight, the weight of the night settling like a dark fog once more.

No one dared to say anything more.

Eleanor didn't feel her feet carry her to her room; she only realized she'd reached the door when her hand slipped on the knob. She shut it behind her with a soft click, then pressed her back to the wood and let the breath she'd been holding shudder out of her. The sobs came in waves, threatening her discreet unraveling. Her hands wouldn't stop shaking.

The kiss replayed in fragments: the hand on her cheek, the feel of his lips, the way his breath mingled with hers. She wasn't sure which part horrified her more, the kiss itself or the way she'd needed it so terribly. The way she'd welcomed it. Her legs gave out and she sunk to the floor, her skirts pooling out around her. She pressed both palms to her face as if it would stuff the memory back in.

"What have I done?" The whisper scraped out of her like something torn loose. Not because it had been wrong—though, God, it was—but because it hadn't meant nothing. She'd seen it in his eyes the second they'd pulled apart, that recognition of hope and desire. She'd stolen comfort not meant for her, all because Elias no longer could.

That was the part that hurt in a way she couldn't quite describe. The guilt felt corrosive, like ink spreading through water. She wasn't sure which version she was mourning anymore: the man Elias was, or the man he should have been. He could have been the perfect husband, and her the perfect wife, and there would be no Greystone manor or mysteries to solve to save the families… just them, and perhaps a cat, maybe a child in a few years. Her body slowly rolled from sobs into just that cold, awful quiet where everything felt too sharp.

Across the room, her eyes found a mirror that had fogged over. For a moment she thought she'd imagined it. The air was cold at this hour; it shouldn't fog. Eleanor stared as the fog on the mirror pulsed, as if something had breathed against the glass.

Her stomach dropped.

"No," she whispered. "Not now."

But the house didn't care what she wanted. It never had. She hugged her arms around herself, curling inward on the floor. Eleanor closed her eyes and wished, with a tightening ache, for morning.

✳ ✳ ✳

The days of July slipped by in a heavy, suffocating silence. After that night, words seemed too fragile, too dangerous to be spoken. Eleanor drifted through the manor's quiet halls, grasping at distractions, desperate to silence the growing dread that clawed at her chest. She floated like a ghost, doing anything to consume her time. She busied her hands with smaller tasks—arranging flowers, polishing silverware, pretending any of these could hold back the growing unease in her chest. But no matter how hard she tried, the manor pressed down on her, an unspoken tension in every corner.

Alaric lingered in the ballroom, pacing like a caged animal

and occasionally pressing his ear to the cool glass of the mirror. Elias buried himself deeper in numbers, the muttering heard from the other side of the door. Both Eleanor and Alaric had taken to putting their heads down and covering their ears whenever they passed the library.

Eleanor's own thoughts paced in endless circles. She wanted to scream, to say something to him, to reach out, to hold them both together, but the words caught in her throat like stones. After that night, speaking to either of them felt like an insurmountable task. So she wandered, a witness to a house that had long ago begun its shift and chosen its meal.

It started on a stuffy summer's day, while she stood folding tea towels in the kitchen. The first suggestion of it was like a blood rush in the back of her head — painful and subtle. A soft drip sounded somewhere behind the wall, water she couldn't quite place. Her heartbeat climbed her throat, each pulse a painful hammering that made her feel faint.

She paused, fingers stilling mid-fold. The kitchen, usually a sanctuary of steady rhythm, suddenly felt oppressive like the walls themselves had tightened, closing in from all sides. Shadows pooled in the corners, as if the house watched her with hungry, unseen eyes. A faint scent of earth and decay drifted through the air, tickling her senses and stirring unease deep within. She set down the tea towel, pressing a tentative hand against the cool plastered wall. The dripping sound faded as abruptly as it had come, but the dampness lingered there, cool and stubborn, long after the noise had ceased.

From that day on, the drips came without warning, echoing from every forgotten corner of the manor. They only began when she was alone, in moments of vulnerability. The soft, relentless trickle whispered from the deepest crevices:

beneath staircases, behind locked doors, through walls long sealed. It clung to her like a shadow, trailing her steps and invading her quietest moments, never granting her a second of peace.

Unlike the brighter days of spring, Eleanor kept her fears to herself. She spoke to no one, not even Winifred, whose presence once brought a strange comfort. It was as though her tongue had glued itself to the roof of her mouth, silencing the words she most needed to say. The manor's silence pressed harder, a suffocating weight that tangled with the soft drip, drip, drip that haunted her every step.

It continued like this even in her quarters. As she lay splayed out on her cold mattress, the relentless drip, drip, drip continued from the corner of her room and threatened to take her sanity from her. It was maddening, and consistent. Then, suddenly, a light flutter by her door.

Startled by the new noise, she rose. The folded page in the crack of her door was yellowed and worn, edges brittle. Carefully, she knelt to retrieve it. It was still warm in her hands, the ink still shining in the candlelight as she unfolded it.

It was a ledger page, filled with neat rows of faded ink—shipments, payments, dates—but what caught her eye was a small annotation in a smaller, more careful hand tucked between the columns:

"You turn away while he drowns in the shadows.
Your silence feeds the hunger that will consume us all."

No signature. No mercy.

Her fingers trembled as she took the words in, letting them seep into her bones. Immediately, she recognized the hand and the paper as her fiance, and if that hadn't given it away, the mad ramblings certainly did. The page slipped from her grasp and fluttered to the floor. Eleanor sank back into her chair, the weight of the manor pressing in around her more heavily than ever. The house was restless, its secrets leaking through cracks and shadows, and she was caught in its grip. She pressed her fingers to her temples as a migraine settled into the folds of her brain.

* * *

Late into the July night, the library was a tomb of paper and shadows. The walls were plastered by this point in clippings: newspapers, scrawled notes, official notices, anything he could get his hands on. He had grown feral in his appearance; his scruff had grown to a short but unshaven mess, his eyes were fire—bright, and his clothing was stained and untucked every which direction it could be. Ink—stained pages were strewn across the desk in clumps and pinned in clusters, documenting shipments and tithes, but also something more he just couldn't pin yet. Elias ran a trembling hand over a faded chart, tracing lines that told a grim story. The air was thick with dust and the weight of years of secrets, each page a shard of a family history bleeding out in numbers.

The sound of footsteps startled Elias from his spiraling thoughts. The study door creaked open, and Eleanor stepped inside, her face flushed with a mix of anger and fear. She held a single, folded page in her trembling hand.

"This slipped under my door," she said sharply, voice barely controlled. "I thought it was from you."

Elias took the page, fingers still stained with ink, and

unfolded it carefully. The writing was small and precise, but unmistakably his. His blood chilled with the realization.

"Eleanor, I… I haven't left this room." He pleaded, his voice small.

A flash of incredulity crossed her face, her disbelief loud in the silence. The moment that stretched between them was louder than any of it, months of mistrust coming to surface. Her gaze bore into him like an accusation itself, stringing him up to be hanged. The gallows awaited beneath him as he scrambled to find his papers among the mess on the desk and muttered, "it's worse than I thought."

Eleanor's breath hitched, and for a moment, her walls cracked. But then she pulled herself together, stepping back as if the truth she'd been avoiding had burned her skin.

"You say you haven't left, yet secrets crawl beneath this roof, Elias. And you shut me out like I'm already gone." Her voice trembled with anger and fear, but there was something more fragile underneath, an aching hope that he might prove her wrong.

Elias' throat tightened as he snatched the papers he's been digging for and desperately presented them to her. Elias's hands trembled as he pointed to the ledger, his voice low and heavy with a mixture of dread and disbelief.

"It repeats," he said, eyes never leaving the faded ink. "Every generation. Losses. Vanishings. Something—… something is bleeding the family down to its bones. And it always starts again."

He traced his finger down the edge of the papers, stopping on entries from before the manor operated. An unbelievable number of bodies, paid to a place that did not yet exist to memorialize them. "See this?" Elias whispered, voice barely steady. "These shouldn't exist. These were recorded before the first blight… as if someone already knew it was coming."

Eleanor stilled, her eyes wide and unreadable. She looked to be a mix of afraid and sickened, and her hands were lightly trembling. Elias had never seen her this unraveled; her face had no light behind it, and her hair was dulled even in the glow of the candlelight. It was the first close look he'd gotten at her in months, and it was cruel and unwelcome.

She swallowed hard and stepped back, folding her arms as if to shield herself from the truth, and from him.

"This isn't some haunted tale," she said, voice brittle. "It's just… paperwork. It's all you have left, and it's driving you mad."

Elias met her gaze, pain flickering in his eyes. There was nothing he could add to make her believe him, or to forgive him. He swallowed. "It's more than paperwork. It's our debt. And it's killing us."

Eleanor didn't react with any warmth. Instead, she gave a soft, "goodnight, Elias," before quietly turning on her heel and leaving the library, shutting the heavy door behind her.

Elias sat motionless long after the door's echo faded, the silence around him now a heavy shroud. The warmth that Eleanor once brought, the quiet steadiness that tethered him, had slipped away, leaving a hollow ache that throbbed beneath his ribs.

He felt the sharp sting of her absence, more cutting than any wound he'd borne before. Her rejection wasn't just a rebuke of his words, but of the fragile hope he'd clung to in the dark. He was alone now, truly alone, swallowed by the cold weight of the manor and the relentless tide of his own unraveling.

The numbers weighed heavy in his hands, taunting him

with every scribbled line. Time and hope slipped through his fingers like ash. These weren't just figures; they were ghosts that refused to rest, debts no forgiveness could touch.

But he was close. If he could just unravel the source, break the cycle, maybe, just maybe, he'd be free. His father's madness wouldn't have been in vain. His mother would smile again. And Alaric… Alaric would find a new torment, a rival he couldn't outshine. Elias would claim the manor, make it right, not just for himself but to prove he was the rightful heir in every sense. And he'd find a way to make it up to her. He had to.

But now, he sunk to the floor in exhaustion and watched the door, hoping she'd turn around. She didn't.

* * *

Alaric lingered in the vast emptiness of the ballroom, the moonlight slipping through the tall windows like pale fingers brushing against the dust-covered floor. The chandeliers hung silent above, their crystals dull and lifeless. The silence pressed heavy against him, questioning his resolve.

His worn work shoes made no grand sound as he crossed the floor, only the soft scrape of leather on wood. It was hours after the workmen had long since departed, leaving the house to its shadows and secrets. In one hand, he clutched a flask, once heavy with brandy but now nearly empty, its metallic chill a brief anchor to the world.

Alaric moved drunkenly, twisting and turning in the pale slivers of moonlight, humming along to a song that no one else could hear—a melancholic melody pulled from memory

201

and loss. The vast ballroom seemed to breathe around him, the walls whispering echoes of forgotten laughter and faded grandeur. In this moment, he was alone but not lonely. He never felt truly alone in the ballroom.

From the shadowed doorway, a figure slipped in, just outside his line of vision. He fixed on it, squinting. The figure was thin, dark-haired, and pale. It wore clothes, but unlike any he has ever seen this particular frame in — an elaborate overcoat with a sparkling trim, matching vest and pants, all in white. Alaric's breath caught, a flicker of joy brightening his weary face as if the night had gifted him a reprieve.

"Elias," he murmured, staggering slightly as he held out his hand, "come, dance with me."

He reached out, arms opening wide, and before he fully registered, the figure stepped into his embrace. The air thickened instantly, heavy and electric, charged with an eerie stillness that pressed close around them. Alaric's fingers dug gently into the fabric at the hollow curve of the figure's back, then found Elias's hand, warm and trembling.

Closing his eyes, he leaned into the moment, letting the silence fold over him as he began to spin slowly, humming a long-forgotten tune that felt like a thread pulling him back from the edge. The ballroom seemed to shrink, the vastness collapsing until only the two of them remained—lost in a fragile, fragile bubble of time.

Their bodies moved in unison, Alaric guiding the phantom in loose circles and soft twirls, the motion fluid despite the ghostly weight in his arms. His breath came steady and deep, and as he inhaled, he imagined Elias's earthy cologne seeping into his veins. It was a balm for the ache inside him, mending the fractures he'd tried so hard to ignore. In that suspended moment, his heart beat steady, whole, as if the world outside no longer mattered.

Then he opened his eyes.

The strong smell of rot mingled with the air as he gazed upon it. The figure in his arms began to unravel, the flesh mottled. Its skin was sagging and drenched like old parchment. The warmth he'd imagined was a cruel trick; instead his fingers brushed against brittle bones beneath decaying flesh.

Elias' form trembled, veins darkened and pulsing with something unnatural. His eyes were sunken and void of life, staring blankly with a glassy, milky sheen. His mouth hung slightly open, a dark stain spreading at the corner like ink. Then, it crumpled against him, decay seeping through illusion and piling to the floor.

Alaric collapsed onto the dust-laden floor with it. The vast, empty ballroom closed in around him like a tomb.

III

Part Three

11

Stillness and Rot

The manor was sleepless again. The flickering candlelight barely touched the edges of the stacks of ledgers sprawled across Elias' desk, their yellowed pages worn thin by decades of sorrow and secrecy. He traced trembling fingers over columns of numbers, each deficit and missing shipment a silent scream etched into paper. The patterns were cruel and relentless—loss upon loss, generation after generation, like a slow poison seeping into the bloodline. Somewhere between the ink and the shadows, Elias felt the weight of a legacy that refused to be denied, and the terrifying truth pressed in around him: the house was feeding, consuming, and he was trapped in the cycle, tracing the lines of his own undoing.

Every book, every generation, every record ended the same way. The numbers always ended the same way: a deficit that no ledger could explain. Shipments vanished into thin air, livestock disappeared from the rolls, and entire villages slipped into silence, erased from records as if they had never been. Each gap was a missing piece in a puzzle that refused to be solved. As Elias examined older ledgers and older still, the pattern emerged time and time again. It would be logged tirelessly by his family until the ink blurred in trembling handwriting, frantic scratch-outs marred the margins, and entire pages were torn away, as though the weight of the truth had fractured the hands that tried to record it. They spiraled into madness, paranoia, and occasionally reckless violence, only for another to take his place in an effort to take his vengeance or even to still the pattern. When it wasn't passed to a son, it was passed to a loved one; the bleed could not be stopped.

Each heir was consumed by the house's hunger, caught in a cycle they could neither see nor escape. The ledgers did not just recount numbers. They whispered curses, tracing a pattern of loss and despair as old as the stones beneath their feet. Elias could feel himself unraveling this time, eyes boring through the pages and setting him on fire. The ledger before him was no mere record; it was a confession written in numbers, a dark inheritance inscribed in ink and blood. The original starvation, once thought a cruel but isolated tragedy, a miscount of grain, revealed itself as the cornerstone of the estate's fortune. It had been a deliberate, merciless foundation built on suffering and silence. This manor had been built on hundreds of innocent bodies who committed the sin of living too close to Greystone.

The pages spun out like a spiraling ouroboros, endless and devouring: feeding, consuming, replacing what was taken, cycle upon cycle. The estate was not just haunted by ghosts; it was bound to them, bound to the debts that could never be repaid. And his own family, haunted by the sin of blind loyalty, leaving generations to go mad in attempts to repent.

Both men were sacrificed. And if they did not act, the curse of it would only spread.

The manor would demand blood.

He thought of Eleanor. He thought of Alaric. His father. His life outside the manor. His life before all this.

His voice cracked, barely a whisper at first, crawling from his lips like a confession to the empty room. "They never stopped feeding… never stopped taking…" He leaned into the pages, tracing in with his fingers desperately. "It's a debt that cannot be paid… but still they bleed us dry…"

Suddenly, he wondered if Edwin had known. Almost simultaneously, he realized he must have. He watched it happen to his father. His father had watched it happen to his grandfather. His own line had become locked within the manor around that same time, every generation. One fractured, the other simply glued himself to the manor as if he had no other allies.

He thought of Edwin's death. Then, he chose not to think of that any longer.

He chose instead to open the next book.

* * *

Eleanor moved through the manor like a shadow trying to hold itself together. The house pressed closer with every step, its weight heavier than grief, colder than fear. Her hands trembled slightly as she arranged the same wilting flowers on the windowsill, the petals curling inward like silent prayers. Only months ago, she had mourned them each time they dried, but she'd given up since, the manor sucking any enthusiasm she had right out of her marrow.

Occasionally, Alaric passed her in the halls and she glanced down, refusing to acknowledge him properly. Her plan was simply not to address him as much as she could manage, and maybe they'd all make it out unscathed. She knew in her heart that it wasn't true, but no one could truly fault her for trying. Instead, proximity became their language: the brush of a sleeve, shared breaths held just a moment too long, glances that flickered with desperate need and equal restraint.

They never spoke of the kiss. The brief, trembling collision of lips that had shattered the quiet between them lingered, a ghost trailing their every thought. In stolen conversations that stretched longer, their voices softened and walls dropped. The facade of civility cracked, revealing the raw, unguarded selves beneath. But these were fleeting moments, and Eleanor left them abruptly and shaken. Any glance that lingered spelled danger.

They weren't anything to one another but a balm in the shape of those who had shaken off their care. Abandoned, tormented loneliness—a club they were the only two members of. Sometimes the silence was intolerable and that constant dripping spun her head into a million directions. Other times, the loneliness was almost peaceful, holding her in its soft, pillowed embrace. Most of the time it was just loud. August went on in a dirge.

One morning, after nights thick with restless dreams and days spent wandering shadowed halls, Eleanor reached a fragile breaking point. The manor's walls felt like they were closing in, breathing down her neck with every silent step. She longed for air that didn't taste of dust and dread, for voices that didn't echo with ghosts. So she made a decision, quiet but resolute. She would step beyond the iron gates, beyond the maze of corridors and endless rooms, and find the town that lay somewhere past the manor's reach. She craved the touch of something real: the morning sun, the hum of life, the simple comfort of a stranger's presence.

Clad in a simple day dress, she slipped through the heavy front doors, which groaned like a reluctant sentinel opening just for her. The air outside was inviting and warm, a breath of clarity after months trapped beneath the manor's suffocating weight. For a moment, hope bloomed in her chest. She hadn't left in months, which was a combined effect of the manor's distance and the lack of staff, who had thinned out over the months.

It was going so well at first. The path ahead was clear, the air fresh and warm with the gentle heat of an August morning. The light filtered softly through the trees, carrying the faint scent of grass and wildflowers beyond the manor's walls. She walked steadily, her hand lifting the heavy iron latch of the gate with a quiet creak. Slipping through to the other side, her sleeve caught briefly on the rough metal edge, but it was no matter. She stepped out with a spark of hope, her confidence growing with every step.

The gravel beneath her feet soon softened into damp earth, the crunch turning to a muted squelch as the terrain shifted. The manor's towering silhouette receded behind her, becoming smaller with every step, as if she were truly leaving it behind.

She pressed on, breath steady, until she looked up again.

The iron gate loomed before her once more, heavy and unyielding. She was outside the gate again.

The path had twisted back, folding in on itself like a cruel trick, trapping her in its endless loop. A cold weight settled in her chest as the manor's silent presence pressed in, watching and waiting. She stilled, heart hammering as the gate loomed before her again—the same, unyielding barrier she had just passed. Panic prickled at the edges of her mind. The path was no longer a path but a trap, folding back on itself with cruel precision. The manor was not done with her. Without hesitation, she turned and rushed back inside, the heavy doors closing behind her with a final, hollow thud. The walls seemed to lean closer, the shadows deepening, and the manor's breath was cold on her neck.

The next sound she heard was a distant call of her name. It was disembodied, floating, and insistent. She did not recognize it. It was not Alaric. It was not Elias. It was not Winifred. But something in the voice, a cadence she almost recognized, kept tugging at her. Foolishly, she thought that ignoring it would quiet it, but it persisted until her curiosity rose above her fear and she pulled herself feebly off the floor of the entry. Anxiously, she followed it.

Every step felt chosen for her, placed by some unseen hand. Every corner she turned led her deeper into the quietest part of Greystone, where the lamps flickered thinly and the air smelled of damp stone. The dripping in the walls had quieted to focus on the call, its magnetic pull drawing her pace for pace, however much she wished to resist. Strangely, she saw no staff as she wandered in a trance. The morning welcomed only her. Then, the door.

It stood at the end of the corridor, impossibly present and unmistakably waiting. A thin line of darkness leaked through the crack beneath it, pulsing faintly in time with the lapping of water just beyond. Her breath wavered, and once more it whispered her name from behind the heavy wood—wet, hollow, and nearly pleading.

Eleanor reached out, her fingertips brushing the knob.

The sound stopped.

And then, as if waking from a nightmare, she tore herself away. She fled the corridor, back through the manor's twisting arteries, past windows reflecting only her own frayed outline. She did not look over her shoulder. By the time she reached the safer, warmer parts of the house, her pulse was still ricocheting painfully through her throat. She pressed her back to the nearest wall, breathing in unsteady, shallow shivers.

That was when she saw Alaric. He stood at the far end of the hallway, halfway in shadow, watching her with an unsettled softness. He looked upon her with the expression of a man who recognized it because he'd known it himself. He gave her a nervous smile, appearing much warmer as he did so.

He didn't ask why she looked so pale. He didn't ask why she was shaking. Instead, he offered a simple, "couldn't sleep?" He stepped toward her, slow and careful, as if she were something fragile left out in the rain. She shook her head.

They found themselves walking together without deciding to. Their steps aligned, their silences aligned, the quick rises and falls of their chests aligned. They wandered into the darker corridors of the east wing, circling around the subject the best they could. Instead, their conversation veered, softly and naturally, into confessions they had no business sharing with one another. Their fears, their exhaustion, their loneliness. The sense that Elias was venturing somewhere that neither of them could follow coated them both.

Every time one of them shifted, their knees brushed. Every time they exhaled, their breaths almost mingled. No touch, but a sharp and unbearable wanting, gathering like static in the charged air between them. The house listened. The day brushed them with its strokes of gold. Restraint became its own kind of intimacy, stretching thin, thinner, ready to tear.

* * *

Something was unraveling inside Alaric, a thread pulled loose by the house itself.

His once sharp, handsome features had faded, as if worn thin by the weight of sleepless nights and quiet fears. The color drained from his face, leaving behind a ghostly pallor that seemed almost unnatural under the manor's dim light. His eyes, once bright and confident, now held a distant glaze, as if parts of him were slipping away into shadows only he could see. The vitality that had marked him —his charm, his careless laughter—crumbled slowly into dust, scattered by the relentless winds of stress and something darker.

One evening, as the night curled around the manor like smoke, they found themselves lingering near the ballroom, two figures drawn by something neither dared to name. Alaric was talking, or trying to. His words stumbled and fell away mid-sentence, his voice trailing into a tense silence as his gaze drifted past Eleanor's shoulder, eyes wide but unfocused, as though he were hearing a secret whispered through the stone.

When she followed his look, he could hear her breath still. The ballroom wall loomed before them, cold and cracked, a silent witness to untold horrors. Alaric's hand moved slowly to press against the mirror, his palm flattened as if to catch a faint tremor beneath the surface. It was a compulsion, really.

Alaric's body stiffened, the color draining from his cheeks. His voice was a hoarse whisper. "Do you hear it?"

Eleanor had shaken her head, eyes wide in fear.

As the nights passed in a haze, he slept progressively less. The nights were haunted by relentless tossing and the faint sounds that seemed to crawl beneath the manor's bones. She caught him one dawn, alone and silent in the bright, sharp morning, his ear pressed against the ballroom wall, as if he hoped to listen his way into understanding, or escape.

"Alaric," she had said, her voice breaking the heavy silence.

He pulled away, face pale but stubborn. "I'm fine," he said, but the lie was fragile.

She watched him, knowing that beneath the surface of his insistence, he was already lost. A long moment stretched taut like a thread about to snap. Then the house groaned a low, mournful sound that rattled the floor beneath their feet. The chandelier above trembled. A slow knocking began again somewhere deep behind the walls, steady and deliberate, like a heartbeat dragging itself from the dark. This time, she heard it.

His eyes caught hers, wide and haunted. Without a word, he stepped closer, the distance between them suddenly unbearable. Without meaning to, he embraced Eleanor tightly, their bodies flush.

"We can't keep doing this alone," he whispered, voice rough with exhaustion.

She didn't answer, and Alaric could understand why. How could she? The truth clawed at his throat like a living thing, and their hands, trembling, found softer resting places. There was no forgiveness here, only the heavy, crushing weight of what exactly they had found themselves in and what was still to come. The fear of surviving this alone tightened his throat and his chest.

She opened her mouth, closed it, then tried again. Tears welled up in her eyes. He'd never seen her cry, or anything close.

"Alaric…" The name landed between them like a repentance. "I don't…" she swallowed. "I don't want to lose you too."

Her voice broke on too, as if she'd been holding those words behind her teeth for weeks, afraid to let it leave her body. Before he could answer, she stepped closer. Her gentle fingers picked up his free wrist, turning it over to press her thumb to the veins there. The blue and purple lines there pulsed—with anticipation or fear, neither could tell. She drew a shallow breath.

"I need—" The sentence collapsed. He watched her face as it searched his and, suddenly feeling too seen, he pressed his forehead to hers. They lingered in ambiguity a moment longer. He felt her pulse stutter under her skin. Both of them hovered on the edge of a knife.

"Eleanor," he whispered, but the name came out cracked, ruined.

Then, something in her broke. Her fingers curled in the front of his shirt, not pulling him closer so much as holding herself upright. That tiny collapse of composure undid him entirely. He answered before either of them could think better of it. His hands found her waist, guiding her back with a gentleness that trembled at the edges. She didn't resist.

Her heels scraped against the ballroom floor as he walked her backwards to the mirrored walls. The light fractured there, making all sorts of patterns on the floor. Her back met the glass with a soft sound. The mirror shuddered. So did she.

"Alaric—" It wasn't a protest. It wasn't permission either. He lifted his head just enough to look at her.

"We don't have to," He whispered, his voice already equally heavy with wanting and dread.

"Please, just—" Her breath hitched. "Don't let me be alone." He caught her face in his hands; it wasn't a claim, but a confirmation that she was alive, real.

It was Eleanor who snapped their restraint. Her hands slid up his arms, clutching, grounding.

He pressed her more firmly to the mirror. It wasn't forceful, but with the kind of urgency that came from a unique kind of desperation. There were no more words as their bodies found an equilibrium. Their lips met with desolation and anguish, but they were warm and moved together, a line taut between mouths. What happened wasn't careful, wasn't romantic, wasn't anything either of them could have imagined months ago. What happened was distorted and desperate, and wholly unavoidable. He kissed her again, slower this time, but with no less desperation.

Her lips parted, and his breath mingled with hers: warm, uneven, almost frantic. Her body arched subtly toward him, answering without words, drawing him in. His hands followed the shape of her waist, the line of her ribs beneath the thin fabric, urging her closer in small, instinctive pulls. Her fingers traced the column of his throat, then flattened against his chest, feeling the stutter of his heartbeat as though confirming he was alive, real, here.

He pressed her more fully against the glass, and the surface gave the faintest, protesting groan. Her breath broke against his mouth, a small, involuntary sound, and it undid him. They moved together not with desire, but a raw, aching need within them. When his hands found her hips, she gasped softly, not in pleasure so much as recognition. He felt her body align with his, her breath stutter, her fingers dig into his back. The moment sharpened; the air thinned; the mirror behind her vibrated as if a second heartbeat lived inside it.

They gave in.

It happened without grace. His hands found the hem of her skirts, fingers shaking as though he were lifting a veil off something dangerous. The fabric whispered up her legs, and he gathered it in trembling fists before pressing it to her chest. She took the burden of it from him, clutching the folds herself, a silent agreement that neither of them dared articulate.

The mirror fogged around the edges. The chandelier trembled overhead. Their movements were clumsy, rushed, shaped by need rather than desire. Her gasp blended with the sound of his breath hitching, their bodies stumbling into a rhythm forged by fear and recognition. There was no sweetness to it, only a frantic pull toward something alive, something warm, something that proved they were still here even as the manor seemed to eat at their edges.

The walls, usually so watchful, seemed to retreat. The oppressive air that had been stalking them for months thinned, yielding space around their bodies. The great ballroom, with all its ghosts and grandeur, folded in on itself until the only thing that existed was the heat of her, the grip of him, the terrible relief of another living soul pressed close.

As they desecrated the room, it felt holy.

* * *

Eleanor rose slowly from Alaric's bed, breath uneven, as if her bones were remembering something she had never known. The sheets slid from her hips in a soft collapse, still warm with the shape of their bodies. Her limbs felt foreign. Not sore, hollowed. As though something had been scooped out of her in the night and not returned. The floor felt hard and cold under her feet, as though rejecting the warmth inside her flesh.

She turned over her shoulder to take in her surroundings, a sickness rising in her chest that felt deeper than any illness. Alaric lay beside her deeply, violently, asleep. His face was turned towards the wall, as if even in sleep he couldn't look at the mess he'd made of her. She didn't touch him. She didn't dare.

The cold followed her as she rose, drifting between the floorboards like old ghosts. Her body drifted, stepping delicately over the scattered trail of clothing on the floor. Her skirt collapsed like an empty husk, his shirt unbuttoned and tossed beside it in urgency, everything as evidence in a night neither of them had intended. She stopped in front of her slip, stepping into it like a funeral shroud. Her dark hair was undone fully, cascading in strokes down her back all the way to the small of her back. She hadn't the slightest idea where her ribbon had gone.

Alaric stirred, eliciting a quick turn over her shoulder from Eleanor. He was still asleep, and for that she was thankful, but he had turned towards her in his sleep. The warm gold of the August morning light danced in patterns on his cheek and his side, silhouetted by the sheets. They said that Lucifer was God's favorite angel, and she suddenly understood.

His curve in the sheets was slightly effeminate, a small

waist and smaller shoulders giving him the appearance of a woodland elf. His blond hair caught the light as if meeting an old friend, the dust glittering in the sunlight around him in brilliant silver and gold. It wove through the strands of his hair and played on his cheek, illuminating him. His brows knitted together as he dreamt, and the expression made her want to wave away any bad dreams he could ever have. She hated him for it, the way he could appear so helpless and innocent when he'd been readily complicit in their sin and betrayal.

Gathering nothing from the floor, she opted to walk to the door barefoot instead. She'd have Winnie collect it later, she decided, unable to look at him a second longer without tossing up the contents of her stomach. The pull at her sternum deepened, a slow invisible hook drawing her forward. She stepped into the hall, the hem of her slip fluttering against her legs, her body cold. She didn't think. Her body moved, obedient to something enormous pressing through the air. The second she left the room, it had returned.

She meandered the entire east corridor with her hands clutching her shoulders, gazing into long forgotten rooms as she passed. These rooms felt so unwelcoming now, so ripped of possibility. The ballroom appeared as a tomb. The paintings of old men and household scenes and even the goddamn Venus looked grotesque. The wallpaper was a sickly olive green that belonged in a mortuary. The worn runner under her feet felt thick with dust and time, rather than well-loved. She drifted, time-worn and weary, as the walls only felt thinner and still thinner.

The corridor stretched before her in a strange, wavering light. The house seemed to breathe in long, uneven intervals. With each of her steps, the humming grew warmer, heartbeat-slow, as if she were walking toward the center of something vast and living. The sound returned. At first only a low hum, almost part of the walls themselves. Then it sharpened, softened, curled into shape. A melody.

Her mother's voice.

A tune from childhood, sung in the kitchen on winter mornings, in the bath when Eleanor was small, in the garden while trimming late blooms. A tune her mother only used when she thought they were alone. The one her mother would use as steam rose from the kettle on cold winter mornings as she padded around the kitchen. A tune private enough to feel like a secret. Never in public. Never with her father nearby. A hope that only they knew.

Eleanor had not heard it in years. She had not dared to try humming it herself, afraid she'd get it wrong, afraid it would crumble in the air if she shaped it with her own voice.

Her chest tightened. Her steps slowed. The melody was too tender and too exact. And for one dizzying moment, the manor felt like home. Not because it was safe, but because it was cruel enough to wear her mother's voice like a borrowed skin. Her eyes welled with tears and she followed it mindlessly. She didn't notice the way her fingers shook, didn't register the faint sheen of sweat on her palms. The pull in her chest had turned sharp, insistent. A door frame appeared in front of her, familiar and wrong in equal measure.

She stopped. Her breath hitched.

Somehow, she'd found her way to the doorway at the end of the corridor once more. Eleanor's pulse stumbled. For a heartbeat she was a child again, small and unsteady, reaching toward a space where her mother was just out of sight. She should have run. She knew she should have.

But months of loneliness had sharpened into need. Years of grief had hollowed her. She stepped closer until the cold radiating from the knob stung her palm. Her breath trembled. The humming softened, becoming unbearably intimate. In the quiet, her mother humming to her alone, the way she used to.

"Please—" she whispered, not sure who she was begging anymore.

Her hands closed around the knob. It burned, It froze. It pulsed. All before the fear could return, before the tune could slip away and leave her with more unbearable silence—

Eleanor wrenched the door open, desperate for anything that felt like truth. The humming stopped the instant her eyes gazed down into that space. Eleanor froze.

Her eyes widened, slowly, then too wide, as if trying to take in something that should not fit in a human gaze. Her pupils constricted to pinpoints. Her lips parted. A soft sound escaped her throat, not a scream, not yet, but a thin, broken whimper as if the air had been knocked out of her lungs. Her fingers spasmed on the door frame. Her whole body leaned back, away, instinct trying to flee while shock kept her rooted. Her breath shuddered once, twice. Then, her face ruptured with understanding, terror shaping itself into something almost physical.

She took one step backward. Then another.

Then the thing—whatever shape the manor had chosen, whatever memory it had hollowed out to fill—shifted. Just a tilt. A lean. A too-familiar angle of the head that turned her bones to ice. Eleanor spun so fast she nearly fell.

Her shoulder slammed into the wall; she pushed herself off it. She fled barefoot down the corridor, her breath ragged, her slip whipping around her legs. She didn't look back. Couldn't. The very thought of turning her head felt like offering her throat to a knife.

She didn't know where she was running—to safety, to a door, to nothing at all. Only away. The sound of her own heartbeat drowned out everything except the soft, certain footfalls behind her. They were too soft for what was following, too close for how fast she was moving. It was almost breathing against her spine. Whatever that thing was, and it was a thing, she could sense its raw need to consume her whole.

The manor echoed with her flight: the violent slap of her feet on the boards, the broken sob wrenched from her chest, the slipstream of shadows that lunged after her. Every picture frame seemed to watch her go. Every doorway seemed to shrink as she passed. Behind her, she felt the moment the thing reached out, the moment it was close enough to grasp her and drag her away. She ran harder, letting the corridor swallow her whole, letting the manor fall away behind her like a closing mouth. The air changed first. In the entry it was cold, real, unfiltered by the manor's breath. and then the door materialized ahead of her like a salvation she didn't trust.

She hit it with her full weight. It gave.

Eleanor stumbled out onto the front steps, the bright morning light swallowing her. Her foot landed wrong on the stone on an edge she didn't see, and a bolt of pain shot up her leg. Something tore. She cried out, the sound sharp and animal, nearly toppling sideways. Behind her, the manor emanated a warm, living glow onto the steps.

She considered turning back. She couldn't. She wouldn't.

She lurched into motion again, half-hopping, half-falling down the steps. On the final one her injured foot buckled;

she pitched forward into the gravel, stones embedding in her palms, scraping her knees. She sucked in a breath that felt like shards. Across her white slip, the blood spread in slow, ruby blooms. The house was still open behind her. She swore she could hear it growl.

She scrambled upright without even brushing the blood or dirt away, and ran. The pain in her foot flared with each step, bright and nauseating, but she ran anyway, because stopping meant feeling the manor's gaze settle on her again. She could hear—God, she could swear she could hear—the soft tread of something crossing the threshold she had just escaped.

The line of trees reached into the sky ahead of her, twisting unnaturally. She plunged into the forest without hesitation. Branches lashed at her bare arms. The world narrowed to breath and pain and the terror in her throat. The forest floor was uneven, treacherous, but better than the smooth, hungry boards behind her. Leaves snapped underfoot, loud enough to betray her, but not louder than the phantom echo of footsteps she imagined behind her.

She didn't stop running until the house's glow was gone behind her. Until she couldn't hear anything but her own pulse in her ears and her ragged breath. Until she leaned against a tree, sliding down until the bark caught her hair, her injured foot trembling uncontrollably.

She had left the manor.

She had left *everything*.

When she finally dragged her gaze upward, past the trembling lattice of branches, the horizon struck her like a blow. It was… clean. Too clean. Suspiciously level, as if something enormous had been scraped away. She couldn't have run more than a few hundred feet, could still taste the house's air in her lungs…but where the manor should have loomed, there was nothing. No roof line. No silhouette. No shadow.

Just an expanse of blank sky, unsettling in its innocence.

The absence of Greystone Manor was louder than any pursuit. The forest seemed to lean inward, listening to the space where it should have stood, as if waiting for the house to inhale again.

As the moment stretched, the manor and Eleanor lost resonance.

It had let her go.

* * *

Alaric woke up with a start.

For a moment between sleeping and waking, he didn't know where he was. Only that the room was colder than it should be, and that he was alone in a bed that had not known warmth in its time in the manor. His breath was ragged and quick, pushing himself upright as his joints protested. The ache of the previous night still mapped across his body in places he'd rather not examine yet.

He blinked to the far side of the mattress. Empty. The blankets were shoved aside, the space she slept in still indented and faintly warm. A single strand of her dark hair clung to his pillow. Nothing of her remained but the evidence of her strewn about the room.

"Eleanor?" His voice cracked on the second syllable. He waited, listening to the creak of the floorboards. Listening for the soft, irritated exhale she made when disturbed suddenly. The manor returned nothing but a long, unforgiving stretch of silence. Alaric's pulse quickened, suddenly worried. Something about her absence felt more final than a simple jaunt to the shops or downstairs for tea.

He swung his legs over the side of the bed and stood, unsteady. He pulled his clothes from the floor, dressing in his shirt and pants from the night before, unbothered by the faint sweat marks lining it. When he turned to the doorway, he noticed it ajar, as if someone had snuck themselves out. He stumbled into the corridor. At the end of it, the front entry door stood open as well, letting in a thin, metallic wind. The sheer wrongness of it took a full breath to register. The manor didn't allow doors to be opened. Not without consequence. Not without intention. A cold dread gripped him.

"Eleanor," he whispered again, barely a sound.

He hurried down the hall, each step feeding the rising panic clawing up his spine. The boards felt softer beneath his heels, as if the house had grown pliant in the night, its attention elsewhere. There was no buzzing, no shifting of walls. Too quiet. Too still. By the time he reached the threshold he felt half-mad with dread. Wind stirred the hem of his shirt. The air outside was brighter than it should have been. He stepped onto the stone landing and froze.

Footprints. Fresh. Immediate. Bare. Small.

Eleanor's.

They trailed down the steps, imprinted in drying blood. The pattern was smeared in places, as though she'd faltered. He felt the ground tilt.

"No, no, no— " He followed them. His feet slipped on the dew-slick stone, but he didn't slow. Each print pulled him forward in a tightening spiral of fear, a path he had no choice but to walk. The trail carried him past the courtyard, through brittle grass, toward the rusted gate of the estate. Her blood marked the world in soft, uneven declarations.

He reached the gate, and stopped. Her footprints ended at the threshold. Cleanly. As though she had vanished into the air. Alaric stared at the empty road beyond, breath shuddering out of him. The morning hung around him like a veil, fog swallowing the treeline and the horizon alike. He clutched the iron bars, knuckles whitening.

"Eleanor!" He screamed, his voice carrying into nothing. Nothing answered.

Only then did he realize the sickening truth: she had not fled from the manor. The manor had let her flee. He shook the gate once, twice. It rattled but did not open. His panic sharpened into something jagged. He didn't care about the half-whispered guilt of the night before. He cared that she was gone. He cared that he had not been spared with her.

A sound rippled through the courtyard behind him. Alaric's head whipped around. A knock.

It wasn't loud nor frantic. But it was deliberate. One single, patient rap that carried through the quiet morning stillness straight into his bones. It came from inside the house. Deep within it.

The ballroom.

His breath caught. He took a step backward. Then another. The fog barely parted around him as he turned from the empty road and faced the manor once more. The manor stood in front of him the exact same as it always had, but he suddenly felt that he was gazing into the mouth of a beast. The air around it had thickened. The windows were too dark, every pane reflective, withholding. Another knock.

He didn't want to go back inside. Something else wanted

him to. Something that had waited for him to step outside and see what had been taken. Something that had allowed Eleanor's footprints to exist only long enough to torment him. His legs moved first in spite of him, thoughts following like a shadow.

He climbed the steps again, crossing the threshold with a trembling exhale. The door shut behind him with a faint sigh of wood. The hall welcomed him with an eerie, tender silence, like a throat clearing.

He followed the sound. Past the drawing room. Past the library. Past the side hall where he and Elias had once fought so viciously they'd broken a mirror. The shard still lay in the corner, its edge dulled with dust, though he did not remember leaving it there. It must have been years since he had. Another knock.

He swallowed hard, stopping in front of the ballroom. Yesterday those walls had seen their collapse into one another. The mirror still bore the ghost of Eleanor's breath, the smudging of her fingers. But the knock wasn't coming from those walls. It came from the walls beside the mirrors, the boarded-up section he'd discovered months and months ago. The section that had sickened Eleanor and barely impressed Elias.

A slow, intentional rhythm—One—two, pause, one. Alaric pressed a shaking palm to the newer, paler boards. The knock returned against his palm. He sucked in a breath. Though it was impossible, it was unmistakably familiar: the cadence of a childhood code he and Elias had used when communicating through the walls while living in separate wings of the manor during storms.

It was Elias' knock.

But that made no sense. Elias was worlds away. Elias didn't know about last night. Elias didn't know Eleanor had run. Elias couldn't be there—

"Alaric?"

The whispered plea curled into the air, a sweetness that invited and curdled. His throat tightened until it hurt. The knock sounded again, firmer this time, urging. The ballroom stretched before him in muted gray, the chandelier swaying though no breeze stirred the air. The mirror where he had pressed Eleanor the night before showed only his pale reflection now— distorted, stretched slightly, as if the glass had not yet forgiven what it had seen.

He should turn back. He should run into the forest as she had. He should call for Elias, for the groundskeeper, for God, for anyone. But the manor pulsed around him like a heartbeat he had once synchronized with as a child. It wanted him here.

Alaric's fingers pressed against the surface, tracing the faint outline of where the panel had once been pried open. He remembered the way Eleanor's eyes had widened in fear, how her palm had curled over her mouth. He remembered Elias walking in lazily, taking one deep look at the passage, then at him, then disappearing down the hall once more. He had told his men to seal it.

With a breath caught between defiance and fear, he crouched and pried at the edges of the boarded panels. The wood creaked in protest but yielded piece by piece under his grip, revealing the narrow opening behind—the throat of the manor's secret. Cold air seeped from it, carrying with it the faintest hint of something ancient and damp.

He grasped a candlestick from the floor beside him, lit it with a match from his pocket, and shone it into the darkness past one remaining board. The narrow passage sloped downward, the rough stone floor curling away into a blackness that seemed to swallow the feeble light. It was an impossible passage.

Then he heard it again. It was soft at first, almost like a whisper in the silence. It sounded like a dragging, slow and wet, like cloth being pulled across stone.

Alaric froze. The sound soaked into the marrow of his bones, stirring something primal. Beneath that dreadful scrape came a faint voice, barely more than a breath, trembling with urgency and desperation.

"Alaric…"

The name curled through the air, fragile as a spider's web, yet impossible to ignore. His heart thundered. Elias.

"Alaric, please—"

The voice cracked, weighted with a sorrow that tightened Alaric's throat. He swallowed hard, fingers trembling as they brushed the edge of the final remaining boarded panel. The pulse beneath his palm quickened, syncing with his own ragged heartbeat.

"I'm coming!" He replied, voice cracking with a mixture of fear and resolve. He set his candle carefully to the floor beside him, the flickering flame casting jittery shadows that danced along the walls like restless spirits.

His hands found purchase on the wood, gripping it with a fierce determination born of years of fear and regret. He pulled as hard as his body would allow, muscles straining against the stubborn resistance. The wood groaned in protest, splinters flying as the boards gave way inch by agonizing inch. Then, with a final wrench, the barrier snapped free. Alaric toppled backward, heart pounding, lungs heaving, mind spinning with the weight of what lay beyond.

Scrambling to his feet, he seized the candle once more and stepped into the dark passage beneath. The air was colder here, damp and heavy with the scent of earth and forgotten time. Each footfall echoed hollow and distant, swallowed by the endless black. The manor seemed to exhale behind him, a shudder passing through its walls, alive and ancient.

His thoughts twisted in a tempest: Elias's voice, the sorrow in it, the desperate plea that clawed at the edges of his sanity. Was this a warning? A call for rescue? Or something darker? Every instinct screamed at him to turn back, to flee into the cold night air, to run until the manor was no more than a fading nightmare. But something deeper, something tied to the very core of his being, urged him forward.

He couldn't leave Elias. Not like this.

The passage stretched ahead, narrowing and twisting beyond the candle's fragile glow. Shadows pressed close, whispering promises and threats alike, but Alaric's grip on the candlestick never wavered.

With one last, steadying breath, he stepped deeper into the abyss, chasing the fragile hope that somewhere, beneath the manor's crushing weight, Elias waited alive, calling for him.

12

September

Elias awoke from a night he never truly slept through, the kind that leaves the body aching and the mind skinned raw. He had crumpled into a particularly welcoming chair in the library. Though "welcoming" felt like mockery, the wall sconces burning out to nubs. His spine protested as he straightened, the upholstery imprinting its plush into his cheek.

The room was dim, holding the pale wash of early morning as though reluctant to commit to daylight. Books lay where he had abandoned them—volumes on local history, family records, half-read letters he'd convinced would keep him awake. His eyes drifted to the clock above the mantel; it was far too late for anyone to still be in bed and far too early for it to be this quiet.

The last tatters of a dream dissolved before he could name it. He rubbed his face with both hands, feeling the grit of exhaustion at the corners of his eyes. The manor felt wrong. It wasn't loud enough.

Usually, the mornings carried the soft bustle of life. Even in his solitude, he'd noticed it: the soft clang of pipes working through the house and waking, the creak of floorboards disturbed by someone's constant pacing, Eleanor's absent-minded humming of a tune as she wandered up and down the corridors, Alaric shouting at a stubborn window latch. But now… nothing. It was a silence so complete that it felt staged.

Elias pushed himself upright and waited for the draft to sting his skin, but the walls held the same stagnant air that he'd fallen asleep to. It was as though the walls did not want him to leave, did not want him to see what had changed. He stepped toward the door regardless, instinct tightening in his chest. Something was wrong, he just couldn't name what.

Even the floorboards felt muted as he stepped into the hall. It felt muffled, as if withholding some deeper sound. He could not place it, but he first felt pulled to Eleanor's quarters in the west wing, only doors from his tomb of the past few months. It struck him just how little space she'd left between them, how perhaps she'd waited for him to knock. Just knock. Now, her door was left ajar.

That alone was enough to stutter his breath. Eleanor never left it open; she guarded her privacy with a mild ferocity. He pushed it wider with two fingers.

Inside the room looked almost carefully undisturbed. The bed was neatly made, her pillows excessively fluffed and her comforter bearing a slight indent, as if someone had sat there only recently. A half-finished cup of tea sat on her bedside table, long since grown cold. Her suitcases were open, and her things were tossed out of it in a haphazard display. The brush on her vanity still held strands of her dark hair. Her perfume, jasmine and coal dust and something softer, was gone. Not faint, but *gone*, like the windows had been thrown open in the night and shut again before dawn, though they were latched now.

A twisting dread meddled with his stomach.

He crossed the hall, drenched in unease as he found Alaric's quarters. This door was in fact closed, but not fully, and there was no sound of stirring from within. It caught against the frame with a reluctant scrape. Elias pushed it open, nearly tiptoeing inside.

The sheets here were twisted, dragged towards the edge of the bed as if he'd launched out of bed in a start. No shoes. No coat. The wardrobe hung open like a jaw. Alaric's gloves lay on the floor, one finger bent inward as if stepped on recently. Elias' gaze drifted lower, then caught. A coldness climbed the back of his throat.

A pile of fabric sat unceremoniously on the floor. He knelt, examining the heap. Folded nowhere, hung nowhere…simply left here. Eleanor's blouse was strewn on the floor, stripped as if done in a hurry. Her stockings lay beside it, one balled and one stretched. Her skirts piled in a careless husk on the floor, and her corset was caught on the bedpost. Everything except her undergarments lay about, everything she may have worn if she planned to leave. Elias stood, placing a hand on the bedpost to steady the world more than himself. His knees felt unreliable, and the room seemed to tilt around him, rearranging its shadows, waiting for his understanding to catch up.

Eleanor had undressed here, that he could be sure of. Alaric had dressed only enough to leave the room. Eleanor had dressed only enough to return to her room. And both of them were missing.

He left the room before the walls could suffocate him.

At first, he moved with purpose, the kind born of denial rather than confidence. He checked the guest rooms, the music rooms, the parlors, the study. He called their names steady, repeatedly, and clinical. Only his own voice answered, swallowed too quickly by the halls.

He pushed deeper into the manor. The east rooms. The various parlors. The corridors lined with portraits of Greystones who had mastered the art of looking disappointed long after death. He called again, louder this time, dread scratching the edges of his composure.

"Eleanor! Alaric—ENOUGH OF THIS!"

No footsteps, no rustle of skirts, no flippant scoff, simply nothing. Just silence. Dense, obedient, rehearsed silence.

He descended the back staircase and crossed through the servants' hall, then doubled back through the gallery, the dining room, the smoking lounge. It should have taken him half the house to get there, but somehow every path led him back in front of the ballroom. He would turn a corner, expecting a linen cupboard or the west stair, and instead see those massive double doors yawning open, inviting him into its throat. He retraced his steps, certain he'd miscounted, though he was surely familiar enough with the layout by now. Took another route. Chose different hallways. Walked quickly, then tried again slowly with deliberate precision.

Every path circled. Every path betrayed him. Finally, he gave up, and he stepped inside.

He drifted to the center of the ballroom, his breath shallow and his hands trembling despite himself. The air felt weighted, as though the manor was pregnant with its usual rot. He took one step towards the far end of the hall.

The ballroom doors slammed behind him. The force of it

echoed off the marble, a violent crack that ricocheted through his ribs. He spun, heart lodging high in his throat. Wind surged through the room, though no windows were open and there was certainly no draft. The chandeliers shuddered, the crystal ringing like bones against itself.

Then— music.

It started thin and warped, like a gramophone needle scraping metal. A melody that might once have been cheerful, now dragged through something rotten and unkind. It seeped from the corners of the room, from the floorboards, breathing through the house. A waltz fractured beyond comprehension, limping, lurching and refusing to die. Elias spun wildly as he tried to find the source, his eyes instead laying on a figure across the room.

It was nearly human in outline and horribly familiar. But then, it was… wrong. It pulled too tall in the wrong places. Its proportions stretched just enough that the eye could not keep balance. Its stance was mimicry; the angle of the shoulders, the tilt of its head. It was the impression of recognition. The silhouette stood perfectly still, except for the slightest, shivering tremor. It was as though it were practicing the act of existing and hadn't quite mastered it.

"Alaric…?" Elias tried, though he knew better.

The figure cocked its head in a way that suggested memory rather than intention, a puppet gesture borrowed from a life it had never lived. It wasn't Alaric's lazy mocking angle, but slow like an animal testing the limits of a body it didn't belong in. The music jutted, skipping a beat. The figure took a single step toward him.

Elias' stomach turned.

It began to fold. Crushed inward, collapsing like a puppet

whose strings had been severed all at once. Limbs buckled at impossible angles, shoulders caving, the suggestion of a spine snapping into itself. It didn't fall so much as implode, drawn back into the floor by something unseen, something hungry. Elias couldn't move. He couldn't breathe. He sunk to the floor with it, a hand over his mouth to desperately keep his breath from touching the room.

It felt like a demonstration, a warning, and a confession all at once. The silence that followed was absolute, as if the manor were waiting to see whether he understood. Slowly, as if debating if they should, the doors to the ballroom creaked open.

***

Elias fled the ballroom without meaning to, his body pushing him through the halls of the east wing and up the stairs, apparently allowing him now to leave after its bragging. He threw himself inside the library once more, slamming the doors behind him with so much force that they rattled a couple books off shelves nearby. Dust motes trembled in the morning light as he lay against them, a compulsion and a premonition hitting him as he entered. The ledgers. Check the ledgers.

He crossed to the desk immediately, fingers fumbling with the ledgers he kept too meticulously. Dates, receipts, staff rotations, supply orders, household schedules— just numbers, all of them. They had shifted several times before this year, and he needed them to explain now what exactly he had just experienced. He dragged one towards him and flipped it open.

Ink. Papers. Columns. Totals.

"Seventeen pounds for coal… five for lamp oil… the roof estimate…"

He clung to them with both hands, his palms shaking unforgivably. If he let his mind drift back to the ballroom, he would have to admit it — the house wasn't haunted or cursed. It was communicating. And worse: it had wanted him to know what exactly it took.

Then, it showed itself. There, in handwriting close to his own but wrong in ways he failed to articulate:

The bastard heir must remain.

The cycle is fed.

The debt adjusts.

Something inside Elias snapped. It was not with the violent clatter he might have expected, but slowly, almost imperceptibly, like the delicate spine of an old book finally giving way after years of strain. A subtle fracture that spread through him, a quiet undoing. He closed the ledger carefully, as though the fresh ink might still bleed from the page, the weight of those words pressing down like cold stone beneath his fingertips. The soft thud of the cover felt deafening in the heavy silence that followed.

His lungs clenched, tightening as if the air itself had thickened, refusing to fill the space between breaths. The room, once a refuge of order and certainty, seemed to contract, the shadows crawling in from the corners, lengthening and deepening like dark ink pooling on paper. He pressed a trembling hand to the edge of the desk, grounding himself against the swell of dread rising like a tide in his chest. The scent of aged paper mingled with something colder, darker, like the faint trace of smoke or dust disturbed after centuries of silence.

Outside the study, the manor breathed in its slow, steady rhythm. But within these walls, the words grew sharper, closer, threading through the air like invisible ink revealing a message only he could read. Alaric was not simply missing. He was an unholy tithe.

Blood for blood.

* * *

The day stretched slow and heavy, folding itself around Elias like a shroud. He stayed in the library, the one room that felt least changed, least given over to absence. Outside, the sky pressed gray and low, its light muted and diffused as if the sun itself were reluctant to intrude on Greystone Manor's sorrow. He sat on the floor with his back pressed to the desk. The ledger was still curled between his fingers as the sun repositioned, and his heart fractured into loose shards.

His shoulders sagged, chest tightening with the slow, suffocating weight of grief. Outside, the wind whispered through the branches of ancient trees, their skeletal limbs scratching at the stone walls like restless fingers. The house itself seemed to exhale a long, shuddering breath that rattled the glass and stirred the shadows. Elias's heart fractured into loose shards, each sharp, scattered fragment of sorrow and fear cutting deeper than the last. He did not move. He did not speak. He simply sat, letting the silence wrap tighter around him, a quiet companion to the echo of loss that lingered in every corner of the room.

A faint humming drifted through the corridors then. It was soft, fragile, and impossibly familiar. Elias caught the melody before he could fully place it: the same tune Eleanor had hummed while brushing her hair, a delicate thread of sound woven with quiet hope and careful habit. For a moment, he truly hoped that she would be on the other end of that door. For a long moment, he simply listened, letting the fragile notes settle around him like dust motes in a slant of pale light. Then, with slow, cautious steps, he moved toward the source, each footfall muffled against the worn floorboards as if the house itself were holding its breath.

He drew to it, like a moth to fading light, stepping softly towards the door and cracking it open only a sliver. The air outside felt thick with something unseen, Eleanor's perfume mingling with it again like a cruel promise. The weight of it pressed down, a chill creeping beneath his skin. No figure met him this time, uncanny or otherwise.

Instead, the sound folded in on itself like smoke caught in a draft. The melody unraveled, dissolving into silence so complete it felt like the very air had been swallowed whole. The quiet that followed was heavier than any sound — thick and pressing with the ache of something lost and unwilling to return. Elias stood frozen, the thin crack of the door framing an emptiness that stretched farther than his eyes could see. From somewhere deeper in the house, a door creaked open: slow and deliberate. The sound matched her exactly. It was almost certainly the gentle, measured rhythm of Eleanor's hand pushing against cold wood, steady and certain, as if she were crossing thresholds on her own terms. Elias's breath caught. He froze, every nerve taut. He turned toward the sound, eyes searching the empty hallway.

Carefully, with precision, the house seemed to rehearse her presence. It shifted around the emptiness of her presence with every creak, every sigh, every whispered breath of memory left in her wake. Elias moved slowly down the dim corridor, the worn floorboards creaking faintly beneath his careful steps. The heavy silence wrapped around him, thick and expectant, as if the house itself were watching, waiting.

Then, a new terror — a soft, deliberate tapping coming from inside the walls. He froze, hands still tracing the wallpaper to steady himself. He pressed his ear against the cold plaster, listening.

One—two, pause, one. A perversion of a childhood pact, made by boys who still believed the world would spare them. The comfort of many a thunderous night. A promise made into rhythm. Alaric.

He pulled back slowly, fingers grazing the wall, and the corridor seemed to grow darker. The house had spoken and now felt as though it were holding its breath, waiting for his answer. The taps echoed in his mind long after the sound faded. Elias pressed his hand against the cold wall, feeling the weight of the manor's whispers pressing in from every corner.

But beneath the ache, beneath the pull of those haunting echoes, a fragile thread of clarity began to form. He would not allow himself to be consumed — not here, not now. Elias resolved to leave. To step beyond the manor's grasp before the sorrow could drown him completely.

Not because he wanted to forget, nor did he want to forfeit, but to survive the mourning of losing all three in one fell swoop. He would carry his grief quietly, like a wound wrapped tight beneath his skin, tending it in his own time, in his own way. For now, the house could keep its echoes. He would walk away. And maybe, just maybe, find a place where the silence was not a presence, but a mercy.

Elias retreated to his quarters, each step heavy, the weight of resolve pressing down like stones in his chest. The door closed behind him with a soft, final thud, sealing him in a small world that suddenly felt too large and too empty all at once. His hands shook as he moved to the wardrobe, fingers fumbling over the worn fabric of his coat, the straps of his bag. The simple act of packing, once so mundane, now felt like an impossible reckoning.

Not because he wished to forget. Nor because he wished to forfeit the memories here. The bond, the loss, all was tangled into every corner of the manor. But to survive, truly survive, he would tend to it in his own way, in his own time. Elias gathered his bags, pulling them through the halls, past the rooms they'd sanctified, past the echoes of their memories, and down the stairs himself. His hand reached out, fingers brushing the ornate brass handle, expecting the familiar resistance of aged iron and worn wood.

The doors did not budge.

He pressed harder, heart pounding in sudden panic. The lock held fast, unyielding. There was no creak, no groan, no sign of surrender. He dropped his bags to the floor, pulling at it wildly, a scream rippling out of him like some tormented beast. Finally, he managed to force them open, the shudder of the sunlight collapsing into an overcast sky. What lay before him, though, was not a world he recognized.

Instead of the sprawling grounds, the towering trees, the familiar sky, there was only a flat gray expanse stretching endlessly in every direction— a fog without depth or shape, a void that swallowed all sense of distance or dimension. It stretched away from him in every direction, an endless sea of mist so thick and uniform it felt less like fog and more like an absence. The void swallowed all distance and dimension as though consumed.

There were no shadows, no shapes, no hint of earth or sky. There was no horizon to rest his eyes on. As far as he could see, there was a muted, featureless, faded gray that pressed in upon his senses. It was heavy and suffocating, stealing air from his lungs as it undulated and danced on the stairs. Elias' breath caught; this was no natural fog. It was silence made visible.

The gray fog before him shifted as he pressed one foot onto the steps. It did not disperse as fog naturally might, but receded in a deliberate, measured motion. It stepped back. It matched him, mirrored him. Each step he took, the void responded in the same way, pulling away in perfect rhythm. The emptiness was alive, an uncanny presence folding around him. It was neither friend nor foe, but something else entirely, something hellish and vile. With every mirrored step, the distance between him and the impossible horizon remained the same. He turned back, measuring his distance from the manor, finding that while he had made it down the stairs, he had not been moving away from them at all.

Panic blossomed in his chest. He broke into a run, feet pounding the featureless ground, breath ragged against the suffocating gray. The fog did not chase. It mirrored, it matched; never chasing, never yielding.

Elias burst through the open doors, stumbling across the threshold as if crossing between worlds. His hands slammed hard against the heavy oak, the sound ringing sharp and final in the stillness. The door crashed shut with a weight that echoed through the manor's bones. He pressed his forehead against the cool wood, heart hammering with bitter defeat.

A crushing realization consumed him, starting on his feet and crawling up his body in a chill. The manor had decided. It would take all three of them, relentless and ravenous with hunger. It would repay its debts with their blood. It would not stop until satisfied, and then it would spread, luring another of their kin into its depths once their skeletons were found coated in dust and left in the corners.

He would die here. They would all die here. Elias looked up, breath still ragged, eyes searching the room beyond the heavy door. But the world he expected — the stairs, the corridor, the heavy doors to the dining room— had vanished.

Instead, in haunting finality, he stood once more in the vast ballroom, impossibly returned. The high, arched ceiling stretched overhead, draped in shadows and pale daylight filtering through stained glass. The polished floor gleamed beneath his feet, cold and unyielding, the echoes of distant footsteps lingering like ghosts.The chandeliers hung silent, their crystals catching what little light remained, scattering fractured rainbows across the walls.

His heart twisted with disbelief and dread.

* * *

The air hung thick with dust, motes swirling in the muted light like restless spirits. The ballroom he was in now felt real, touched. The floor was coated in dust, and the mirrors were smudged. It felt as if he were no longer in some cruel nightmare, but instead a reality far worse. It seemed no soul had been in the room in at least a few days.

But the floor told a different story. The dust was disturbed., broken and scattered beneath his gaze. His eyes lifted to the mirrors, where a faint but unmistakable hand print still smeared along the glass. The print was blurred at the edges, as if someone had pressed their palm hard against the surface, either to steady themselves or to hold back something unseen. It lingered there like a silent plea or a frozen moment, catching the dim light and casting a faint, haunting shadow. Elias swallowed, his eyes tracing the walls and stalling.

The damage was ungodly. Several wooden panels had been torn free, hanging askew or lying broken in jagged heaps along the baseboards. The sawdust scattered the floors, footprints punctuating it as if marking their humanity. Then, they descended a narrow staircase — one half remembered and unacknowledged mere months ago. There, they vanished.

Elias stepped forward slowly, drawn irresistibly toward the heavy oak door. The air around it seemed to thicken, charged with a silent urgency that made his skin prickle. He lifted his hand, fingertips trembling as they brushed against it. It was warm and alive with a subtle heat that pulsed beneath his touch, unlike the cold, unyielding surface he had expected. A shiver ran through him.

A cold draft leaked through the narrow gap between the door and its frame, slipping inside like a living thing.

The air around Elias pulsed faintly, a slow, monstrous heartbeat vibrating through the walls and floor beneath his feet. An oppressive weight settled over him, cold and relentless. Sick to his core, Elias staggered slightly, the room tilting. His body froze, muscles taut and trembling. Palms slick with sweat, throat tightening until each breath felt like glass scraping past. The silence around him stretched thin, broken only by the rhythmic thudding echoing deep within the manor's bones: an invitation.

For a long moment, he stood motionless, caught between the unbearable pull of the house and the instinct to flee.

Then, from the other side of the door, he heard a familiar and gut wrenching sound. It was a voice. Choked, as if caught in a throat too tight to form words properly, ragged with the weight of something unbearable. Broken, fracturing like cracked glass, splintering into desperate fragments that barely held together. Fragile and raw, trembling with the thin, tremulous pulse of pain and fear, like a candle's flame flickering against a gathering storm. His throat grew tight. It was a voice he knew in his bones, one he heard in the most horrifying and soothing of dreams.

It sounded like Alaric.

Despite the terror clutching his heart, Elias inched closer once more. His breath hitched in his throat, hands shaking as he reached for the door once more. With a slow, trembling push, he opened it.

A rush of cold air spilled out, sharp and biting, flooding the corridor beyond like a sudden winter storm breaking through a shuttered window. The chill wrapped around him as he pressed inward, one uncertain footfall after another. For a moment, the world seemed to hold its breath, caught between the warmth he had just left and the endless shadow waiting beyond the threshold.

The walls were rough-sewn stone, slick with creeping moss and patches of stubborn mold, blotching the surface like bruises against the cold gray rock. Faint, flickering light from a single sputtering lantern revealed heaps of forgotten crates and rusted tools, the scattered remnants of years locked away from the world above. The floor beneath him was patchy and cracked, the earth breaking through the stones there. A faint drip echoed somewhere in the shadows, steady and relentless, like a metronome counting out the promise of time passing. The chill seeped into Elias's bones, an oppressive, suffocating cold that spoke of silence and secrets buried deep beneath the manor's grand facade. Here, he felt the manor beginning to close its jaws.

Hopelessness began to grip him, sure he'd been lured into the manor's most effective trap of the evening, when he heard another choking cough from deep in the bellows. As quickly as he could, he tore down the winding passages, pausing only to hear another cough echo and tracing its direction.

Elias's footsteps slowed as he entered a wider subterranean chamber, the narrow cellar corridor giving way to an uncanny stillness. A faint, phosphorescent sheen hung in the air, casting an otherworldly glow that shimmered pale blue and sickly green against the damp stone walls. The light seemed to pulse softly, as if breathing with the chamber itself. The air was cooler here, heavy with a scent both earthy and faintly metallic, like iron and wet stone mingling in silence. His eyes adjusted to the dim light, and when they did, Elias saw him.

Alaric was slumped against the cold wall, body curled in on itself as if trying to fold away from the world. His breathing was shallow, ragged, and barely more than a whisper of life. His skin, where the glow illuminated it, looked pale and translucent, his veins like fragile threads beneath its surface. His clothing clung to him, drenched and heavy with water and the shocking red of blood. Shivers wracked his body, small, involuntary tremors that spoke of shock and exhaustion. Elias stepped forward, dropping to his knees beside Alaric, voice trembling as he called his name.

"Alaric."

The faintest flutter of recognition passed across those pale features, a flicker of warmth in the cold shadows. The air hung thick and silent around them, broken only by the soft, desperate rasp of Alaric's breathing, a fragile tether between life and something darker lurking just beneath the surface.

His face was pale, etched with shadows deeper than the dim light could reach, every breath trembling with silent dread. Slowly, his trembling hand reached out, fingers curling weakly around Elias's wrist, seeking something solid, something real. He clung to him, fragile and desperate, and Elias' other hand found the line of his jaw and cupped it as gently as he could manage.

For a moment that felt too final, neither spoke, heavy with the weight of a near goodbye neither could say aloud. The shaking that wracked his body softened slightly, a fragile thread of calm threading through the storm within.

Then, softly, "Guess it isn't finished with us." He offered a dry laugh, which rolled into wet choking. Elias pulled him to his own chest, holding Alaric in the darkness as if he'd evaporate before him if he didn't keep him in his grasp. Alaric's breath steadied, and his heartbeat followed suit, proving his life. His pulse, however, echoed in the walls around them, an uncanny reminder. Elias gripped his arm tightly, hauling him upright with a firm urgency and a newfound determination.

"Alaric, don't look back," he ordered, voice low but unwavering.

Alaric's knees buckled, but Elias caught him before he could fall, steadying him against the cold stone wall. Together, they stumbled toward the narrow staircase leading back up, each step heavier than the last.

Beneath their feet, the pulse deepened, swelling into a slow, relentless drumbeat that echoed through the walls and climbed behind them like a rising tide. It grew louder, closer, filling the air with a dark, living rhythm that seemed to reach for them with every breath. Elias forced them forward, dragging Alaric beside him, desperate to outrun the house's hunger before it closed its jaws for good.

They burst out of the chamber and into the narrow corridor, stumbling forward as the cold air bit at their skin. Before they could catch their breath, the door slammed shut with finality, sealing itself tight. The pulse that had chased them stilled abruptly, sucked away into an oppressive silence that settled like dust in the air. Only their ragged breathing disturbed the stillness, harsh and uneven as it was. Elias sprawled out on the cruel parquet, his hand clutching to Alaric's like a lifeline. Both men lay there for a long while, their bodies bowed beneath the weight of a moment that lingered like a whispered psalm.

13

The Final Benediction

Elias coaxed him upright by degrees, one arm braced around Alaric's back, the other steadying his trembling hands. Alaric's breath hitched as the world reeled, but he didn't pull away; he leaned into Elias as though that small point of contact was the only thing tethering him here.

"Easy," Elias murmured, lowering him against the wall. "Just stay with me."

Alaric was pressed with his back to the mirror, still breathless but alive. His skin was drained of vitality and his muscles appeared to be weak. From his scalp and through the roots of his golden hair dripped a distinct crimson, something he didn't acknowledge but Elias fixated on as he took in his form. His hair itself was pushing every direction, messy and unkempt, clotted with dried blood where it wasn't knotted in itself. He shuddered lightly.

Elias crossed the room for a basin of rainwater that had collected in a small ceramic bowl. He ripped a piece of cloth from his shirt, sacrificing it as he dipped it in. When he returned, Alaric's eyes finally fluttered open at the sound of his footsteps, unfocused but searching. Elias knelt, pressing the cool cloth to his forehead. Alaric exhaled in another shiver, something like relief relaxing the edge of his jaw.

"Didn't think I'd see you playing housewife today," he muttered weakly, trying for a smirk that never quite formed. Elias' jaw tightened with restraint. He wasn't expecting Alaric to thank him, but the least he could do is pause his teasing for an hour or two. Elias ignored the bravado and worked patiently, wiping the dirt and cold—sweat from his temples, his cheekbones, the hollow beneath his throat. Alaric didn't speak again; he only watched him with a dazed, wounded sort of trust.

When he deemed him steady enough, Elias left the room to locate some food from the kitchen below. The halls were steady and consistent now, even as he looked around corners, half—expecting to find something inhuman around them. The manor seemed to breathe a sign of relief, or rest in the calm before the storm. He couldn't be sure which.

He found some herbed bread and filled a glass with water from the pump at the sink, the first draw tinged with the mineral smell of the pipes that accumulated in the night. He found some stale broth covered with a cloth on the stove, hoping desperately that it wasn't terribly old, and some preserved berries in a jar in the cupboard. It wasn't quite a meal, but with the absence of any staff that he could see, it had to make do. The silence was accusatory; their absence emphasized every step he took and the rattle of dishes, as though it ate directly through him.

They ate side—by—side on the ballroom floor, their knees nearly touching. The food tasted flat, metallic, and almost unreal after everything they'd survived. But the act itself felt anchoring, an undeniable return to the living world. Alaric's hands shook as he lifted the bread; Elias pretended not to see and quietly slid the plate closer. For the first time in days, or maybe even months, it just felt like a room.

Alaric let out a faint breath. "If I live through this, remind me to demand a better dinner." His face was sunken, resigned, but still peaceful.

"You were always impossible to feed," Elias said, and his voice was softer than he meant it to be. A ghost of a smile twitched at Alaric's lips. The laugh that followed was barely more than a rasp of breath, but Elias felt himself being welcomed in. Wordlessly, placing his bread back down briefly, Elias dipped the cloth once more into the bowl between them, wrung it out, and pressed it gently to Alaric's forehead. His movements slowed without meaning to, something instinctual and familiar. Alaric blinked mid—chew, watching him with that half—conscious, hazy focus.

"You're doing it again," he murmured. Elias slowed, his eyes focusing on the man instead of his edges.

"What thing?"

"That… fussy hovering you used to do. When we were boys." His eyelids drooped as if the memory itself tired him, but his voice held a faint warmth. "Whenever I got scraped up or fell from the terrace wall, you'd reach for water and a cloth before I even stopped bleeding."

Elias felt the breath leave him, his heart hammering in his chest: this time, the excitement of being seen. The memory rose, quick and immediate: Alaric, twelve, wild and grinning as he dangled from a too—high ledge. Elias, terrified, angry and already reaching to steady him the second his footing faltered.

"You were reckless," he managed.

"And you were always there to…un—reckless me." Alaric gave a weak shrug. "Some things don't change, I suppose."

Elias looked down, his hand hovering above Alaric's temple. The man had betrayed him, hurt him, haunted years of his life, and yet here he was. He leaned into his palm without thinking, trusting Elias even in a place that had only hours ago tried to kill him. Alaric's expression eased; not much, but… enough. Enough for the knot between them to loosen only slightly, a mistake and a balm.

Alaric shifted slightly, wincing. Elias continued to tidy his companion with equal hesitancy and reverence. A silence stretched thin between them, as if it were testing their strength. Beats passed — quiet, heavy, and warm at the edges.

"Do you remember the time the kitchen door jammed and we had to climb through the pantry window? I tore my coat, and you swore me to secrecy." Alaric offered suddenly. The memory was so jarring and vivid that Elias stalled, cloth in hand.

"You threatened to tell the whole staff unless I gave you my half of the tarts." Elias teased, smirk tugging at the corner of his mouth. It felt foreign, but so, so welcome.

"I stand by that negotiation."

Elias exhaled through his nose, almost a laugh. "You were insufferable."

"And yet," Alaric rasped, "You climbed through first." Elias paused, realizing that he had — without hesitation, without thought, just to make it easier for Alaric to follow. He often did things just to make it easier for the other. He still did, without realizing, as though Alaric was not independent but instead a part of him. He did so even now, as he let his bread go stale just to keep Alaric from bleeding out inside their sanctuary.

"I suppose I did, didn't I?" He admitted quietly.

A small, startled sound escaped Alaric. It sounded so weak it resembled a sigh, but it was unmistakably a laugh. It surprised them both, and both of them fell into laughter together, despite there being really no joke particularly apparent. For a moment, grief loosened its grip. For a moment, they remembered how to be them: Not Thorne and Greystone, but them.

Elias sat back on his heels, staring down at him, and the house felt strangely distant. A soft, shared warmth rose in the silence. Not quite a truce, but something older and still alive. Elias didn't name it, nor did either of them dare to.

But the laughter filled the ballroom.

* * *

Minutes stretched into hours as they sat together on the floor. Alaric never described what had rendered him in his current state, but he described as much as his mind would let him conceptualize. The underground had been loud, incessant, and violent in nature. It would lead him one way only to injure him and turn him another; eventually, he had given up and slumped against the wall, hoping for death to find him there. As the time plunked achingly, Alaric's pauses grew longer, his movements grew slower, and he slumped down onto Elias, falling asleep.

Elias rose slowly, careful not to disturb Alaric's fragile rest. Cradling him gently, he lifted Alaric's weight and began the slow, unsteady walk back through the manor's twisting halls.

Each step echoed hollowly in the oppressive silence, Alaric's head lolling against Elias' chest. His breath was uneven but constant, his eyes fluttering open only long enough to keep time for his steps as exhaustion claimed him. Elias' arm tightened around him unconsciously, a silent promise.

When they reached Alaric's quarters, Elias eased him down onto the bed, pulling blankets gently over him. The familiar room felt foreign and cold, shadows stretching long across the walls. Elias lingered, brushing damp hair back from Alaric's forehead, making sure he fell asleep completely. Alaric's breath softened, slipping into deeper rest, but the lines of tension in his face never fully eased. Elias sat on the edge, fingers tracing idle patterns on the blanket, heart heavy. It had cracked him open in a way he hadn't expected.

Eleanor. God, if he were a better man, he'd be frantic. But worry wasn't quite the shape of what he felt for her. He'd seen the signs for months; the slow, polite distances, the way she'd already seemed half—gone even as she stood in front of him. Her absence now felt like the completion of a process already in motion since the first day they crossed that threshold. She hadn't been taken from him; she'd been drifting away anyways, piece by piece. He had been bracing for it for longer than he thought.

But Alaric vanishing from his world wasn't something he'd ever expected. The shock of nearly losing him struck him deeper, under the marrow and the sinews. Alaric was his last tie to a version of life that made sense, the last person who knew what he'd been before Greystone twisted them both into its strange orbit. Someone who, despite everything — despite the lies, the rivalry, the unsaid things— still felt like the one person who saw him. Someone who loved him, perhaps, even in his tangled sort of way. Elias bowed his head, his hand placed gingerly on top of Alaric's. Eleanor had left. Alaric had been stolen.

Elias stayed beside him for a long time. Long enough for the dust to settle and for the adrenaline to reassemble into something soft and trembling. When he finally stood, it wasn't to leave, but just to move. He began tidying in small, compulsive gestures; he folded and refolded a blanket by the edge of the bed, straightened books on the bedside table, pulled the curtains open before deciding the light was wrong and closed them again. He kept tidying, even when there was nothing left to fix. Elias smoothed the last fold of the blankets, still feeling the weight of the man's head on his shoulder from hours earlier. He tugged the curtains open again, restless.

The light didn't change. He tugged them closed again. The light still refused to waver. Beneath him, the floorboards underneath him gave a subtle knock.

Elias's body moved faster than his mind. In a second, he was beside the bed again, shaking Alaric awake. He stirred, rising groggily, rubbing sleep from his eyes. His breath hitched, his fingers curling weakly in the sheet, wincing as if remembering pain. Before he could explain, the knock sounded again — slower, heavier, intentional. He turned to the weaker man, whose eyes were wide, catching something familiar in it. His voice was papery and raw when he spoke.

"It followed us up," he whispered with a finality. Elias swallowed, feeling faint as his heartbeat throbbed in his head.

"Alaric... what followed you?" Alaric didn't answer at first. His throat worked as though swallowing back a scream. Another sound rose — a dragging scrape, deep in the walls, something shifting its weight. His eyes were lucid in a way

Elias hadn't seen in months.

"I saw them," he whispered. "Under the floors. Under the earth. I saw the names. Stacked and marked. All the heirs. All the sacrifices. What my father owed. What yours owed. What Edwin tried to stop."

Elias' pulsed hammered. "And what did he try to stop?"

Alaric's breath caught — too sharp, too fast. He tried to turn away, but the movement cost him; he sank back against the pillows, expression twisted as if he were remembering something that still had its hands on him.

"He tried to stop the count," Alaric murmured. "He tried to stop the house from choosing." His eyes were half—lidded, unfocused, but the dread behind them was horribly clear. "He knew one of us would inherit. He knew one of us would…feed it."

A chill tightened around Elias' ribs. His blood ran cold as he grappled with this new understanding; the house was no longer passive, it was a predator, and it was starving.

"It's choosing… between us?"

Alaric shook his head weakly, a small defeated movement. Elias felt something inside of him shift into an indistinguishable horror he had no name for. "What do you mean…?"

"When I was under the floor," he whispered, "I saw a new column in our records. New spaces were appearing. Blank names…but waiting. The house isn't only feeding on heirs born into the line. It's widening the family. Claiming anyone tied to Greystone by blood or bond or burden." His breath hitched. "It's growing hungry, Elias. And when a line doesn't produce children, it takes whatever else it can."

Elias felt the room tilt. He leaned on the bedpost to stabilize himself. "We don't have children," he said, barely forming the words. "Neither of us—...there's no heir."

"That's the point," Alaric breathed. "It won't let the line die. If the family won't continue, it will create one. It will pull in anyone connected to us. Eleanor. Servants. Anyone who stayed long enough. Anyone it can brand as part of Greystone's debt."

A cold, insidious sickness crawled his body, right underneath his skin. Alaric shifted, his hand finding the others', a gesture of grounding more than care. "Oh, god— Eleanor, I—"

"Not just her," Alaric rasped, gripping Elias's wrist with a sudden, surprising strength. "You don't understand. It doesn't need her to be here to be taken. It only needs her to be yours. And if it can't reach her, if it can't have her, it will come harder for us." He paused, watching Elias' face carefully. Elias stared, stunned. This wasn't inheritance. This was consumption.

"Elias... what do you remember that you know is truly yours?"

The question hit him like the closing of a hand around his throat and equally violently. For a moment, he could only breathe in shallow gasps, as if the room had thickened into something heavy and wet. Alaric's fingers were still hooked around his wrist, a grounding promise while his mind drifted far away and they both trembled.

"What kind of question is that?" He breathed, sounding wholly unconvincing that he didn't have a clue. Alaric swallowed, his eyes flickering with something resembling grief and fear together.

"Down there, I saw things no one should see..." He began, his voice wavering with memory. "Pieces. Moments I knew weren't mine. Whispers that weren't voices. It shows you what it feeds on. What it plans to feed on next."

Elias' eyes began to well with tears, bred of anxiety.

Alaric continued, voice raw: "It showed me your name. Over and over. Not the man you are, just the heir. Just the offering. And the house… it's been rearranging you, Elias." He shook his head, breath catching. "Not fully. Not yet. But enough for it to try to write memories over yours."

A cold pressure rose in Elias' throat. He stood abruptly. The room swayed around him, but he pushed through it, pacing once, twice, before stopping beside the door.

"Elias?"

"There's something I need to show you." He expected Alaric to protest; he barely had the strength to sit upright. Instead, his gaze flickered towards the corner of the room, where the shadows had begun to pool once more.

"Then we shouldn't stay here. I'm coming." He said with a tone of certainty that transcended his fear. Elias swallowed and opened the door. Alaric rose with difficulty, but followed towards him, met by Elias' arm holding him upright. A faint draft pushed past them, as though something had been waiting on the other side.

"If it's been rewriting my memory, it'll be rewriting the records too."

They walked slowly down the hall, Elias keeping one steadying hand at Alaric's back. The corridor felt unusually long, the air thick and unmoving, as though the manor were holding its breath. Each step stirred a faint echo, one that didn't quite match the rhythm of their footsteps. Alaric stumbled every few steps, catching himself on the wall, and Elias walked carefully to steady him.

Noon had begun to close in on the manor, but neither could

be sure anymore if that was accurate or a trick of the beast once again. The haze of fog through the windows appeared sentient, its ebb and flow at the horizon a warning and a reminder. Alaric's breathing rasped softly beside him. He was awake, barely, but the weight of exhaustion hung to him like a wet cloak.

After a long stretch of silence, his voice came in a near—whisper, as if traveling a great distance to reach him.

"Do you remember," he murmured, "the night we snuck out of the west wing to watch the meteor shower from the east balcony?"

Elias let out a soft, surprised exhale. The answer was that there wasn't a way he could possibly forget it. A fondness warmed his voice.

"You dragged me out," he said, smiling slightly but still more than he had in a long time. "Told me the sky would fall if we slept through it."

Alaric gave the smallest hint of a smile. But then, mid—step, he slowed. Stopped. His brows pulled together, confusion tightening the fragile lines of his face. "Elias, that's... that's not right."

Elias frowned gently, feeling caught in a lie he had not told. "What isn't?"

Alaric's gaze wandered unfocused across the shadowed hall before settling on him again. "You were the one who woke me. I remember you shaking me, telling me you'd seen a streak of light already."

"No," Elias said, soft but certain. "You were the bold one. You dragged me." Alaric's expression darkened — not in anger, but in hollow fear.

"Elias," he said again, slower this time, as if testing the shape of the truth. "I was terrified of being caught. I never would have dragged you anywhere at that hour."

Elias opened his mouth, then closed it again. The memory rose behind his eyes, clear as polished glass: two boys snuck from their beds, the hush of night around them, the chill of the balcony, the sky scattered with fire. But the scene trembled like something seen through heat. One details wavered, then another, then—

Who stepped out first? Which of them had whispered he dare? Which had pulled whose hand? The questions pressed into him like a cold hand against his throat. Behind them, the row of candle sconces flickered in perfect unison, flames bowing left, then right, as though stirred by a breath they did not feel. Elias swallowed hard and tightened his grip on Alaric's arm, steadying him, and himself. The memory still shimmered faintly in his mind, resisting clarity, a beautiful thing being quietly rethreaded.

"Come on," Elias urged, guiding him onward. They moved forward again, slower now, the hallway stretching ahead like a vein narrowing around them. The manor seemed to lean closer with each step, listening, adjusting, readying. Elias could feel it as their past was rewritten as sand in an hourglass turned by somebody else's hand.

✳ ✳ ✳

The library greeted them with a hush that felt deliberate. Elias pushed the heavy door open with his shoulder, guiding Alaric inside. The smell hit them first — old paper, burnt cotton of melted candles, dust, and the faint underlying traces of mold.

The books were just as scattered as he'd left them, and the work now suddenly seemed to futile in retrospect as Elias' eyes scanned over it. He sighed, almost in apology. Alaric sagged against the nearest table, breath trembling. He was awake, but only in the loosest sense, held together more by will than strength.

Elias moved quickly, gliding to the desk on the far end. Everything there remained how he had left it, but faintly wrong. The spines, once cracked and brittle, now seemed a shade darker. The pages, though he'd left them open, now rested closed, as if the house had tidied itself up behind his back. He could feel warmth from the nearest one and he recoiled.

Alaric watched silently, his eyes hollow but alert. "Show me," he coaxed. Elias hesitated, but pulled the nearest one closer and opened it. The pages sighed before him. There it was — rows of names, marriages, heirs, dates. The Greystone and Thorne lines, though never married, wrapped around one another like two mangy trees. At first it had looked like a genealogy, but he knew better now. It wasn't a record. It was a tally.

He turned the page and froze. Alaric noticed instantly, catching the moment his breath faltered. "What is it?"

Elias lowered the ledger to let him see. Their blood ran cold.

Their names were in the margins. Faintly, at first, as if smudged. Then again, darker. Then again. Dozens — hundreds— of repetitions. Layered over one another in places in a frantic hand. Sometimes Elias' name appeared alone. Sometimes Alaric's. Sometimes both, intertwined, dates reaching into times that had not yet occurred. Some lines had been crossed out. Some underlined. Others had been rewritten over and over again until the ink pooled thick and black like dried blood.

"That's what I meant," he whispered. "That's what I saw. Below. Carved into the walls. Etched into the stone. You and me. Names repeated because it doesn't care who we are, only what we owe."

Elias staggered back. His heartbeat thundered in his ears. He snapped the book closed and dropped it unceremoniously, watching horrified as it clattered to the floor. "What do we do?" His voice cracked. "Alaric, what do we—" He stepped back further, crashing into the desk as he did so. Alaric reached his hand out, unsteady, grasping Elias' shaking wrist. His next words came with a resolute certainty that suggested he'd only been waiting to suggest this very thing since the moment he'd come up.

"We burn it."

Elias looked at him for any trace of uncertainty, and upon finding none, he knew he was right. The house had written them into its story. And they would need to destroy the story to be free.

14

L'Enfer

Dust hung thick in the stale air, catching the pale, dying light like forgotten memories trapped in glass. Surrounding them was centuries' worth of relics, towering nearly to the ceiling, some only accessible with ladders. The tables were coated in thick layers of wax and dust, scattered with the remains of research that no longer mattered.

On the mantel of the hearth, photographs of Alaric and previous heirs as children taunted them with lost legacies. Against the wall leaned the painting of them as boys in the meadow, a sickening reminder of days passed in a funeral shroud drop cloth. Eleanor was right to call it a mausoleum all those months ago. The room felt thick with the weight of their decision.

They spoke in hushed voices as if the manor could hear them, their backs pressed to the desk. They felt less exposed here, in a place where the manor refused to look for them. Elias stared at the corners of the ceiling, watching the shadows play there, far from him.

Elias's gaze settled on an old cobweb, its spirals sagging from the ceilings. "Remember that night in the library? When you tried to hide my book just to annoy me?"

Alaric's lips quirked, a faint warmth beneath the usual sharpness. "You caught me, of course. And you pretended to be furious, but you read half the book anyway."

A quiet chuckle slipped between them, fragile and brief.

"I don't think… we knew how," Elias said, quietly, as if the house could still hear him. "To be close, I mean." A pause. "I don't think we learned how."

Alaric's eyes met Elias' for a moment — unguarded. His smile faded into silence, the weight of what was lost hanging in the air between them.

Alaric's voice was quieter than before, almost swallowed by the stillness around them. "There's too much… silence, here," he admitted. A shadow crossed his face. They fell into a delicate tension, words stirring slowly at first, then growing with urgent clarity.

"We can't just burn everything," Elias insisted, his fingers tracing the worn edges of a cracked ledger. "There are pieces worth saving… fragments of who we were, who we still are. If we let it all go, what remains?"

Alaric's eyes sharpened though his voice remained steady, "What remains is the curse that we carry, that our goddamn lineage—…" He paused. Sighed. Pushed a hand through his hair. Winced when it caught a clump of dried blood. "The roots run too deep. If this house stands, it drags us under it. Or worse, anyone we choose to care about." Their gazes locked, two halves burdened by the same truth.

"But the memories…" Elias pressed. "They're not just shadows to me. They're why we keep fighting, they're… real."

Alaric's voice softened, a crack showing through his usual restraint. "Some memories are chains. Flames waiting to burn us if we don't learn to let go." Grief tangled between them, loud in the study room. Light played on the tables, a promise and a threat. Elias didn't respond, just bowed his head in defeat. The manor was a dying, mangled thing, but it was theirs.

Their Acadia had once surrounded them with the promise of sanctuary. Its trees had provided them sanctuary from the lives outside, the meadows vast and warm in the summer light. Every summer, Elias and Alaric had bounded joyfully through the halls, marking it unaware, faithless and pure. Giggling, Elias had chased after Alaric for what felt like miles through every room. Alice and the white rabbit, determined and doomed. And now, they'd set fire to it all, damning their entire paradise the day it turned on them. It felt like giving up on the place that had held them safe, until it didn't.

Alaric's fingers moved before his voice could catch up, reaching out with tentative hesitation. His hand brushed against Elias's, the touch light but electric, a fragile tether amid the weight pressing down on them.

The rough callouses of Alaric's palm contrasted with the warmth beneath Elias's skin, a subtle grounding in the cold stillness. Time seemed to slow, each heartbeat thudding louder against the silence. Neither spoke. Outside, the wind whispered softly through cracked panes, rusting dry leaves like parchment. Hands clasped, warmth blooming in the cold, a silent vow.

The light in the window had not changed nor moved in hours.

* * *

They moved slowly through the dim rooms, their footsteps muffled by years of dust and silence. Books lay forgotten in corners, their pages brittle and yellowed, ink faded but still holding the weight of countless names, debts, and secrets. Elias picked one up reverently, the leather cover cracked beneath his fingers, the scent of old paper rising faintly like a ghost's breath.

Alaric traced the carved edges of a heavy chair, its wood worn from generations of use. He traced the entire room as he collected, his fingers pausing over a worn porcelain vase and lingering on faded patterns lost to time. They gathered what they could carry: the ledgers, a handful of heirloom furniture, small trinkets tucked away in drawers. Each piece was carefully carried to the center hall of the house, where the pyre waited like a silent altar. As they placed the relics one by one on the growing pile of dry wood, a weight settled on their chests. These were not just objects, but pieces of memory, grief, and identity laid bare for the flames. In the stillness before it, they found a fragile quiet between them. Words felt heavy, so they spoke little, sitting close in the flickering candlelight. Shadows danced softly on the walls, casting their small sanctuary in a gentle glow.

At one point, Elias shifted closer, his knee brushing against Alaric's. Neither pulled away. Instead, they shared a brief, searching glance before Elias reached out almost without thinking, tucking a loose curl behind Alaric's ear. The touch was light, tender, and somehow more intimate than any words could be. Alaric's eyes met his, steady and unblinking, as if measuring the weight of the moment. Neither moved to pull back. Instead, the distance between them shrank, breaths growing slower, deeper. The flickering candlelight cast a warm glow across their skin, the quiet heartbeat of the house wrapped around them like a fragile cocoon.

They separated just as quickly, both surprised and unsure how to follow it. Elias tried first.

"Um— The… kerosene. We should probably—…" He stuttered, his face hot and his heart hammering in his ears. Alaric nodded, his eyes on Elias as he stood, their understanding louder than it had ever been. There was an unspoken promise between them, delicate as a thread spun from twilight, yet fierce enough to hold against the gathering storm. It hovered in the spaces between their words, in the quiet brush of skin, in the shared breaths they neither pushed nor pulled away.

The manor seemed to lean in, its ancient walls holding their secrets close, as if listening with bated breath. The silence stretched, thick and expectant, as though the house itself awaited the choice that would unravel everything and yet, somehow, offer a chance at something new.

In that moment, time slipped, fragile and suspended, balanced on the edge of what was and what might be.

Hours later, as they gathered near the pyre they build, his hands trembled too violently to lift the smallest relic. Elias caught his gaze; there was no denial left, only quiet surrender. Alaric didn't need to speak. The fading color in his cheeks, the way his body sagged, made the truth undeniable. The curse wasn't just on the manor. It was in him, draining life with every passing moment.

Alaric sank onto the edge of the pyre, fingers tracing the rough wood, his breath uneven but steady. The room felt smaller somehow, the shadows closing in with each flicker of the candlelight. Elias swallowed hard, the words catching in his throat. "We'll make it out," Elias said, voice softer now, more uncertain.

Alaric gazed up at him, wordless, ignoring his trembling hands to give him a tired smile. It wasn't reassuring. Elias sank beside him. Outside, the world held its breath, and inside, the weight of what must come settled quietly, without need for explanation.

* * *

Silence draped the manor like a shroud, holding its breath before the first spark whispered a promise of oblivion. They knelt before it, their own unholy altar, breathing one last shallow breath in the world before it would take the legacy. It almost felt pathetic — if it could be destroyed so easily, why had they destroyed themselves for it too? The air felt still and reluctant, like a cornered animal.

They had poured kerosene through the halls and the corridors all throughout the house. The east and west wings were all dripping with it; the beams and the walls almost looked like they were sweating. The sharp reek of it lingered on their clothes, their throats, lingered on the backs of their tongues. Floorboards groaned with anticipation, as though they were waterlogged not from age but with saturation of all the things that had crossed it. Everything glistened, slow rivulets gathering at the baseboards like the house was leaking its own lifeblood.

Nothing burned yet, but the house held its breath. Alaric

269

stepped forward first, the lantern in his hand rattling faintly as the glass tapped metal in short, uneven bursts. Elias came to stand beside him, the two of them framed in the glistening dark like trespassers at their own execution. For a long moment, neither of them moved. Elias lifted a hand to wipe his face, then let it fall — his hands were already slick.

"It's ready," Alaric said, somber and almost apologetic. Elias nodded.

There was no ceremony to it. No final declarations, no last words. Just a small, decisive shift as he tilted the lantern, just enough for the flame to catch the waiting sheen on the floorboards.

The fire took instantly. A thin line of orange unspooled at their feet, racing down the corridor as if the manor exhaled and offered itself up. They didn't look away.

It began as a low thrum below the floorboards, something they mistook for them contracting in heat, if they hadn't known better. The flames climbed the kerosene—slick beams in hungry vertical sweeps, and with each surge of heat the manor seemed to push back, shuddering like a creature roused from a long, resentful sleep.

Shadows convulsed along the wallpaper, warping into shapes that shouldn't have had the space to form. Elias felt the pressure behind his teeth, behind his eyes, a desperate rhythm pounding to be acknowledged. Alaric swayed once, as if caught by an unseen current, jaw tightening against whatever rose up from the depths of the structure. The fire roared through the entry, down every hall as it caught. Elias barely had time to look up before a burning beam snapped loose and plunged downward, smashing into the floor where they'd been standing seconds earlier. Embers exploded across their boots, skittering like sparks kicked from some furious forge.

Alaric grabbed his arm. "Go—"

The rest of the sentence fell away in the noise and chaos. The house was collapsing inward, each breath of flame pulling the manor tighter to itself. They ran, their boots slipping on the slick floors, air thick enough to scald their lungs. The corridors they'd soaked were now a gauntlet of fire, every doorway a mouth of heat. Smoke coiled around them in hot, grasping ribbons. Elias didn't dare look back. He could feel the house folding, see the walls shuddering in the periphery, hear something; voices, wind, memory rose in the flames. The corridor split ahead — one sagged while the other side burnt. The smoke turned everything into a moving blur, heat pressing at their backs in sharp waves. Elias coughed, stumbling as the floor lurched beneath them. Alaric stopped, steadying him deliberately.

"Elias," he urged, and something in his voice cut straight through the roar of the fire.

Elias tried to pull his arm feebly, his pulse in his head throbbing and echoing in his ears. Alaric planted his feet, refusing to move even an inch. "Alaric— Don't stop, the exit— we're almost out!"

But Alaric had gone strangely still in the flickering dark. His eyes shone with a clarity he'd only seen in the rarest, most dangerous moments of his life. The pulse shook the house again as it screamed like a wounded beast, prepared for the slaughter.

"I think…" Alaric said, his voice low and rough, "I think this is how it ends." He paused, eyes locking with Elias'. "The only way it ends."

Elias stared at him, horror rising. "No. Don't do that. Don't pretend you know what this house wants. It doesn't want a damn thing—"

"I know," he continued, almost gently. "I don't think it wants me. I don't think that's it. But a sacrifice out of love…" He said, almost to himself, "might overwrite the greed."

Elias blinked, choking on smoke and disbelief. "You're not certain. You're not—"

"No," Alaric said. "I'm not." Then, softer: "But you'll live."

The heat intensified, flames licking the walls like desperate vultures picking a bone clean. The manor groaned above them, the ceiling beginning to bow. Elias grabbed Alaric's sleeve desperately, fingers trembling. "We go together. Or not at all."

Alaric's expression twisted in pain, fondness, and regret held in one impossible moment. "You idiot," he whispered, almost laughing. "You still don't get it. Let me choose for once."

The ceiling cracked with a deafening pop. A burning beam crashed down between them, forcing Elias back. Alaric seized the split second of separation, throwing him towards the surviving corridor with more strength than made sense. He fell, clashing into the wall with enough force to knock the air from his lungs. Through the thick smoke, Alaric took one intentional step backwards.

"You live," Alaric said, fierce and final. He took another step back. "That's the only way this balances."

Elias reached out, breath shallow, but the floor beneath Alaric gave first, shattering in a burst of flame and collapsing into the inferno below. His form dropped out of sight as the pulse collapsed into one long, echoing shudder. Then, Greystone Manor began to collapse in on itself for real.

For a second the world went entirely silent. It was so silent, he could hear his own heart cracking down the center. A thunderous crack rolled out from above him, shifting, groaning, and beginning to fold. The pulse that had been battering the walls was now a constant whine, destabilized, like a death rattle. The heat drove him back. His eyes watered, the smoke clawing at his throat. Another beam split, spraying embers across his shoulders. The corridor behind him buckled, cutting off any path but one.

He had no choice, and no time. Elias staggered down the narrow, burning passage, barely able to tell where the floor held and where it had already begun to sink. The manor's structure was failing in a chain reaction, each collapse triggering another, like the house was tearing itself inward. A section of ceiling dropped behind him, close enough that the gush of heat surged him forward. His lungs screamed and his vision tunneled as he desperately pushed through it. One arm outstretched to feel along the warped wall and the other clutched his ribs where the force of the last shove bruised him through.

He made it into the entry, where the door frame sagged and melted. Elias braced a shoulder against the door, once a prison bar, and forced himself through. He stumbled into the evening just as the roof of the east wing folded inwards on itself with a devastating roar. Cold air hit him hard; it was too clean all of a sudden. He collapsed, exhausted and injured in the wet grass there, coughing until he tasted blood.

Before him, Greystone Manor burned in roaring, furious sheets. The flames devoured its heart, cruel and unrelenting. The pulse in his head had faded now, ebbing into the noise of cracks and collapses in the wood and stone. Elias stared at the inferno, just waiting for something. Any proof that Alaric was somehow alive, that this wasn't real, that a terrible nightmare had consumed him.

Nothing came. Only fire. Only ruin.

And, impossibly, the hollow, staggering quiet of freedom.

15

January, 1884

He passed quietly and easily through the morning hush. The local cafe windows were fogged with the arrival of customers, and he slipped into his usual corner quietly with the ease of habit. It was a modest little place, smelling of cardamom and yeast, with a bell over the door that never rang the same way twice.

He ordered without needing to think, the waitress greeting him with the familiarity she reserved for only the warmest strangers. He liked it this way. Steam curled from his cup as he opened a dog-eared paperback, the spine worn into something soft, almost shapeless. Some mornings he read. Some he wrote a few lines in the journal that lived permanently in his coat pocket: nothing remarkable, just scraps of thought, small observations, names he hadn't said aloud in years.

Elias breathed into the quiet and let it hold him. It wasn't happiness, not exactly. But it was life. A gentle one. Made up of paperbacks and coffee. His fingers absently traced the worn cover when a weathered hand dropped a small, sea-stained volume beside it.

"Thought you might like this," the voice uttered, soft and steady.

Elias looked up, meeting the man's soft gaze. His hands were calloused from work, and Elias hadn't seen him in months, but that was the way of things out here. People came and went near-constantly, dropped in to see anyone who mattered, and shipped off again until the next time. He liked these sorts of friends that didn't ask him to be anything.

"Thank you." He responded, warm. The man sat across from him, the chair making a rough scrape on the wood. Between them was a thick copy of Alice in Wonderland. How banal. His mouth must have betrayed his tinge of recoil, because the man glanced toward the window and nodded, changing the subject.

"Have you seen him?" He asked, his tone haunting. Elias didn't have the slightest clue what he meant, his eyes following the gesture. Elias closed his journal slowly, feeling the pulse of the sea crawling in behind his ears.

"Seen... what exactly?" He tried, cautious.

The blacksmith's gaze didn't waver from the misty shoreline. "They say there's a man. Or no, a figure. Sometimes it's there at dawn, or dusk, standing just beyond the breakers. Doesn't move, doesn't speak. Just watches the sea, like it's waiting."

Elias swallowed hard, the salt air filling his lungs sharper than before. "A man?"

"Or something like one. Folks around here have been saying it must be a ghost, never able to go home, and never quite gone."

He met the man's steady eyes again. "Do you believe it's real?"

The moment stretched between them was wordless and

heavy with anticipation. His throat went dry, and the pulse behind his ears had moved to his neck. The man shrugged, a tired smile tugging at his lips. "Does it matter? It's just a bloody ghost story."

Elias nodded slowly, a nervous smile crossing his lips as he gazed out to the fog and the endless deep.

He thanked the man with a brief nod and stepped outside. The morning chill still clung to the air, but the rising sun had begun to warm the narrow streets of the village. He moved slowly through the familiar lanes, the worn cobblestones uneven beneath his boots, until he reached the small cottage that had become his refuge.

Inside, the quiet was different. The weight of solitude pressed to him, but it was his. His books littered the desk and his shelves, haphazardly organized but never forgotten. He read for a while, but his mind kept drifting back to that morning's conversation. When dusk fell, painting the sky in muted shades of purple and gold, Elias wrapped a thick coat around his shoulders and stepped outside again. The village had settled into its evening rhythm, smoke curling from chimneys and lamps flickering behind curtained windows.

He stepped out cautiously, the familiar crunch of sand and pebbles keeping him company. The sea stretched out before him, vast and unknowable, its surface catching the last light of day. Elias paused at the water's edge, letting the cold breeze carry away the weight of years. The fog started to roll in, carried by the waves. Here, he fixed his gaze on the horizon.

He wasn't sure what he expected to see, just that he needed to confirm it for himself. Something in him pulled him to the water's edge, willing and waiting for something unknowable. He inhaled, the salt air sharp and cleansing.

In the swirling mist, a shape began to take form. First, indistinguishable, then still and silent. It watched the gray horizon before him, its silver edges mingling with the oncoming moonlight. It didn't speak, or move, or *do* really much of anything. Elias' heart tightened with something quieter than fear. When it turned, there was no face, only a hollow where eyes might have been, and yet it watched him with a weight that pressed deep into his bones. The figure didn't move. It didn't breathe. It simply stood there, a sentinel between water and sky, waiting.

Elias's heart pounded — loud, ragged, and uneven — but it still wasn't fear that gripped him. It was a quiet reckoning. A recognition. For a long moment, they held each other's gaze across the mist-wrapped shore, bound by loss and unfinished stories.

The sea whispered behind them, endless and patient.

For a moment, two ghosts stood at the end of the world.

About the Author

Vida Rose writes stories about beautiful places with terrible secrets and the people drawn back to them. His work weaves together gothic mood, emotional intimacy, and supernatural unease, often exploring the quiet spaces where longing and dread blur and how our emotions can sometimes feel otherworldly themselves. Outside of writing, he divides his time between haunting local bookstores, collecting obscure folklore, and watching way too much 80s cult horror. He currently lives in the Pacific Northwest, where he writes late into the night with a playlist of indie ballads and the mews of his two cats.

You can connect with me on:
🌐 https://vidaroseauthor.com

www.ingramcontent.com/pod-product-compliance
Lightning Source LLC
Chambersburg PA
CBHW071545110726
47908CB00007B/2002